JILLIAN E THOMPSON

Melody of Redemption

Lullaby Series, Book 1

Acknowledgments

There are so many people that I would want to thank for making this book possible. First, my oldest son, Eason, for being the curious child that you are and asking me one day while we were driving what the words to "twinkle, twinkle" the lullaby song were. You are the reason that this whole book came to life. Second, my friend in New Zealand, Mollie Smith, for being my sounding board and letting me rant and rave about everything and anything that had to do with this book and even the things that aren't. Third, to all of my students that I have taught and had the pleasure of working with. Your enthusiasm about my book has made me feel joy. That is the entire reason that I write, to see the joy in children's faces as they enjoy a good book.

Most importantly, I want to thank my husband, Cliff, for being the rock under my feet. Without you there to keep me tethered to the ground, I would have floated away long ago with my imagination. You understand my passion and let me have the time to focus on it. I wouldn't have been able to finish this book without your support. Thank you for being everything to me and being the one to let me have the time to develop and create this remarkable world that Mary Beth and the others live in.

Lastly, to those kids in the maes, "scout's honor."

Prologue

The air whistled around me, and heat enveloped me as I shifted again. I could feel every jolt underneath me, each movement bringing me closer to fulfillment.

My body shook with the impact as I hit the ground running, faster and faster, escaping. What I was escaping, I couldn't determine; all that mattered was that I had to escape them. It didn't matter how fast I ran or the distance I attempted to put between us... it was always too close for comfort. There was no way to escape.

"Where do we go?" I hollered to him as we rounded another corner, the dirt flying as our feet pounded against the ground. My heart thumped erratically as the sounds of branches breaking around me. "They're going to catch up," I shouted as we rounded another corner.

"Don't give up, MB. They haven't gotten us yet," a voice replied. A nameless person running in front of me. "We'll be okay if we get there; just don't stop running."

I panted with exertion, my sides aching as I attempted to keep up with the person before me, but it was useless. I was never going to make it. As I went crashing to the ground, rocks jabbed into me as the footsteps got closer. I closed my eyes, knowing that this was the end. He was never going to come back for me.

I jerked up in the bed, my heart pounding like I had been running a race in my dreams. *What the hell was that about?* I questioned as the sweat dripped down my neck. The room was stifling hot, and I slid out of the bed to open my window, willing my heart to slow down as I approached it. I tried to recall the details of the man in front of me. But to no avail, I couldn't remember any details about his appearance, only that he had been taller than me. Not that it was a huge detail almost everyone was taller than me.

I sighed as I watched the moonlight begin to fade in the night sky outside my window. The coolness of the night rested gleefully against my heated skin. I glanced over at the alarm clock at the edge of my nightstand: three forty-one; the numbers blinked at me. Well, at least it wasn't too early. I pushed myself away from the windowsill and headed towards my closet. I might as well prepare for the day; the dream lingered as I pulled on my clothes. Somehow, I knew that something—everything—was about to change.

I

Mary Beth

Act I – The End Begins Here

One

As I rose from my bed, the moon was fighting to keep the sun at bay. It wasn't dawn, and I had places to go and things to do. The lights in the house were still dark when I opened my bedroom door. I sighed with relief; it was always easier to get to the hunting grounds if I didn't have to stop to talk to anyone first. I opened my door as silently as possible and crept down the hallway, adjusting my bag, trying to get it into that sweet spot where I could move freely without anything dropping. I paused as I glanced in at my sweet twin sisters and the devil that they called my little brother before heading down the stairs. Mom and Dad would wake up soon, but they wouldn't panic. It was my habit and had been my habit for years, so it wouldn't surprise either of them if my bed was empty. I wanted to get out onto the open field before the other hunters in the village got up. It was always a race to get out there before anyone else. Resources were limited, and if you didn't get up and at it, you lost your chance for real meat. We could have the synthetic shit anytime, but everyone in our home was looking gaunt.

As I reached the bottom of the stairs, I grabbed my bow that leaned against the wall as I walked to the front door. Shutting the door was always a challenge; the house was decrepit, old, barely holding on, but at least it was something to protect us. The shit had hit the fan long ago; the world turned sideways and hadn't been the same since, but I managed to get it to shut without too much noise.

We were forced to live in these communities now; hell, they weren't communities… It seemed more like a prison. Walls surrounding us, what they considered the hunting grounds were little more than dead grass and barren trees within a three-mile radius of a wooden fence. I was convinced the wall was broken in many places; otherwise, we wouldn't have fresh food… unless… I had to shake myself out of it. I was a conspiracist. I was truly confident that the world was out to get me; it didn't help that it affected a lot more than just the environment when the world went sideways. It has modified many of the children in the world, including kids like me. I always wondered if they were placating us to keep us from asking too many questions. But there were… there were so many questions.

There had always been promises the world was going to get better. Promises for families would be taken care of. It was all just a bunch of lies; there was nothing to take care of us. I was pretty damn confident of that. The government didn't do anything.

I remembered when we first came here after the explosion; Mom had been heavily pregnant with the girls at the time, and Nick had only been four. Dad had been working that day, so Mom took us all to the mall to celebrate Dom's last day as a freshman. I choked up; Dom was a sore topic, and it always hurt to think of him. My brother had been the world to me, and with him gone, I perceived the gray shadows more than ever before. He had been…

Shaking my head, I brought myself back to the present. The air was thick and oppressive under the dark skies. It was harder to breathe now. The entire world had changed, and it wasn't for the betterment of mankind.

I drifted through the streets, trying to avoid any open windows or lit rooms. I didn't like the way that people stared at me. It was another significant reason why going earlier, rather than later, to hunt was my habit. I could avoid everyone for a bit longer. It was also best to avoid certain areas that I knew would generate significant sound such as the marketplace. I wasn't welcome there anymore, but then again, none of us affected by the destruction of our world were welcomed in most places around the village. We were outcasts, even in a world that should be working together to be stronger than ever.

I knew it would lighten up here in the next hour as the sun broke the horizon's surface; however, I couldn't even clearly remember what it looked like. The skies were nasty. Opaque, all we ever glimpsed, was the residue of the sunlight but never the sun.

During the early morning hours, I could find more animals as they came out to play. The heat and oppression that came with the heavy air weren't as bad at night, or in the wee hours of the morning, so that's when I took my chances.

The walls around the village they built to "keep the world out" were thick and tall, and the barbed wire lined the top. I could never figure out why we were keeping the world out, and none of the teachers would answer my questions when I asked about it when I attended school here. This is why I considered we lived in prison; it reminded me of the movies we used to watch when I was a child. I think they were deliberately keeping us in, but then again, *I'm a conspiracist*. I was sure that everything that the government did was to harm the public more. Hell, I wasn't even sure what the world looked like anymore, let alone the beautiful lands of Colorado that I had grown up in. The bombs had destroyed a substantial portion of the state around us, and the government considered it a safe area, but I didn't wholly agree with them. I was confident that the government had been part of the "bombing" by China. There was no way that the craters and destruction around me were caused by bombs dropped by the planes over the country. Even if it was targeted bombs, I still don't believe it would have changed the world this much.

I was confident that there wasn't a safe place for anyone. Whatever had been in those bombs—radiation, drugs, chemicals, or whatever—it had done something to us... Well, the kids that were close enough to be in the disaster zones. I looked down at the callused turquoise bumps on my hands as I walked along the streets quietly.

How could they say that we were safe when there was such prejudice against those who had no control over where they had been when the bombs went off? They thought the Civil War was destructive, but this was a thousand times worse.

Finally, reaching the gate, I noticed no one was manning it yet. I was in luck! Maybe this time I could get out and in before having to deal with anyone considered a guard of the settlement. They weren't guards, at least in my opinion. I considered them "bullies," the sort that push people around and use whatever power they have to make people feel inferior, which generally meant me and others with the same physical affliction.

Shaking myself loose, I began walking steadily towards the settlement entrance. Adjusting my bow, I pulled my pouch from my side until it was in front of me. The heavy smells of sage, thyme, mint, and lavender floated to my nose as the pouch's cover slid a little from the movement. I'd used this same pouch since I was ten and followed Dom when he hunted. The gut-wrenching pain, the panic, and the betrayal blew through me like a cold wind. I clutched my stomach as it rolled around I remembered how his disappearance had affected all of us, how I had gotten into trouble for what I did to help him. I stopped short, attempting to catch my breath; the panic attack was close, and I had to find something else to think about. The smells permeated the bag permanently, reminding me that I should probably gather more herbs along the way.

Nearing the edge of the guards' station, a dull sign caught my eye. It was written long ago, back when they first made these communities… It was just some old wood that someone had written on in paint; the paint was peeling in places, so the words didn't always show the proper way, but I knew what it said; I had it memorized.

"Hey, you," a voice called out. I glanced behind me to note that someone was walking up towards me, and I quickly pushed myself through the gate. I wasn't ready to talk to anyone; it was my quiet time.

Hunting is allowed in settlement perimeters. Hunt: Rabbits, Birds, and Deer. Contact the guards if a bear is found within the perimeter gates. The words were etched into my mind as I almost sprinted out of the gate. I never understood why we had to get the guards if a bear got through; I could have handled it easily.

I hated, positively hated, that damn sign. I hated the limits of this stupid place and the rules that the governing body put in place after the blast. But most of all, I hated the narrow-minded views of the people, those who considered themselves our saviors, the people who sold materials or food. It all came back to appearances and how we were judged on what we appeared instead of who we were. I felt more like an outcast daily than I was here, and yet I couldn't leave my family alone in this place. Nick was already getting to that age where the mutations started to appear for me, and I was worried he would get it a lot worse than me... not to mention our baby sisters. I dreaded thinking of how the group mentality would impact them when signs started to appear with them.

I pulled my hood above my head as I walked along with the vast blank lands by the gate to the wooded, fielded area. I prayed that the person who yelled at me wouldn't come back.

"Hey," the voice called again, and I swore internally. It simply wasn't meant to be.

"What?" I snarled; I wasn't in a good mood now. I had lost the peace that I wanted this morning.

"What time was your slot?" I didn't bother to turn around. "You know, you have to check in with the guards, right?" Did this person think I was stupid? I never checked in with the guards in the morning; they knew I was out here. It was my routine, even though it was technically against the rules.

"Don't worry about me." I said, "I take care of myself and everything that I need to." I kept walking; if they wanted anything to do with me, they could attempt to follow me. Otherwise, I was happy to lose them on my way to my spot. After a while, I didn't hear anything, so I sighed in relief that they had decided to leave me alone.

I focused on the surrounding grounds, thinking about how the grass didn't grow as thick anymore, but with the vegetation there, it was quiet. Not to mention that the area that I always went to wasn't very popular with the other hunters. It was a great spot with herbs and other great natural remedies. It attracts other things, like animals, because of the natural growth there. Maybe today would be a good day, and I would catch something. However, on the off chance I didn't, I could at least collect something worthwhile to bring home.

Dropping my hood, I pulled my hair back and put it into a ponytail, hoping that it would lighten some weight. I had never cut my hair; it was always something Mom said would make me feel good about myself, but I sporadically wished I would.

The air was chilly despite the oppressive feeling it gave my skin; it was a heavy, cold blanket around me. This feeling rarely left me alone when I was awake. The air felt so dense out here, so different from what I remember as a child. I could feel the cold, but it never truly felt like I was cold because it was thick against my skin.

My long ebony hair shifted uneasily against the bare skin of my shoulders, weighing heavily even in the ponytail. The occasional breeze drifted across the plain, lifting a few strands to float against the wind, but it did nothing to help the weight of my hair or the thickness of the air against my bare neck.

I sighed as I looked out at the dead grasslands before me, my ears open to any sounds that drifted up from the grounds. Usually, there would be a lot more going on now, with the sun barely coming up and the light floating through the opaque skies. I wished I could see the sun, just a little of the brightness so it wouldn't be so gloomy. My brothers would argue with me whenever I said I wanted to see the sun. They would tell me that the sun was just playing peek-a-boo with everyone. I had never been more optimistic that there was something that made it hard to see anything in the skies.

Stealthily, I walked the grounds as time passed by. *Maybe today wouldn't be a good day for hunting,* I thought. I started rooting through the dry grass, looking for still edible herbs. At least, this way, I thought, the day wouldn't be for nothing. Stuffing the herbs into my pouch as I found them, time passed by even quicker than before.

Eventually, though, as I cocked my head, the soft sounds of a rabbit's pitter-patter drifted over the silent grounds.

Well, well, I smiled. *It's about time.*

I reached across my shoulders for the bow that rested in its case on my back. I had been hunting with this bow since I was eleven; it was the deadliest weapon in my hands. My father and brother had both attempted to teach me to use knives and even a handgun. I could use either of those weapons; however, the bow made everything I targeted fall to the ground when I aimed at it.

The pale tone of my right hand clashed with the turquoise bumps as the contrast shone under the morning glare. Compared to the dark colors of the government-issued clothing, I was a bright light of whites and blues on the plane. Even though I had been forced to wear the clothing, the holes and patches my mom had to make on them helped cover the lightness of my skin when I was on the prowl.

Silently, the deadly weapon slid from its case. Reaching with my other hand, I pulled on the bright orange feathers of the bolt, dragging it out of the quiver. Steadying my hands, I primed my arrow into the notch in the bow.

I scanned the horizon as I continued to listen to the pitter-patter of the rabbit's hops, placing the location of my prey along the Northeast boundary wall. Suddenly, the flash of black and white among the tall, dead weeds alerted me to its whereabouts. Threading the bolt through the taut strings of my bow, I aimed.

Looking through the scope, the rabbit's outline fell into focus as I pulled tightly on the grip of the crossbow.

Swish. The air vibrated as the bolt glided through it and jetted from the bow. The strings slapped against the grip, biting my fingers, and I pushed the crossbow down. Following the path of the bolt's bright feathers, I watched as it headed straight toward the rabbit.

Ears twitching, the rabbit glanced up as the bolt flew closer to its target. I held my breath, hoping that the rabbit hadn't noticed, but luck was not on my side as I spotted the twitching of the rabbit's ears. It had heard something. Fuck. The thought crossed my mind, and I prayed.

Please, please...

It was pointless, as my eyes squinted harder, attempting to focus on the minute animal over fifty feet away. Suddenly, the wings released themselves from the back of the rabbit, and the animal started to hop. As the rabbit took flight, the bolt whizzed by the flocking rabbit and embedded itself in the boundary wall.

"Son of a bitch!" I swore as I watched the bolt waver in the board of the boundary wall. What the hell scared it away? I attempted to listen to my surroundings as I clenched the crossbow tightly in my fist, my fingernails eating into my palms. I was pissed. This was a pointless excursion. There was nothing, no sound whatsoever, except my breathing in the field. I angrily stomped across the yellow and dead grass as I reached the lonely bolt.

My pouch, full of herbs, slapped against my waist. The rod's blackness stood out starkly against the weathered board. I knelt on my knees angrily, placing the crossbow next to me. I grabbed the bolt with one hand and braced myself against the boards with the other hand. The grass crackled under my knee as I began to pull on the bolt.

At least I won't have to share it when I return to the border. I thought, trying to be positive, as I tugged on the bolt. I was trying hard not to think of how ravenous the girls would be without the extra food. I continued to try and unwedge the bolt from the board, landing on my butt with my feet, bracing the board as both hands tugged at the stuck bolt. As the bolt slid out of the board, I swore again. Why didn't I attempt harder to learn knife throwing or shooting the gun again? This was the most challenging part of shooting the crossbow.

Bolts weren't a commodity, and I couldn't simply leave them behind. Even though not everyone hunted in this "new world," they would gladly take my arrow if I left it; it could be used for something else, of which I was convinced. The only kinds of weapons you recognized anymore weren't as wondrous as my bow that my dad had salvaged from the wreckage of our home, so unless you owned a gun, you were better off with a quick hand and a knife. I was lucky to have been trained in every weapon, so I could handle my bow and anything else thrown at me.

The last few inches were torturous as I pulled harder. As the board released the bolt from its clutches, I tumbled backward. Landing hard on my back, my pouch slapped the dead grass, and the handle of a hunting knife I had clipped to my thigh dug into me. As I held the bolt aloft, the dead weeds and grass snagged in my hair. Gazing up at the bolt from my prone position on the ground, I smirked; at least it came out.

A heavy clapping filled the area, and I looked back toward where I came from. The man talking to me earlier stood there clapping at my expense. "Well, that was entertaining."

I stared at him. *How the hell did I miss him back there?* His easy grin looked like it could easily be contagious. His dark skin had a luscious sheen to it, and it was so dark that I couldn't determine whether he had mutations or not on it.

"How did you get there?" I demanded, dusting myself off. His laughter was light and easy, a sobering chuckle that reminded me of another sound at a different time and place.

I stood up, wiping my clothes off as I went. The entire time it was silent as I waited for the man to respond. Yet, the man was gone when I was done cleaning my clothes from the messy, dry grass that had stuck to them. My mind was in a daze. I'm a pretty good hunter; I can hear what most people can't, but how did this man disappear without a sound?

"Well, I guess I'll head back," I spoke to the dead air as I picked the twigs and grass from my cloak. I didn't know where the man had disappeared, and I wondered if he was still watching me somewhere around there. *It was disturbing.* It wasn't the first time a man had accosted me on the hunting grounds, but it was the first time that a man had just disappeared into thin area. I talked to myself a lot; otherwise, the silence I dealt with regularly would have driven me insane. Yet, in this instance, I felt like I was still talking to that man even though I couldn't see him. I didn't recognize him at all, but he felt familiar.

I started to pick up the last few herbs that I could see.

Otherwise, today would have been another pointless day. I tried to fine-tune my hearing to see if I could hear where that man had disappeared. I pried out my sack and put the herbs inside when I was done.

I was still a mess; I could feel it in my hair. So, I stood there and shook my head. The long locks of my hair flew around, pushing some loose twigs and plants out of my roots, some falling out of my ponytail. Pulling my band out, I ran my fingers through the ebony strands, untangling the wild pieces of the world from my hair, as I walked to my crossbow. As I bent forward for the crossbow, my hair flipped over my head, creating a curtain around my head from the ponytail.

Two

A twig snapped behind me.

Startled, I grabbed my crossbow and swore internally. The herbs had spilled all over the ground in my mad attempt to pull my bow out from under my sack. It was still empty, and I quickly glanced around me, so I picked them up. I was mad and confused, but mainly I needed to cool my jets before returning home. Not only that, but I could see the shapes of bodies as they moved around the edges of the boundary walls. There was no hurry. I preferred not to deal with them yet, even though I swear that one had just been here. It was like having teeth pulled whenever I had to deal with the "security" of the settlement. They were assholes; they didn't need a uniform to be that; they simply were. The words were truths, but it didn't feel right when thinking of that man I had just seen.

There were so many on the ground from my attempt that I was almost mellowed out by the time I had picked everything up. I pulled off the ratty cloak from my shoulders as I put the crossbow back into the case, slung the bolt back into the quiver, and adjusted my pouch before pulling the cloak back on. I don't even know why I had the cloak anymore. It had belonged to my brother once… I guess I just couldn't give it up yet. It had been part of some cosplay things he had done, and I guess he had liked it so much that it became his signature look. He had been such a dweeb, but then again, I guess that drove me into a dweeb too.

There was such love and sadness whenever I thought about him. I always felt like I was adrift in the sea, the way my emotions whiplashed between happiness and sadness when it came to Dom. Tugging on my cloak again, I smiled at an image of him racing around with the cloak flying behind him as he pretended to be a wizard. I chuckled to myself, reaching up to wipe my eyes, the moisture soft against the skin of my eyes, accidentally touching the turquoise bumps that brushed against the sides of my eyes. I could only imagine they glistened in the few patches of morning light that drifted through the hazy skies as they were illuminated in any type of light.

I pulled the hood of the cloak over my head, tugging it down over my face. I wanted to avoid being noticed. I didn't. It didn't help that I could feel the sweat rolling down my face from the heat of the almost-hunt and the dank air.

I pulled on the oversized black tee shirt, attempting to straighten it, as well as the ratty cloak, trying to cover the sights of my mutation before the prying eyes of the village caught a glimpse of me. Not only were the bumps along with my fingers and my eyes, but they also trailed along my upper arms and shoulders. I don't understand why I got the bumps. Mom has pictures of me before the bumps, and I never had them before. I had to cover them the best I could whenever I came into the village, or something awful could happen. It's happened before. It was a horrible reaction to something out of my control, but it was a compassionless society. No one cared about those damaged by the bombs; they altogether feared them instead… They feared me. It was best to be invisible as much as possible when I went through it, and people were out and about.

That was one of the reasons why I always tried to get out before the sun was elevated; I was aware that they would be staring at me once I got in. Or even something worse. I shuddered at the thought of the hands that had pulled on my clothing, trying to rip it, barely a few months before when I had gone hunting. It had been one of the worst experiences I'd had in a long time, and it made it a terror of mine to go out into the settlement without my dad or brother with me. Not that I wasn't a badass by anyone's claim, but there was no respect for people like me within the settlement, and there were fewer and fewer of us monthly. I couldn't help but wonder if something was happening to us… There went my conspiracy theories again.

I continued walking along the worn path of the grasslands as the buildings began to loom bigger and brighter in front of me. Even being depleted and lacking fresh paint, the buildings were brightly colored even with the dimmed colors from years of minor to no care. The dome of the farming section shone in the hazy morning light. I never could understand how they got the farms to work when there was no real sunshine, but we got food weekly from it. Maybe the dome had some artificial light, but it was as see-through as a window. I didn't understand it, and Dad always refused to explain it.

Lost in my thoughts, I shivered as goosebumps rose alongside the turquoise bumps on my arms. My hunter instincts hackled, and I quickly turned around to face the boundary fence. I had felt this way a couple of times in the past; however, the number of times I'd been so thoroughly aware of my surroundings had increased in the last six months. I knew something was out there; I wasn't sure what it was, though. I was certain that something or someone was watching me.

As I began to scan the fences, an icy, cold dread filled my veins as I stared at the boards. I hoped bandits would not try to get in, or something else. Bandits had rushed us before… that was why there were so many guards around the boundaries now. It was terrifying when they entered, but they got them off the property. We haven't seen them since. I prayed that there was nothing or no one there as I continued the search of the fence for the item or person that caused my instincts to kick in.

The discomfort eased as I reached the last section of the fence and saw nothing to raise an alarm about. Oh, well, I thought as I turned back to the settlement. I started to hum a song, a nursery lullaby that had always eased my mind, as I quickly glanced up at the dirty and hazy opaque skies. It was the same song that I always hummed… the same one constantly on my mind. It was my coping method. It kept me from being deranged.

Twinkle, twinkle, little star, How I wonder what you are... The words were from the melody my mom had always sung to me as a child. It drifted through my head as I attempted to clear my mind. Singing a lullaby had been her nightly ritual with Nick and me before the girls were born, although the song had changed over the years. I think she endeavored to have something different for each of us. Something to make us feel unique. First, she would sing the song Mockingbird to Nicky, making sure he was deeply asleep before she'd put me to bed, singing about the stars after reading me a goodnight story. The story was always a bonus for me. I was such a bibliophile that it was the only way she could get me to agree. I smiled and tried to relax as I continued to near the settlement entrance from the hunting grounds.

I tried so hard to let go of the narrow-minded views of the people in the settlement when I came to hunt. It was the only time I didn't feel I was being judged for being alive. Yet again, I was about to experience that narrow-mindedness as the guards came sharply into focus behind the sign that dominated the wall before the gate entrance to the settlement from the hunting grounds.

Fucking terrific.

A small crowd of people gathered around the entranceway. The sharp black colors of the uniform, the vibrant yellows that designated them as the menial guards they were and not a higher rank, stood out in the hazy light from the sunless skies. Coming closer to the entrance, I watched as the crowd slowly dispersed from the conversation or activity they were doing; instead, the guards started to wander around and circle me. Yet again, I was faced with the fact that I was a caged animal. Nothing more and nothing less, well, maybe less... They tried hard to make me feel that way, but I continued to stare at the glass as half-full. They were idiots, and I was brilliant just like Dom had always told me when I was a kid and the kids were bullying me at school.

However, that didn't mean I would put myself in a position of confrontation. If anything, I shut down even more. I knew that the bumps of my mutation raised my cloak in those areas, and I tried to pull the cloak closer together without moving my weapons. I tried for years to wear nothing but long sleeves, but Colorado's dense weather and sweltering heat made it impossible to do it for long. So, the short sleeves of my shirt provided nothing around protection, nothing to block their eyes from focusing on my mutations as my feet slowed down, dragging as the gate got closer and closer.

From within the group, I spotted the dark, curly head of someone I had once been friends with while at the school, where the settlement was mixed well among the guards. His hair wasn't as shaggy as I remembered it to be. Not to mention that he no longer had the malnourished effect many of the kids in the settlements had when we were going to school. His olive arms had muscle and depth that hadn't been there before, and I almost drooled at the sight of such a well-defined form. What was I doing? I shook my head and focused on the other aspects I missed. I noticed he had turned out to be charming with some food in his stomach. He wasn't as defined as other guards, and luckily, he wasn't as heavy as some. He must still be new.

So, when did he join the guards? I pondered as I watched several of the older guards start to pull him towards the front, towards me. I sighed.

Damn, initiation time, I assumed, as Conrad stood in front of me. Why do they always get the new guards to harass me when I go out? This wasn't the first time the latest guard had stopped me, and I half-hoped that Conrad wouldn't fall into the same narrow-mindedness that affected the guards within the settlement.

"H-h-h-halt," he stuttered. "Please…" His timbre voice trembled with the pressure of the guards at his back. I was starting to feel more hopeful. He recognized me; that was clear to perceive. His brown eyes were pleading with mine, but why was he pleading with me? Nervous ate at my stomach.

His eyes slowly lowered to the ground, shame filling their depths. It was apparent that he still wasn't comfortable with this new position. Or maybe he remembered we had once been friends… back before my bumps had appeared.

One of the guards, his hands meaty and thick, pushed him violently forward, as though reminding him that he was still on probation. Just like every other guard that had come before him, and I knew that he was going to give in. The push gave him the charge, the reminder that he had to perform to the expectations, so his statement filled with courage as he continued. "Place your weapons and all your baggage on the ground."

Even with that encouragement and the remainder of the guards at his back, his expression was grim. Oh, yeah. I thought. He remembered me. I started to pull off my bow and quiver, my hood falling backward as my cloak moved around. My mutations were out for anyone to see. They would all find a way to make me miserable; that much was obvious. So, I went into survival mode, ignoring the look of disgust and focusing on the lullaby instead.

Twinkle, twinkle, little star.

I wondered where I had missed the signs that he was considering going for a government position. But then again, I hadn't spoken to many of my friends since the mutations had singled me out at school and pushed me into servitude.

How I wonder what you are.

The guard continued to circle like vultures as my layers of weapons, and my pouch was torn from my body like dead skin.

Up above the world, so high.

Anger boiled my blood as the guards swooped down and began searching through my meager possessions, as though there was something inside the bags they could seize for themselves. Maybe that is how they got to look so chunky and muscular… They got to steal from the meek and poor. Conrad stood to the side as the rest of the guards continued their search for my belongings. At least he respected me that much, I guessed. The lullaby continued to bounce through my head as I breathed deeply, trying to calm myself and lower the sound of blood pounding through my ears.

As I pulled myself together, I said, as calmly as I could, "I didn't catch anything in the fields today." I pulled my hood up over my hair, trying to cover myself again. I added my physical armor as I emotionally armed myself for war against these idiots.

The surrounding guards laughed, as though I was telling them a joke. "There is nothing there but some herbs I found."

"That's for us to determine," the guard with the thick, meaty hands snapped as his eyes glared up at me from the inside of my pouch. He had knelt as soon as my bag had hit the ground to search it. It wasn't like he needed any more food. The rest of his head was buried in the worn leather, as though he thought there was a hidden pocket within it. I had decided the last time when he had torn my clothes in his haste, to grab my catch then that he was going to be called Sir Thick-a-lot due to his thick behavior and fatty hands. He was a complete idiot.

"Where are you hiding it?" he growled, his impatience seeping through his words as he threw the pouch at me. Some herbs fell to the ground as I caught them. *Yup, thick, dense, stupid behavior.* I reflected as the lullaby continued to sweep through me, calming my nerves.

"I told you, I didn't catch anything today."

"We watched you shooting your arrow. Where is the prey you hit?" He demanded. "Where did you hide it?"

A shout of agreement surrounded me as the other guards joined in with his demand. *They had nothing better to do than to spy on the people hunting. Don't they have some type of job to do?* It was infuriating that they would spy on me, yet simultaneously I knew, deep down inside, that they did it because they thought I would do something due to my skin.

I hope you haven't died. My rendition of the song echoed slowly through my head as another guard threw my quiver at my feet, and they crowded around me. I was starting to get nervous; however, witnessing my weapon thrown so carelessly to the ground antagonized me. They had no respect for the belongings of others.

I bit my tongue, however, because I couldn't afford to have Mom and Dad pay for me to get out of the barracks again. The last time had cost them food for a week.

"You have to be hiding it somewhere!" The guard who threw my quiver exploded.

A chuckle erupted in my throat, cascading out of my mouth, at the frustrated look on his face, it was priceless to witness the guards so wrapped up in the meager possessions of a simple teenager in the settlement. They were so entitled!

Holding back my smile, I sought to choke down the laughter. "Nowhere, I've told you." The words slipped like honey from my throat, hiding my laughter in them. "I only found these herbs during my time slot this morning." I pointed to my pouch, which one of the guards still held aloft. "Besides, your man earlier should have already told you that," I smarted.

Sir Thick-a-Lot got up in my face. "Who do you think you are?"

"I'm no one. Never have been," I replied. I was getting tired of these guys already and just wanted to get back home to eat breakfast before I had to get to my master's, I mean work. It was always the same old, same old topic with the guards, and I hated every minute they took away from my life.

My head quickly jerked to the side as his thick hand landed on my cheek. I could feel the burn and sting of his strike as I rolled my head around again. I bit my lip. I could already feel the swelling. My hood fell to my shoulders as my eyes met his. He smirked at me.

"You think you're important, don't you? Well, you're not," I could hear the guards muttering to themselves as they watched the interaction between Sir Thick-a-Lot and me. The murmurs echoed as Sir Thick-a-lot's breath blew hot and heavy in my face.

"Do you want to lose your place? Mutant? You are no one, and you better learn to listen to those that control you." His words echoed in my head. "Or maybe some more time in the barrack would better suit you."

Those that control you... I fumed, You will never control me, you bastard! Breathing deeply, I tried to avoid breathing the disgusting air from Sir Thick-a-Lot and calm myself before responding. The threat of the barracks was precisely what I needed to remind me that I wasn't doing this alone and that my actions had consequences.

Consequences that affected more than just me.

Minutely, I nodded my head in "understanding" to get him out of my face, although my throat burned with words that I knew I could never say.

Conrad stood to his right side, shadowing the guard, as he held my crossbow out for me to grab.

"Now, mutant, you are going to go home and be a good girl, or you will lose your place the next time you speak out against a guard."

Pushing me backward, Sir Thick-a-Lot stepped away from me. I stepped around him, trying to appear placid to avoid causing Mom and Dad any harm, not to mention the girls or Nick. Even though I desperately wanted to seek my vengeance against the idgit, I knew that the food was more important than his petty behavior. Keeping my family safe was more essential than striking the idiot down where he stood. My hunting knife was a sharp reminder that I could cause him some severe damage at any given time, but this moment was not that time.

Sauntering over to Conrad, I grabbed my bow out of his hands. He reached toward me, as though he was trying to find a way to apologize for the harsh treatment I'd received, but I brushed him off. He could have done something earlier. It reminded me that no one wanted anything to do with me anymore. His brown eyes looked at mine; shadows of rejection and failure flashed in them.

Steeling myself against those eyes, I pushed around him, "Whatever."

Grabbing the rest of my belongings, I stomped away from the group of guards, heading to a small clearing, and tried to gather myself before entering the village. There were a few empty houses out this way, places for the guards to rest I had always assumed, but people would sometimes hide out in one of the houses for thorough gossip to spread. I could barely remember if anyone had lived in these houses when we first came to the settlement. I glanced around quickly to make sure no one was there before pulling my hair back into a ponytail and putting my hood up before rearranging my gear again. I didn't need any trouble when I reached the marketplace, and hopefully, no one had caught the incident with the guard just then. A flash of gray passed my eye, and I swore internally.

Damn guards always cause trouble. Now I'll have to deal with the single-minded idgits in the marketplace. Someone had been watching, but I could only hope I got out of the marketplace before they spread anything to the vendors.

Taking a deep breath, I strode into the marketplace of the small village, where I could already see it was bustling. It wasn't much after nine in the morning, but the vendors were already out setting up their booths, and the early risers were promenading around the streets, heading from one vendor to another. As I mingled with the crowd, I kept my distance to avoid any unwanted attention.

My home was on the other side of the marketplace, past the collection of broken and rotten buildings that the government called our homes in this disgusting settlement. Some areas, several stories high, where the unmarried youths who were no longer eligible to live with their parents were considered apartments. They were nothing more than a hovel.

Yet, the people who served the government in a military position received better treatment than any one of us. Their homes were closer to the dome and the farms providing food. They received the freshest foods, while the rest got the scraps. No one was treated fairly if they didn't have a connection. Especially those of us who suffered from the radiation and tragedy of the nuclear bombings almost ten years ago. We were the lowest of the low.

It all disgusted me so much, and yet, there was nothing that I could do about it. I was still a kid. I had another year left before they would force me into the apartments and away from my family.

The lullaby began to dance through my head as I thought of the atrocities that we, that I, had been forced to suffer through.

I hated every minute I had to stand in the village's marketplace. So, I tried to focus on getting home without worrying about haggling with anyone for the meager possession of herbs I had acquired during my hunt. I will deal with that later. My stomach rumbled, reminding me why I wanted to get home so quickly. I was starving.

As I walked, I did catch a glimpse of the bulky frame of Joaquin in the crowd; however, he had enough haggling going on around him that I would happily go see him without everyone else watching me.

Other hunters were trying to bargain for household essentials and food with the meager food provisions we could bring into the village. I was glad not to join them in their haggling at this moment.

I draped my cloak over the handle of my knife, pulling it tight against my leg, as I forged a path through the thickest crowd around me. The person who observed the interaction with the guards must have already started talking about what they believed they knew, as the villagers' eyes began to trace my motions through the square.

I sighed; it was already hard enough trying to get around the marketplace without bringing attention to my oddities, without being talked about. The few stares I could endure came from the surrounding merchants, burned through my heavy cloak, and flushed my cheeks. I cursed mentally. I was so tired of being put on display, of being the person that they degraded throughout the settlement because I was different from most of the other people within. Putting my head down, I tried to hurry through the marketplace to the edge of the town square, where I could distinguish the crowds that started to thin out.

Glancing through my bangs and around the edge of my hood, I looked at some crumbling buildings instead of focusing on the death glare I discerned from some stares focused on me.

I paused mid-step as I regrouped my thoughts. Do I want to ignore the opportunity to speak with Joaquin for a trade?

Turning slightly, I glanced back at the sturdy frame of the only merchant who would deal with me. He had always been decent with me in the past, although things had started to change with his bargains. I felt he wanted something more out of the deal than I was willing to trade. I touched the rough hide from my pouch, filled with sage and thyme, and wondered if anyone else would be willing to deal with me for such valuable herbs.

Nah, it wasn't worth it. The stares were enough without adding his odd behavior into the mix. I decided and shook my head; I started up again. Nope, I decided firmly that there might be someone else who is willing to trade fairly with me. Simply from the stupid radiation that I was exposed to as a child, everything was so much more. It was toilsome, regardless of which way I went.

I pulled my crossbow firmly across my midsection, reciting

my oversized shirt and cloak tense against my skin and the bowstring. Glancing around me, I noticed the stares of some older women nearby. My cheeks burned as I glanced down; I should be used to the eyes trailing me by now. It didn't do me any good to yell at them; it would only cause them to go get the guards, and I couldn't afford another barrack trip.

Hurrying my steps, I finally reached the outskirts of the marketplace, where the crowd was almost non-existent. Sighing, I finally relaxed my muscles and shrugged some tension out of my shoulders. I peered through my bangs again as I tried to determine the best route home, the one with fewer interactions, and finally turned left and headed towards my home.

II

Dom

Three

I watched as she walked around the grounds, gathering the herbs, before spotting the rabbit. Her ebony hair was a family trait, and tracing her when she had her hood down was a lot easier. Watching her with my cloak caused a variety of feelings within me. Sadness and joy were the most prominent.

This wasn't the first time that I'd watched over her while she hunted. She needed the protection, even if she didn't know it. She was careful in the settlement; I'd seen her be cautious with the vendors and how she changed her route every few days. It took a while for me to get to know all of them, but she still had a pattern. One that I was convinced that someone else had noticed. I wanted to protect her and them all, but ultimately this was a lot safer than where I had spent the last five years.

As the rabbit took flight, I watched her stomping to the bolt. It wasn't too close to me, but I still moved and tried to maintain the mandatory distance I had promised to keep while she was within the complex. The rabbit's shadow floated along the ground as it moved away from her field of range.

I chuckled. This wasn't the first time that she had missed

her prey. She was always a comedy when upset, but she was always something to watch. I watched as she fiddled with the crossbow, her knees in the tall dry grass, trying to adjust the strings or something else.

The clapping was unexpected, and I searched for the noise source. There he was. *How the hell did he get down here? I thought he never left the mountains.* A sense of dread filled me. If he had come down, then something was about to happen. I could feel it in my bones.

She said something to him as she sat there. Then, she stood up and shook out the rest of the weeds and grass that filled her clothing. But her words fell deafly as he took flight and disappeared as he had never been there. I burned with the injustice of it all. *How fair was it that he could leave, yet Lizzy had to remain there?* She glanced around for him before she finished her morning routine.

I wished more than anything to know how to use a crossbow. I would have shot him out of the sky, but I'd never learned how to use the crossbow; I was more adept with a gun, any gun, as long as I kept aware of my surroundings. But a weapon was telling, and I couldn't tell her I was out here. It might do more harm than good.

I watched silently as she collected her scattered gear from the ground. Picking up her herbs, my eyes scanned the surrounding horizon, ensuring it was still safe for her. It would be unlikely for her to be unaware of her surroundings, even though I was pretty confident that she was paying more attention than I assumed she was. Yet, I still swore internally as I watched her take her time with each little item that was strewn about.

God, MB, hurry and finish. You are being much too slow. You'd swear you were still ten years old.

I lowered myself to the ground, my arms hurting from holding myself above the fence, and landed on a stick. The resounding noise hit her ears as I heard her arrow sliding into the cradle of the bow. Fuck.

I stood still until she finally relaxed, finished picking up, and turned towards the broken buildings and the large glass dome that dominated the small settlement.

She sighed heavily; I could hear each little noise as her chest rose and fell with each deep breath; it penetrated the air, dead silence otherwise unbroken. I could imagine each action as the sounds reached me; I didn't dare try to stand against the fence again. I could see her going through the motions, just as I remembered her and her routine from when we used to go hunting together a long time ago.

Not only that but as I finally peeked over the top, not too much; there wasn't enough time before someone would be coming to the side I was at. My head was barely visible above the fence, with my fingertips white against the weathered boards. Just as she started to walk towards the perimeter fence, her head whipped around as though she was scanning the fencing that I stood behind. *Damn, she had been checking her surroundings.*

Moving quickly, my head disappeared behind one of the larger poles of the fence by the time her gaze reached the spot where I had stood. I held my breath and counted to thirty before peering through a hole in the wooden plank. She was nowhere near where she had been, and I swore again. Grabbing my bag from the ground, I rushed along the outer perimeter to catch up to where she was.

III

Mary Beth

Four

I watched as the paint peeled from the rafters as each house deteriorated before me. Our house wasn't much better, but it was two stories and kept us as safe as possible. My route had taken me along the backsides of the buildings surrounding our home, so I neared the kitchen instead of the front door, just as I'd intended.

Through the cracked walls and broken windows of the building, I could hear the scraping of dishes in the sink. I sighed; I guess I wasn't as quick as I wanted. But then again, I had given up once the damn rabbit took off. I could have been much later, and having the guards try to shake me down when I got back didn't help much, either. I wondered what leftovers might still be available as I put my hand on the doorknob.

Heaving the door open, the only solid thing in our entire building, or so it seemed, I entered the kitchen. The sounds of dishes hitting each other in the water abruptly stopped as I stepped on the stained, cracked linoleum. Expectant purple eyes glanced up at me from my mom's short, wiry frame at the edge of the sink. Her five-foot-three was dainty compared to my five-foot-ten one, which was probably still growing, but who knows for sure. Her hands floated in the dirty dishwater of the sink as she continued to gaze at me with hope shining brightly in her eyes. Furthermore, her eyes were so bright; maybe it was just today that they seemed much more colorful than ever.

I know she didn't mean for me to feel like I had to take care of the family. None of them did. But I still wanted to make things better for us. I felt like it was my duty. I felt like I was the reason or one of the reasons that we struggled so badly. I knew my bumps had made it hard on the family since they started appearing about a year and a half ago. That's when the food began to "unfortunately" become more burdensome to produce, and since we had such a large family, we had been hit the hardest by the food shortage.

My eyes watered; I felt like such a failure. I turned away, trying to remain calm. Acid churned in my stomach, and I made a quick about-face away from where she could see me. I could see that the glimpse of the flickering light of hope within her eyes was withering before me.

Damn.

Gulping, I turned and pulled the crossbow over my shoulders and leaned it against the broken wall. The case was dark against the hallway door in the kitchen. After I balanced it perfectly against the shattered remains of the wall, I began to pull my pouch over my head. The heady scent of thyme and sage mixed and brought me peace before I heard her footsteps echo on the linoleum floor. She was never one to quit, and I guess that's where I got it from. I pulled at the pouch and held it in one of my hands.

With a sigh, I waited for her to come closer, and yet I still pulled my hood closer to my face; I didn't want anything to betray the mark of that brute's hand. It stung even after almost twenty minutes.

As one of my mom's slim hands landed on the bare skin of my shoulder, where my cloak and t-shirt had fallen off, the other reached around and pulled me towards her. Turning, I looked at the ground, and her hand finally pulled the hood away from my face.

"I wish you wouldn't hide your beautiful face, Mary Beth." Her warm tone filled me with peace. She cupped my cheeks tenderly, wiping the tears as they fell. My cheek stung, but her gentle care and love improved it a little. She said nothing as she looked at me; I could feel her eyes on me as I continued to look at the ground. Her following words ate at my soul, though, as she continued.

"But, I take it that today was unsuccessful." The pouch slid from my grip as the warm feeling of the tears continued to fall on my cheeks.

My shoulders heaved hard as I sought to control my breathing, the movement rocking her hands as I held in the wail of disappointment that became trapped in my throat. I tried so hard to fall in line, to be the perfect person, but I wasn't.

I didn't fight with the guards anymore because it cost too much. We had suffered that week with me in the barracks. I couldn't chance my temper getting the best of me and setting us into that predicament again.

I tried to grab the falling bag of herbs with shaking hands as the tears continued to stream down my face. My mom's hand grasped the pouch as it fell, and I tried to focus on the leathery hide, seeing the blotches of my tears staining the flap. Sniffling, I tried to calm myself and pull it together before anyone else came down the stairs.

Releasing the sob in a nervous sigh, I shook my head in the

affirmative. Her hand fell from my shoulder, and she joined her other hand in gripping my pouch. I had always been so good at reading people, especially those close to me, and I knew that even though she never really expected me to be perfect, she needed me to be in many ways. Guilt tore through my defenses as I watched her fight the disappointment and despair that swallowed her frame. Her hands fell limply to her sides; the pouch fluttered, herbs spilling all over the floor.

"Oh well," her voice tried to be nonchalant despite the emotional war in her eyes. We'll have to make do with the delivery this afternoon until your next catch."

She failed miserably at being nonchalant as the worry dripped through the spacing of her words. Stepping away from me, she turned back towards the pile of dishes that waited patiently by the sink.

"Mom," my words shook as I turned and reached for her hand. "Let's not waste them. We could still use them," I pointed at the spread of plants on the floor, "I'll go trade them later. Besides, I have another time slot tonight; I can take Nick with me."

"No," she said sharply as she faced me, pulling her hand away from mine. You will leave Nicholas alone; he is still too young to be out hunting those wild creatures."

What about me, Mom? I've been doing it since I was ten; how is Nick still too young? I ached to say the words aloud to her. I wanted her to acknowledge that I'd been so much more than a child for a long time.

She turned away from me and dipped her hands in the slimy, soapy water of the sink as she fished another dish out.

I took a deep breath, and I pulled myself together again. It would be better not to fall into this argument again with her;

it was always the same. "But, Mom…"

"But, Mom… what?" My dad's tenor tone echoed from the doorway of the hall. I jumped at his voice; his footsteps had faded into nothingness over the years and surprised me every time.

His dark hair, peppered with gray, stood out messily from his head as he tilted his head at me. Almost all of us kids had gotten his hair; only my twin sisters had favored Mom in the hair department; they were light brown. I smiled crookedly at him, glad to see him before a fight broke out between Mom and me.

"Dad!"

"Hey, kiddo. What are you doing? Huh, giving your mom a hard time already this morning?"

Teasingly, he pulled me towards him and under his arm. After he gave me a noogie, he planted a kiss on my forehead. "What's this?" He cupped my cheek gently, which forced me to show him the swelling redness of my face. "What happened?"

"Nothing, Dad." I snapped at him. I was thankful that he had noticed; at least someone had, but I knew what trouble it would cause. "Nothing at all happened except for Mom trying to keep Nicky from going hunting. Other than that, I'm not giving her or anyone around here a hard time, Dad."

Giggling forcibly, I replied. "Besides, how often do I have to tell you that I'm too old for you to keep doing that?" I had to get the conversation away from my face and towards a more neutral topic.

I tried to look disapprovingly at him, the playful one, which forced another smile onto my face. It was playful and sarcastic all in one shot. When I went hunting alone, I had perfected the art of deception regarding the guards' brutality.

"However…" I trailed off, "Maybe you can help me convince Mom that Nick's old enough to hunt with me. You both know I've been training him since he was nine. Besides the times that he's gone with you, of course."

Nodding, my dad's hazel eyes twinkled in the lazy light from the room's windows; he smiled at me.

"Well…" he glanced over at the silent frame of my mom, "He is turning twelve soon…"

I smiled as I watched my mom sigh in defeat. "Fine, but you better both be careful then." It was always so much easier when Dad joined in with the conversation. I swore that Mom and I clashed more lately than we had ever clashed in the past. I couldn't help but wonder if it was because I was getting older or if it was because she was worried that I would do the same thing as Dom.

Her purple eyes were cloudy, and there was never a time I wished I could remember her beautiful blue eyes. We had some pictures from my birth and their wedding with her eyes as blue, but something had happened to them, to all of us, when we got caught out in the city when the bombs landed.

"You know I will!" I replied, "I have always been careful when I go out hunting." Smiling, I tried to encourage her to trust in me as I took another step toward a more adult role. "And we will bring something home, too, I am sure of it!"

"You're just as stubborn as your old man," she tried to say sternly, her smile still on her lips. I couldn't stop you when you were ten; I tried every day."

Yeah, Mom, you did, at least for a little while. But Dom had taken off before that, so what should I do? I thought I had to do something because you and Dad were so broken by him leaving.

The pattering feet echoed around the tiny kitchen room as the feet pranced around the hallways. Turning my body sideways in my dad's embrace, I watched as the twins rounded the corner in what, I assumed, was in front of Nicholas.

"I'm going to get you!" He screeched at them from somewhere further away while they giggled, running towards where Dad and I stood.

The girls circled us, pulling the long sides of my cloak around them, hiding underneath from their big brother. I gazed lovingly down at my twin sisters, Eliza and Morgana, and their precious hazel eyes as Nick finally busted through the doorway.

Crashing into our group, mainly Dad, Nick wickedly smiled at me before backing up. His glasses lay crooked on his face.

"Eliza... Morgana..." His changing voice warbled.

The girls giggled under my cape as they huddled close to me while Dad stepped away from our growing group. Nick untangled himself from Dad, who then walked toward Mom. Nick's smile slid across his face deviously as he inched closer to me. A finger to his lips as a request for silence from me was all I received in greeting this morning. Dad circled her waist as she stopped to watch us play.

"Gotcha!" He yelled winsomely as he hugged the three of us tightly. I gasped playfully, pretending to be winded by his strength.

"Ni...ck...y..." His name slid out extendedly. He released his hold a little, worried that he had hurt me, and that's when I struck! With the hold on my arms loosened, I reached around his waist and started tickling him.

"Come on, girls... Help me out!" I called.

The girls giggled as they joined in on the tickle fest I had begun. His laughter soon joined the girls' giggles as he fell to the floor. Jumping on him, the girls continued their assault on their big brother. I slowed my tickling hands as I let the girls take over for me. I watched the attack as I stepped backward before anyone could reach me.

Mom's and Dad's laughter joined mine as we laughed with them as the tickle battle continued. The kitchen was peaceful and happy, watching as Nick received the assault of a lifetime from our little sisters, as though my failure this morning had never happened.

My stomach gurgled loudly, loud enough for Mom and Dad to hear it, as she slid a plate towards me. The girls continued their assault on Nicky as I chewed on the toast that was left for me. The crumbs fell to the ground as we enjoyed our time as a family. There wasn't much time left until we had to separate for the day.

Five

Boom! Boom!

The noise of someone banging at our door vibrated throughout the house. Everything had been fine until that sound interrupted our precious family moment. Everyone's laughter disappeared in synchronization, and our heads swiveled down the hallway.

"I'll get it," I said, dropping the remainder of my toast, and pulled my hood up again. It was my safety net, my feet dancing around the tangled mess of my siblings on the floor.

"Mary Beth," my mom's voice traveled with me warningly as I walked through the doorway and headed down the hall. It was always like she didn't trust me to be polite to company whenever we would have it, and it annoyed me to no end. However, I waved back at her, telling her that I was fine and that she was okay to continue cleaning the dishes from last night as Dad stepped away to gather provisions for his day at work.

Bang! Boom!

The pounding of the door was a heavy sound that continued to echo throughout the house as I walked through the hallway toward the living room. I'd already been here once today, and once again, I wished we had finer things. But there were countless families like ours. Everyone had lost so much. There were hundreds around in the state, at least that is what we were told, yet this is where we ended up. Almost everything that we had owned was gone after the bombings; we were lucky enough that Dad had managed to salvage what we had.

The knocking persisted, so I yelled, "Hold on, I'm almost there." Under my breath, I added, "If it was such a damn big deal, then why didn't you come around to the kitchen like a normal person?"

I stopped quickly in front of a broken mirror and looked at my reflection. The handprint did not stick out as much as I thought it did initially, but the turquoise tone of the bumps was even brighter as they stood out sharply against the slightly inflamed skin. The bright blue eyes that reflected at me were stony as I wondered who could knock at our door this early in the day. Few people would come to the front door and continue to pound on the door when a normal person, any of our neighbors, would go around to the kitchen. It was often where we hung out before the day began. I think a lot of the families on our block did that.

Yet recently, I noticed that we didn't have many visitors to our home. I had begun to blame myself for this. There were only so many reasons that a person would stop calling on another family, and it was usually one of two things: either there was a fight between the families or something else made the person uncomfortable when they visited.

I wished people would simply realize I'm still the same as I have always been...

Walking away from the mirror, I pulled my hood tighter to my face as I reached for the door handle.

Opening the door, my face fell to the floor, becoming an object instead of a person for the visitor entering our home. It was my automatic response. I just knew that they wouldn't even acknowledge me otherwise. We were no longer considered "human" or "normal" if anyone looked at our faces; this was something that I had noticed happened a lot to other people and that the radiation had changed. I'd seen it in action at the marketplace, the school, and even my job because we weren't the same as the rest of society.

"Can I help you?" I asked, my head still in the subservient position. It was awkward; I should have felt free to answer the door and be myself, but I wanted to make people comfortable so that they would continue to visit Mom and Dad. I didn't want them to get lonely.

"Yeah, take this…" the deep voice of General Barnes demanded while pushing a heavy cardboard box into my body. My body swayed with its weight as he pushed me aside with it, coming inside the house.

Quickly, I pulled my arms around the box before it fell. Steadying the box and trying to control my emotions, I told the general to head to the kitchen, where everyone was. Looking over the rim of the box at the dark features of the general, I watched as he nodded curtly and sharply turned towards the hallway. It wasn't his first time in the house; he had been here several times. Including the day that Mom and Dad had to pay to get me out of the barracks for fighting with the guard upon my re-entry into the settlement after the hunt. I'd almost lost my crossbow that day. Kicking the door shut behind me with one of my feet, I tried to shift and balance everything as I pushed the door firmly shut with my butt. The box was heavy, and I was tempted to put it down but then realized what it was, so I continued to carry it as I moved towards the kitchen.

"Good morning, Mr. and Mrs. Johnson," intoned the general as he came to attention in the kitchen doorway, causing me to collide with a wall as I turned, doing my best to stop before hitting him.

"Ow!" I muttered. My foot pounded from the collision. "Sorry." *#Sorrynotsorry*, as Dom used to say, I wasn't… What was the bright idea of stopping in the middle of the hallway?

"Oh, Casey!" my mom exclaimed. Please, please, come in and take a seat."

The general walked further into the room, and I could see Mom giving Nick the stink eye as he quickly vacated his seat and stood behind the girls. She wavered between the sink full of dirty dishes and showed the general the empty chair.

I growled under my breath; I hated how they catered to him. *He was pompous and so rude! Besides, he was never friendly enough to call them by their given names; why should they call him by his?* I didn't understand why they acted this way with him.

Dragging myself away from the distracting thoughts that poured into my mind as I gazed at the scene over the edge of the box, I tried to rearrange the box in my arms. Quickly, I walked around his timber frame and placed the box on the empty counter space before my grip on the sides of it failed me.

"Thank you very much, ma'am. I don't have much time for idle chitchat today; however, I did bring your food supplies for the week." His Yankee tone, something my dad often called the inflection of his voice, seemed to be spoken softly, but the greens of his eyes were tricky as gems. "As you can see, there isn't the normal amount that your family would get," he stated as he gestured toward the box I had just put down. "I try very hard to always be open and honest with y'all, so I stopped by. I fear that I have some bad news for your family."

Mom gasped as he finished, and I rushed to her side and held onto her arm as she wobbled. *What bad news could he bring this time?* He was always the one that came to our family with bad news. First, when Dom had run off. Then, Mom and Dad had told me that he informed them of my arrest and imprisonment in the barracks, and now this... What would it be this time?

"What is it?" Dad echoed my thoughts as he stood from his spot at the table; the remains of his breakfast sat at the vacated spot at the table as he walked over to the provision box. It was heavy, that was true, but the general was right... It wasn't as heavy as it usually was.

Moving my arm, I wrapped it around Mom's shoulders as I squeezed her from the side. We may have differences, but she was my mom, and I loved her dearly. On the other side of the room, my dad squared off with the general, who now stood slightly behind where my dad had been sitting at the table. I thought he'd only done that once before as I watched the general give him his full attention. Dad was not a very confrontational person, and yet, for his family, he would do anything that I knew.

The general's emerald eyes hardened into an even darker green, like a gemstone within his eyes; his square-jawed face showed so much weathering. I watched as the general's lips became slits as he squared up. By the stormy look in his eyes and the hardened features of his mocha skin, I could tell that his news would probably devastate my family. Was there anything that this man couldn't destroy? He was an absolute terror, an evil that was bound and determined to make my family as miserable as could be. Why was he so determined to destroy us? We had nothing to do with his past. It had affected us as much as it had affected him. He needed to let it go. The lullaby began to pulse through my head, a gentle humming, a reminder that I needed to remain calm. If I let my emotions cloud my judgment now, I would never know why he came.

"As you may have noticed, Michael," I gasped as my dad's name rolled off his tongue; this was something big. He never called my parents by their given names: "The dome has become overwhelmed by the demands of the settlement's increasing population. There is no way that the workers in the dome, as well as the limited materials that the government sends us monthly, can meet the needs of the people. As a worker in the dome, you must have noticed this."

He paused as my dad nodded his head in agreement.

"The settlement council recently met regarding the overwhelming demands of the people, and some tough decisions were made. As you may know, the materials are not coming as often as in previous years. As well as the increasing population, the council decided that we would have to cut back the number of provisions that the larger families in the settlement received. I've already delivered this news to several of the families in the settlement, and some have decided to modify their rations to support their families. However, several families have made a tougher decision."

His eyes landed on me as his words settled heavily in the air. I turned away, heat flushing my face. In times like this,

I wished that I didn't have any mutations or issues and was like everyone else in the settlement; then maybe I wouldn't get the attention.

At that moment, I truly felt that he had picked our family for many reasons. Our history with General Barnes was filled with pockmarks. I just wasn't sure what the issue was, but we were often one of the first families to receive bad news. Compared to the other kids I had gone to school with, we frequently got more bad news than most. As for tough decisions, we only had two. I could leave our family and live in the apartments, barely making it alone, or I could go. Those were the only options that were ever available. *It would be me, or it would be my mom?* Dad was too important as a worker to be forced to leave, and they wouldn't let Mom live alone. *Fuck.* This was not how I imagined this morning going. I was being forced to decide because I knew, internally, that neither Mom nor Dad could make that kind of decision without some significant emotional crisis.

I could feel Mom shaking in my arms, like a leaf left in the turbulent winds of the hurricane his words caused. *Double fuck.*

I held on to her tighter, trying to ease her shakiness until we could talk about what we would do. *What would I do?*

I knew what I had to do. I already had a plan in my mind that they would never agree to. But as I glanced at the thin frame of the girls sitting at the table with Nick standing behind them, my plan thickened in strength on what was needed. Despite my unwillingness to leave our family alone, I would do anything to ensure they were safe. That had always been my goal and would always continue to be my goal for my family.

Meanwhile, Nick had covered the girls' ears with his hands and pressed them against each other to avoid hearing anything potentially threatening from the conversation, and I smiled inwardly at his attention to detail with the General in the room. He knew it was something big, and, being wise beyond his age, he knew that if the girls heard and understood, we would have significant tantrums.

Dad strutted over to him, gasping, as he said, "You cannot expect a family to…" His words trailed off, and his eyes clouded as he stood before the general. He seemed lost in a haze of red, not noticing how the girls watched his every move. Their eyes trailed after him. He was bowing up, anger etched lines across his weather-beaten face, his hazel eyes darkened with the intensity of his emotions.

The general cleared his throat; the air in the room had thickened with his announcement of the council's decision.

"Of course, the decision is yours to make. However, if you decide to make such a decision, and one of you decides to leave this settlement… Well, there is the Leaving Ceremony…"

His words dropped like acid on the broken tile floor. I watched Dad's fists clenched and unclenched at every word he uttered. He looked so mad that he could have punched him. I was hoping to see Dad do it. The jerk deserved it! Maybe I was biased, but whenever I had to interact with him, he managed to piss me off.

A cry of despair escaped my mom's lips, pulling my attention away, as her tiny frame started to sink to the ground as though an anchor was pulling her down.

"There will be no such thing!" I could hear Dad exclaiming, "No one in this family is leaving! Now, get out before I throw you out."

I held Mom's frame together and slowed her as we sank to the floor together. I glared at the general, daring him with darkened eyes to say another devastating word to my family.

My dad's hands clenched tightly; his expression looked like the occasional wicked rainstorms pouring down on our village. The general excused himself as he stepped around Dad; the heat of my glare and the deadly look on my dad's face must have hurried his parting words. He quickly marched back out of the kitchen door, using the rear entrance that I had initially come in through. The more sensible route.

I rocked with my mom as her body released racking sobs; the sounds of anguish escaped from her choked throat. My dad glared at the nothingness behind the table, glaring into it as though the General was still standing there. Nick had pressed the girls' faces into his stomach, and tears ran streaming down his face, steaming up his glasses, as he watched Mom and me on the floor. Our morning had been turned upside down, and now I had to be the adult again while trying my best to keep my emotional roller coaster in check.

I continued to rock her body, both seeking and giving comfort while trying to think of how I was going to pull this family together… and how I was going to tear it apart by doing the appropriate thing.

I felt the hot wetness of tears fall on my cheeks as Dad continued to stand knocked for six, one hand clenching and unclenching on his sides, as he tried to control his emotions. Mom's cries echoed in my head, even as she was sheltered within my arms, as the anguished noises faded into nothing. Meanwhile, the lullaby continued to play in my mind, a constant reminder that I had the strength within me that made me into a stronger person because of what this woman had given up and done for me as a child.

Even with such intense emotional outbursts from my family, I knew the general's suggestion had merit. I was seriously considering it. I'd seen other families do it, although it was usually the oldest person who left to give the rest of the family a chance. There were a couple of kids who ended up being adopted by other families because they lost their parents to the demands of the settlement. Every so often, when the kids looked normal and had a functional job within the settlement, they could separate and have their places, but I knew that wasn't an option for me. I had to figure out something. Otherwise, Mom and Dad would start cutting back on their portions. *They'd get sick and die, then where would we be?* I know they had done it multiple times when the hunting wasn't going well or if there was a food shortage. It wasn't a long-term solution, though.

The idea also troubled me deeply as I thought of the many people we had watched leave through the gates into the wastelands of Colorado. The leaving ceremony was always this big deal, and everyone celebrated, and it was like a party, well, without the food. I'd heard rumors that other times, people left as well. Times that they didn't make into public knowledge. Yet, we had never seen anyone who had left the gates after their departure, and I was sure this thought had also crossed my parents' minds. Maybe that is what troubled me so much about leaving. *Would my idea be possible if I went through those gates? Was there any hope? I didn't know.*

However, in my heart, I knew that rationing our food would be a greater evil than someone leaving. Everyone didn't realize I intended to go; this was my calling. I had to do this to protect our family. I'd find a way to make it work, and then I would. Even though I knew it was for the best, my heart was breaking, and it would be a massive fight when I told Mom and Dad.

Six

Moments, *no years*, passed by in silence; only the sniffling of Mom's tears broke through the tormented room before I started to gain some sense of necessity.

Nick, my precious brother, protected our sisters with sweet words of nothingness whispered into their ears as he rocked them in his arms on the floor across from me. I watched as their trembling bodies lessened and slowly steadied. Nick's jade-green eyes wandered over to us; the questions in his mind were burning through the lens of his glasses. I knew he wanted to be involved in the decision, but it would have to wait until the girls were at school or occupied.

Just wait, I mouthed to him, gesturing towards the girls with my head. *Can you take care of them for a little while? Maybe get them out of here*, I gestured towards the door with a jerk of my head, *play with them or something, please?*

He nodded dimly, jerking his head towards Dad. *What about him?* He mouthed. Our system of talking to each other never involved any spoken words.

Don't worry about them now; I'll take care of it. I mouthed back, gesturing towards the small frame of our mother that still resided in my arms.

I gave him the evil eye even while my eyes were still wet; he knew what to do. This was one of those moments that I couldn't be happier that we had learned to lip-read when we were younger. Otherwise, this would have been a painful experience attempting to talk while keeping Mom and Dad out of it.

Our parents were frozen in shock, and I needed my nosy little brother to take the girls away. I would take the general up on his offer, but they wouldn't accept it. That's why I needed Nick and the girls out. They didn't need to see our fight, *and boy, it was going to be a fight.*

He nodded again; his eyes burned holes through mine as he gently pulled the girls from the kitchen towards the hallway. Sighing inwardly, I knew that I would have more questions to answer when I went to find them afterward, but I was thankful he didn't try to lead them around Mom's broken form that still resided in my arms.

Her tears had slowed, and the racking sobs had softened over the time it took for Nick to disappear out the front door with the girls on his heels. I smiled softly as I heard the door shut behind them, glancing up at the still form of my father, his hand still balling up and releasing as he stared into the blank area of the kitchen.

At least he got them out of here, I thought, trying to be positive as the thought ran through my head. The lullaby was already fading, and my smile disappeared.

The soft melody of the lullaby eased some of my anxiety throughout the encounter with General Barnes and helped me fight the overwhelming worry that still existed about the situation and my role in it.

I shook my head, pulling the thoughts and ideas together

before I tried to speak them out loud to my parents. I knew the Leaving Ceremony was still several days away, and I began to plan my way of joining them the next time it was allowed so that we all got some closure from it, as I untangled myself from Mom. That is if I could convince them that it was the best plan. The settlement always had one Leaving Ceremony monthly to allow families to say goodbye correctly. If I couldn't convince them to do it that way, I would have to resort to other means that would be more painful for everyone involved, but I would do it for the greater good of our family.

Once I could sit on my knees, I started to pull her up alongside me. Dad's soft breathing was my only clue that he had not passed out in his spot and was slowly, but indeed, calming down. Meanwhile, his eyes were still glued to the space by the table.

As mom stood up with me, I gently walked her over to the table and into a chair. Her head fell into her arms as she rested on the chair. The tears had abated, but the silent sobs still racked her shoulders as she sat there. I was thankful for the little things. We were off the floor, and she wasn't making those anguishing sounds as she had been.

Seeing her tiny frame shaking the table but still standing, I rushed to Dad's side to bring him back to the present.

"Dad?" I paused, waiting for his answer. "Dad?"

When he continued to stare blankly, I used the only word I knew would bring him back around. "Daddy?" I hadn't called him daddy since the day that Dom left us. That's when I had to grow up and be more than just a child.

The whispered word shook his frame as his eyes finally released the air, seeking my eyes beneath him.

"Daddy, we need to talk about this. Are you going to be able to do it? Do you need time?"

I grabbed his hand. Worry outlined his face as he moved his eyes past me to see Mom shaking the small table.

"Where is everyone?"

"Nicky took the girls out. We need to talk."

He nodded, agreeing that the conversation was necessary, but probably more along the lines of him telling me not to worry about it. That was his automatic response whenever there was an issue that he didn't want me to worry about. But I did.

I was pretty sure he had no idea what I was about to drop on him.

I watched as he brought his chair around to straddle Mom's shaking form. He wrapped his arms around her, laying his head on her back. I watched as he whispered to her, her shaking form quieting as his words registered in her mind. Her head tipped up and turned, and she glanced up at him, her eyes filled with unshed tears. She nodded as she straightened and rested her head against his shoulder.

Once they were settled, it was like all of my nerves went into overdrive. I began to pace the floor, a million words and thoughts running through my mind, as I waited for them to completely calm down. I wasn't much calmer than them, but I was determined to make them see my point. I may only have been over seventeen years old, but I was a tornado ready to blow through this conversation.

I tried to think of which approach would make them stop and see that any other alternative would harm the girls and us more than if I... Well, I couldn't even think of the words without grimacing. It wasn't like I wanted to leave; I swallowed hard as the word settled in my brain: my family.

The settlement I would happily leave behind and never even think of again, but my family was all I had.

The girls' hazel eyes flashed in my mind; I saw them grow so slowly and malnourished with even more rationed food than we currently possessed, and the thought was horrifying. They would wilt away! I thought, biting my lip. Or worse, if one of them left or if they both lowered their portions, we would eventually be without a parent. I couldn't have my siblings live that way.

I searched for the right words until I heard Dad clear his throat, warning me that he was slowly losing patience with my pacing. Mom's sob had stopped during my lost time in thought, and she sat with her head on his shoulder, staring at my moving frame. I tried to stop my wandering feet, but I felt helpless, hopeless that they would not listen to my words.

"Stop, Mary Beth." His authoritative tone and the touch of his hand halted me in my tracks as I passed by their chairs.

I glanced at him, not at them, and a shock went through my body. This would be one of the last times I would see them. I didn't want to remember them with such harsh features on their face, so I slowly sat down at the table facing them.

The looks on their faces, the worrisome features on my mom's face, and my dad's determined glare made me wonder if they had an idea of what I was planning or the reasons behind my pacing. Doubt began to creep in.

"Daddy…"

"Don't daddy me, Mary Beth. You look like you are thinking of something awful. Just awful. Whatever it is you are thinking of doing, don't. Absolutely not!"

"But… but… Daddy…" I tried to edge my thoughts in.

"Mary Beth, do you remember the pain we all went through when Dominic went missing? Do you want to send Nicholas, the girls, and us through that again?"

Damn. I thought, how can I be so transparent? The black hair and jade eyes of a maturing young man flashed behind my eyes. Even though it had been almost six years since he left us, since I last saw him, his absence was a hole in all our hearts. I strengthened my will, resolving to change their minds. Pushing thoughts of Dom away, I cleared my throat to try again.

"Daddy," I continued to use the term I had grown out of years ago, trying to soften his heart, "can't you see that Eliza and Ana are starting to wilt away? There isn't enough food in the house for all of us. We must consider all the options that the General gave us. Even if…"

He glowered at me, halting the words as they left my lips. Tears started to gather again in the red rims of Mom's eyes. It was obvious that they were already thinking of the different options and weren't happy with any of them. They surely didn't want to hear about them coming from a seventeen-year-old's mouth.

I thought this wouldn't work; maybe I'll have to be more covert about it. I will have to do much more work to figure it out without them knowing unless they are willing to start listening.

So, I cleared my throat and tried again, "Daddy, there haven't been as many animals coming into the boundary walls lately. We're starting to suffer from this dingy area the government gave us. Besides, Nick can do much of the hunting now since you said he could come with me tonight. You said he was getting old enough. Besides, he is getting to be as good as I am about spotting the animals, and he almost always hits his mark." I rushed through my words, being that tornado that I always thought I was, almost stumbling over them to get them out before I was interrupted again.

"Stop! Stop, right there, Mary Beth Johnson." His voice was filled with anger. "Do you want to kill your mom and me with worry? Do you want to go out there and die? This conversation ends now!" His words echoed off the walls as his fist slammed into the table.

Mom and I jumped; the table wobbled under the pressure of his fist hitting it so hard, and I swore I saw Mom swallow hard. I know that I did. My shoulders dropped, my head falling into my palms as my elbows met the tabletop. Under my hood, the loose strands of my ebony hair closed my face off from them as tears gathered in my eyes. This wasn't a good idea. I'll have to do it another way, a way that I didn't want to, but there was no other choice now; yet, I wasn't a quitter, so I had to try at least one more time.

Sniffling, I tried to think of how to convince them this was the right move. "Daddy, the general said…"

He stood up, gently removing Mom's head from his shoulder, before walking over to me.

His steps were no longer silent; instead, they sounded so menacing that he neared my chair with the footsteps echoing in the broken room around us. I glanced up from my hands to see his hazel irises as they stared down at me. My turquoise irises clashed with his as I tried to win the war that his eyes had started. His lip curled, and I shrank back, again dropping my eyes to my hands. Admitting defeat was never a strong suit of mine, and this issue was too strong to let go; as I opened my mouth to say something else, he interrupted me.

"You will help your brother watch your sisters until it is time for you to go to work and Nick and the girls to go to school. When it is time for everyone to leave, we will continue the day as normal. Do you understand me? This is a conversation for your mother and me."

I nodded my head mutely in agreement, anger burning my blood as I stood up and backed away from his presence. Without looking at him or Mom, I turned and fled through the hallway to the front door. I was so mad at being dismissed like that. Blood started pounding through my ears as I slowed down and stared into the mirror that I had used to check my appearance only minutes before.

As I neared the front door, I could hear his voice and Mom's muttering. "She doesn't..." and "questioning the General" were among the phrases that drifted to me. I could hear the chair scraping, and I could only assume he pulled it out to sit in.

I was tempted to stay there and listen to the words I could hear, but as I headed towards the torn but comfy blue cushions of the couch, Dad called out, "Mary Beth, I haven't heard the door open and close yet!"

Why won't they listen to me? Argh!! I wanted to scream.

I growled and stomped over to the door. Pulling it open with all my strength, it slammed against the faded wallpaper.

I yelled back, "This is stupid! You should trust me!"

I continued to stomp as I went through the doorway, and the dusty steps of our front porch greeted me. I shook my head in anger as I slammed the door shut behind me. I hated how they didn't trust me to make good decisions. I hated how they never allowed me to be an adult or listened to my opinion on anything!

Seven

'll do it anyway. I'll give you a reason not to trust me since you don't want to listen. Oh, I was so mad. I was angry enough and determined enough that as I stomped down the steps, I knew what I would do. The stifling air, a tornado of flickering particles, moved the dirt as my feet shattered them around the porch steps.

I just have to figure it all out before I do it. But I'll have to do it soon. Otherwise, I'll never get it done; something will get in the way. I mean, I've heard of them letting out people without the Leaving Ceremony, but it is usually people who have been put on trial for something. I wondered if I could get in with that group. This meant that I would have to be nice to someone on the guards to get in and do something about getting out.

I plopped down on the last step of our porch, pondering how I could get away without anyone noticing me. My head fell into my hands, and I started thinking of the time slots I was allowed to hunt; I wondered if it wouldn't be a good time for me to sneak away then. But I needed a distraction to get everything ready. A sinister smile widened on my face, my eyes lighting up with the thought of how I would get the distraction I needed, but would he do it? Would he possibly be willing to get into trouble to help our family?

Standing up, I turned back towards the house and started racing up the stairs. However, as I paused on the little porch of the house, I turned back and looked back at the settlement. Could I possibly get away with it? Was it even possible? Shaking my head, I couldn't let the negative doubts get to me now; I turned around and opened the door slightly.

"Dad, what about the herbs?" I called out to him in the house. I was thinking about work and how to use the herbs to prepare everything for my departure, but I still have something left to get for the house.

"Don't worry about it now," Dad shouted.

"Fine!" I yelled back, angry that he was shutting me down again and so quickly, too, as I slammed the door behind me again and headed back towards the hunting grounds. I was going to get Conrad to help me; he owed me for the bullshit he pulled this morning. We used to be friends, and now, as my friend, he would help me help my family.

I backtracked through the settlement, going every way but through the marketplace, even though that would have given me a straight line to the guards. I checked along the way for wandering guards, trying to see if I could find Conrad without having to go around all the assholes that do everything they can to make me feel insignificant.

Fate must have been on my side; as I rounded the next corner, I could see his trim frame leaning against the frame of one of the homes. I sighed with relief as I wandered closer to him, blending in as much as possible with the surroundings. As I came closer, I could hear him talking to someone.

"Yeah, I used to know her." His voice was rough around the edges. I wondered why it had gotten so haggard. "They said that I went too easy on her."

"Well, did you?" A girl's voice responded, and I slowed down. Who was he talking to?

"I might have been." He sighed, "I don't know. They ensured that I wouldn't ever go easier on her again." I saw a hand touch his cheek, swiping tenderly down the side.

Fuck, what did they do? Maybe he wouldn't help me, especially if the other guards were roughing him up because of what had happened between us. I stopped, sliding up to the side of a building behind them, something that wouldn't be easy for them to see me. I didn't want more trouble than necessary, and if he was agitated, I might get that trouble.

"You should report them," she said, interrupting my internal dialogue. I watched as her hand dropped to the side of his arm. "They should have never done that to you."

"It doesn't matter," he insisted, "They think all the mutants need to be destroyed. It's bad enough when the outsider groups attack the dome. But all the mutants within the settlement will put us in danger." The panic in his voice rose.

"What do you mean?" Her voice trembled. "We've always had the mutants here, even when the outbreak started showing. Don't you remember that?" Her voice was so familiar, I could almost place it, but it slipped away again as Conrad answered.

"Yeah, and how fast did they disappear? Even the girl that General Barnes was engaged to marry disappeared. If there are any signs of mutants, we are supposed to find a way to discourage them from staying. Those were my orders."

Elizabeth? What did she have to do with mutants? I know she and Dom had been close after we came here. I had always assumed that they ran away together after that day he got me into trouble. It was one of the reasons that I loved/hated him so much. That was the reason that I always assumed Barnes hated our family. I'm sure that Dom stole her away from him. I was getting distracted thinking about the past and missed an essential part of the conversation, as the next thing I heard was him telling the girl to be careful as she walked away.

Well, I thought, *here's my chance.* I popped out from my hidey-hole and walked towards Conrad, who still had his back to me.

"Hey, Conrad," I called out, trying to act casually. However, my act was not very good, as he quickly turned around and gave me the stink eye.

"What do you want, MB?" He asked. I smiled internally; at least he remembered my nickname. "I've already done enough for you today."

I felt like laughing. *What did he do?* I was tempted to ask him but had to focus on what I was there for. "Not really, you haven't. There is one more thing you could help me with."

"And why should I?" He demanded as he turned around and bowed up to me.

"Because it will get you in good with the other guards." I deadpanned him. He looked flabbergasted as I stopped in front of him.

"How do you think me helping you will get me in good with the other guards?" His eyebrows rose with shock as I stood confidently before him, hand on hip, letting my hood fall in the full glory of my mutations.

"Because you are going to get rid of me." I smiled. He looked at me questioningly but nodded slowly in agreement.

"Okay," he rubbed his neck slightly, "What's your plan?"

Eight

After talking with Conrad, I almost skipped as I headed down the empty lane of homes, where I knew Nick would take the girls to play. I hoped they were still there.

It was the only area in the whole settlement where the children usually went to play. The area used to be well taken care of. There was a playground in the center of the houses; now it was falling apart and more useful for games of hide-and-seek or tag.

The other kids would come out to play when it was later in the day; it wasn't quite time for school to start so that they would stay in as long as possible. They didn't like the murky mornings as I did, but then again, it was almost mid-morning. So, I walked along the rocky path toward the middle of the lane. They stopped mending the roads after the first year we moved to the settlement. I went back and forth between the broken sidewalks and the hard black pavement of the street. It wasn't like we used cars very much anymore. We didn't need to add pollution to our list of problems.

As I entered the empty lane of houses, the area was silent. I listened closely, and the crunching of dead leaves and pebbles, mixed with giggles, filled the air.

I smiled as the girls and Nick came into view. Instead of approaching them, I stood in the shadows and watched them momentarily, my shoulder propping against a wall. Nicky was a great brother to them and me, and I just hoped he would understand what I was asking of him. I sighed and thought of how similar this was to what Dom had done to me, yet there was a difference. I wouldn't be leaving them without something, a promise to return.

Nick stood in the center of the lane, his face crammed in the trunk of a dead tree with his hands twiddling behind his back. Eliza and Morgana stood to his right side as his voice started to count out numbers.

"One, two, three, four..."

The girls giggled again as they raced around the tree, trying to make as much noise as possible, so he didn't know exactly which way they were going. They split off when they spotted me. They glanced around me at the crumbling remains of houses on this lane before they looked at me for guidance.

"Five, six, seven, eight..." Nick continued to count.

I looked at my twin sisters and watched with amusement as they realized they would be caught unless they found a place to hide. Still too distracted to fully join in, I started pointing at random hiding spots around the buildings, but I was willing to help them out a bit. After considering several options (a darkened spot by a set of stairs, the corner of a building, and the overturned trash barrel at one residence), the girls separated.

The comedy of their antics was inspiring and helped release some tension I had been carrying. They scattered and tried to find a hiding spot before Nick stopped. I laughed silently as they flitted from place to place, unsure whether they would be safe.

"Nine... Ten... Ready or not, here I come!" Nick shouted as he jumped around.

I glanced out of the corner of my eyes to see that the girls had finally settled down by the darkened stairway, huddled together. Even though they had the chance to win apart from each other, they still stayed together. They were always better together than apart. The winds grew in velocity, almost malevolent, as Nick jumped around. It was going to be stormy today. I should remind them to get in before it rains. The rain was acidic, not horribly so, but enough that they would get a slight burn if they stayed outside in it long enough.

When I saw his gaze land on me, I smiled and winked at him, hoping to maintain the lightened mood. It was nice to see them playing together. I don't get to watch them as much now as I used to.

He glared at me through his glasses as he walked around to find the girls. *Damn,* I sighed; *he is going to hold it against me.* Nick continued to look around for the girls.

I reached out for him as he walked past, grabbing his arm as I slid to the ground. I didn't want to fight with him, but we needed to discuss whether I would make my plans work. I tried to beg him with my eyes to speak to me, but he just sighed as he pulled his arm away and turned toward the playground. "Eliza, Morgana..." he called out, "can you go see if Annabelle is free to play before school?"

The girls crawled out from their hiding spot and nodded their heads. They weren't giggling now, and I felt defeated. I had been trying for so long to keep them away from the terrors and worries that we faced. Now they were being forced to watch me beg for them to survive, even if they didn't know that. Fighting against the building winds, the girls smiled as their hair went wild.

"Sure, Nick..." Eliza agreed as she pulled on Morgana's hand, and they headed away. They stopped over where their bags lay on the ground. I could hear them whisper back and forth about Annabelle and how she was so lucky not to have older brothers or sisters.

Tears started to fall and glistened against my cheeks. My eyes followed the girls as they left. Then, I waited for Nick to acknowledge me again. His glasses slid down his nose, which was slightly crooked from some roughhousing we had done before, nothing that couldn't be fixed with a quick bend. Our bones weren't the strongest. I heard it had something to do with vitamin D.

I observed him pushing them up with a finger. I saw him deflate, his resentment easing over time, and what felt like hours—though it was probably only minutes—passed before Nick finally glanced over at me through those thick frames. My tears had dried on my cheeks.

"Get up, Mary Beth. Stop being such a drama llama mama."

I struggled onto my feet as Nick walked away from me. Wiping my face quickly, I tried to rub my tear-streaked face clean, as it gave me a chance to compose myself. After I took some deep breaths, I stood.

"Come on, let's go talk." He led the way, and if I wanted him to help me, I would have to let him feel in control for a while. It didn't mean he would control everything when I told him my plan.

I followed him at a slower pace as we walked away from the playground and toward the center of the settlement. I watched as the shadows of the houses followed us. It wasn't long before I figured out where he was taking me. We came to one of the empty doorways to the school building, or at least the house that we called the school building. It was probably an old warehouse or business; it was well-sized but not very personable.

It was still shadowy inside as Nick opened the door and motioned me inside. I shuddered as I entered the building.

I hated this place, and it certainly wouldn't have been where I took him to talk about what had happened this morning, but I wouldn't argue with him about that. It was private for the moment, which is all we needed.

Nine

"Nick," I exploded as we finally settled in a classroom; it had been building since we left the playground, "you heard the general. We either have someone leave or ration our food even more than we already do. He hates us!" My hands flew as we faced off in the tiny room. I could finally release my anger and frustration, which I had a lot of directed at him, Mom, Dad, and everyone. I just hated who I was because of everything.

"Stop," Nick interrupted me, "Mary Beth, just stop, okay? We both suspect that he blames us for what happened, but he hasn't done anything wrong to us. It's always from the council, remember? He said that the council made the decision."

"Who says he didn't influence their decision on what families needed to have their food rationed?" I grumbled, "I just can't bear to see Eliza and Morgana become any thinner. They are already so frail-looking as it is." We all suffered in some way from the environment, but it didn't mean I had to like it.

Nicky pushed the glasses up his nose again, turning around on the desk he had sat on and looking out the window.

I paused mid-step as I watched him. I tried to think of how to tell him my plan. I was the adult in this; I had been the provider in so many ways for so long. He was going to hear the truth, and he was going to have to accept it.

When Dom left, he was too young to honestly remember much of what happened… I couldn't just get up and disappear without someone knowing, someone to help me from the inside if I needed it. I turned and faced him, standing proudly. Despite my doubts, I needed to show him that I was strong enough to do this.

"What's the plan, Mary Beth?" He demanded, his temper flared and faltered. "Are you going to leave us with nothing? Like Dom did?" Nick challenged me. I knew he was brilliant, but he also knew my plans before I made them, which wasn't cool. I was so jelly that he could make everything come together without much information.

Yet, I stared at him, speechless. He was more worried about me than our little sisters… *Really?* My blood boiled as my anger and concern grew, but I ate my words as I took a deep breath. I had to be strong and mature, even though I didn't want to be.

He sat nearly off the side of the desk, his body facing me while his legs dangled over the ledge of the desk. I let him be agitated as I turned away from him and paved the floor.

"I'm going to sneak away tonight," I stated firmly, "and join the group leaving. I don't know what's out there, but I gotta go. I can find something for us, but I need to leave. I must go before Mom and Dad realize what's happening." I was confident that I was making the best decision.

He jumped off the desk at my statement and got up in my face as he exclaimed. "That's stupid, MB. Are you trying to tear the family apart?" He huffed. The pain in his face stopped me long enough for him to grab me by the shoulders and shake me.

"Don't you realize it will kill them if you disappear? Are you trying to make us orphans? They already lost one child." Tears had gathered in his eyes as they shone out from the thick black frames of his glasses, almost even with my own.

I hadn't realized how much my baby brother had changed in the past several years. He was no longer just a boy; he was becoming a man.

"Are you just going to leave? Take your stuff and go? What do you want me to cover for you? Is that it? You're going to make me the scapegoat?"

My idea didn't sound so good when he put it that way.

"Really?" I gritted through my teeth. "That's what you think I'm doing?" I stared him down hard.

"Go hunting without me tonight," I announced. "We already had a spot reserved. I'll pack my satchel while Dad's at work. I will offer to take the herbs, but Mom wants to trade them because she has been getting better deals. Hopefully, I can drop it outside my window and pick it up tonight. When it is time for us to go hunting tonight, I'll go out with you and grab my bag." I paused, taking a deep breath before continuing. "Then, I'll go to the other entrance and leave with the group going out. I got someone to tell me where to go. It is supposed to be a termination group of inmates and the elderly, but I got someone to get me there."

He nodded slowly, his eyes clouded over. I continued, "I'll write a letter and leave it in my room. You'll go and hunt. I'm sure that you'll find something good tonight. When you get home, tell them I told you I had to run and get something and never came back. Don't tell them the truth. Mom will check my room and find the note." I stopped, knowing that the following words would hurt me. Even thinking about them was painful.

"I need you to hold everyone together for me, please. I'll come back when I find a viable spot for us." I promised as I held his eyes.

He continued to stare at me like I was evil incarnate, and I began to doubt that he would agree to my plan.

I told him that I wanted to get us all out of the settlement, which I totally did, but I had to find somewhere safe first. I didn't think he completely understood that yet, though. I also had to find somewhere where we could find food.

I waited; the desire to pace was maddening, but I needed him to know I was serious, and the pacing was the opposite of what I wanted him to see. The emotions crossed his face: anger, confusion, sadness, and resignation. I held my breath as I watched him reach that stage. What's he going to say? The thought crossed my mind as I prayed for his assistance. The soft melody of the lullaby played in the back of my mind as Nick opened his mouth to speak. It brought peace to me as I stood there trembling with worry.

As soon as his lips opened, they closed again. Again, I watched as the opposing thoughts warred in his head. Biting my lip, I prayed for him to see reason. It was torturous to wait to see what he would say, but I desperately needed him to be a part of this, or it was bound to fail.

Finally, he nodded, but even with the nod, his eyes showed the worry and fear that came from the troubling thoughts I had given him by asking for his assistance. He wasn't entirely on board yet but was at least one foot in.

"Nick," my voice trembled. Nicky, please, please support me on this," I begged him. I have to do it. I have to make sure that everyone is taken care of. The only way I can make sure that everyone has enough to eat is to sneak away." I tried to stop him from overthinking it as I continued pleading my case.

I watched as he bit his lip as he contemplated my words. There wasn't much evidence. Yet, I had promised him that I would return eventually. It was more than Dom had ever done for us. I could see that my words had merit, but he was still tempted to say no, and it shimmered in his eyes.

I grabbed the edge of the nearest desk and pulled myself up. I stepped away from where we had sat, huddled on the floor. I watched the emotions continue to run across his face. I hoped that my promise was enough and that he would agree. Otherwise, I would have to go with another plan, and I didn't have one now.

Ten

"MB..." Nick began. Suddenly, however, the sound of footsteps echoing in the empty corridor of the school caused him to pause mid-sentence.

The white-haired head of the only middle school teacher in the community poked her head through the door as I turned away from the window. The rickety desk supported my weight as I leaned against it as she glared at me.

Damnit! What's that old battle-ax doing now? She had been a pain in my ass and was just as biased as everyone else, in my opinion.

"Mary Beth," her voice scratched at my ears, "and Nicholas Johnson." She looked at us each as she said our names. Her brown eyes were condemning. Her thin lips puckered as the spittle came out of her mouth when she spoke.

I couldn't stand how squeaky she sounded, like a dog toy stuck in her throat. It totes did. It was the worst voice I had ever heard. Maybe it was because I hated her. She was the one who had sent me away from the classroom when my bumps started to show. So worried about contamination, I laughed inside; it isn't like I am contagious, nor have I ever been. But then again, when my bumps started to show, I became more resentful of the settlement and how little they helped people.

I felt like yelling at her that my contamination was all over her room. Ha!

"Shouldn't you be at your position now, Mary Beth?" Her eyes were like lasers as she stared me down. Damn, it was bad enough that I was considered unequal for education because of my mutations, but did she have to be so controlling of everything else?

"As for you, Nicholas," she began to say to Nicky. However, Nick was quick to shut her down.

"Mrs. Jamison, I was just getting ready to tell her..." Her laser eyes landed on him, and his speech halted.

Sighing, I rolled my eyes, and secretly, I was glad I didn't have to have her staring me down all day in class. However, my pleasure didn't last too long, as she turned back and focused on me again.

"Again, Mary Beth, I'll ask you... Why are you not at your placement?"

"Mrs. Jamison, I..." I tried to answer, only to be cut short by her squeaky voice again.

"I suggest you leave and get there before they notify the guards that you are missing."

I growled under my breath, nodded, and turned towards the door. She backed away quickly as I neared the door. I smirked inside as I gave her the most pleasant, innocent look I had. She backed away from me until I was on the other side of the door. *Ha! You're scared of me, old lady, man... I wish I'd known that a long time ago, I could have made your life hell for sending me away.* I couldn't help but think of all the fun ways I could have messed with her. It was too late, but maybe I could leave Nick some ideas.

"Nick," I called as I turned, stared her down, and glanced at my brother. "You'll think about what I said?" I had no choice but to give him any additional time now. I just had to hope for the best.

"Yes, MB. I'll do it. We go out at six tonight, right?" My heart pounded loudly in my ears. Did I hear him right? His eyes were hard, a look I wasn't used to. Especially coming from him, I had to do a double-take to ensure I wasn't seeing things.

"Yeah, six o'clock," I said, one foot on the edge of the door. "I'll be ready, I promise."

"Yeah," he said indifferently, "I bet you will be." His words weren't very happy but weren't wholly sarcastic either. I guess it was a happy medium.

I sighed and placed my hands on the door frame. Mrs. Jamison's eyes widened as she took in my stance. *Hell, yeah!* I thought. *She was probably dying to sanitize the hell out of this classroom immediately.* I chuckled and slid my hand down to the doorknob, where it stayed.

"Are you sure you're ready to go hunting?" I asked incognito, just trying to take more time and leave more contamination all over the door. He nodded, not saying a word until I turned away.

As I walked out the door, Nick called me again, "MB."

"Yeah?" I asked as I stood waiting.

"Don't forget what I asked you to do." He reminded me, and I smiled. *He was in. He'd agreed to it... But would he go through with it?* That thought stayed with me as I left the building and returned to our home.

IV

Dom

Eleven

It was hard to get into the village. They had made it hard for anyone or anything to get in if they didn't want it to. However, I'd been doing this for years and knew all the secrets that they attempted to hide.

I watched through the cracks in the walls as she moved along the streets. As she passed people, I saw their jeering faces. *What idiots!* I thought as I moved along with her towards the house.

The house was disgusting. It had always been, in my opinion, but then again, most of the houses within the settlement were. I was lucky today that she had gone along a path that was easy for me to follow without going into the settlement. I had almost been caught once and had become more vigilant since then to ensure they never got the opportunity to take me in. I would become a science experiment. He could just kill me on sight, too. *I mean, I, technically, had stolen his fiancée.* But that was old news; maybe he had let it go. I could only hope.

I watched her enter the house. I waited and observed the house for a while. I paced back and forth between spots where I could see both the front and back of the house just to perform my routine check. I knew I needed to hunt for myself here soon, but I wanted to ensure everyone was okay before I left. I checked in on the family at least once or twice a week. I used to watch them every day when I came back, but after nearly getting caught, I had reduced it to what I was doing now.

I sighed. It seemed like it wasn't so long ago that I'd been home. That I had been inside the walls that now kept me out or attempted to keep me out. It was more of the guards that kept me out now. They had shot at me twice, missing both times, but they were around. When I saw him, I glanced around to ensure that none of them were close. *Shit, what was he doing at the house?* He was carrying a large parcel; it had to be the weekly provisions. My lips curled in disgust and anger. *That man was the devil.* He had no conscience or good bone within him. That is why Elizabeth had left him. *I just happened to be the one that she confided in. That was all.*

I laughed a little. *I had to keep telling myself that.* She was always a sore spot of thought and discussion for me.

The box looked heavy in his hands, and I chuckled to myself. I hoped it was heavy. He moved it back and forth, from one shoulder to another. His deep green uniform was crisp; I could see the lines on it from where I stood. His olive head gleamed, and I wondered if he waxed it to keep it looking so shiny. After a minute, I saw the door open, and her covered head popped out to greet the man. The man didn't even wait to be greeted properly; he pushed the box off onto her and barged into the house.

Yup, world-class asshole! I thought as she struggled to get a better grasp on the box. I could see her as she leaned against the door. She must have been able to balance it a little because she turned around and headed back inside. The door slammed, and I wondered if she kicked it shut behind her. I waited. And waited. And waited. Nervous ate my stomach. It was not a good sign if he was still in the house. I knew something was happening; I just wasn't sure what. I sure didn't want to leave if something was going to happen. Barnes was not a good man, and if he was in there for this long, something significant must be happening. It couldn't be good. I was eager to see him leave. Then, I would stay a little longer to see what happened. If everyone came out and acted normal, then I could go on with my day. And if not, I would be eating from a can tonight and not something fresh.

Minutes passed in silence as I continued to watch the house. As I continued to pace back and forth, I almost missed it as Barnes went out the back door and stomped away. *That was not a good sign, not a good sign at all.* I was used to him marching; he was a military man. *Stomping? That was momentous.* I was tempted to follow him, but then a preteen boy pulled two little girls after him and headed in another direction. I smiled; Nick was growing so big. He had to be at least five-foot-eight or nine now. He was a giant compared to the twins. And it had been a long time since I had seen the girls. The girls had only been about two years old when I had left. They all had their bags for school, so maybe it wasn't as bad as I thought. Yet, no one else was coming out, and that was unusual. As much as my siblings and Barnes tempted me to follow them, I stayed. MB was too responsible not to go to her job. She had learned that from Dad. So, something was up. I just had to wait and watch.

Twelve

Finally, she came out of the house. I could almost see the steam rising from her ears as she slammed the door shut behind her. Questions filled my head. *Did they fight? What were they fighting about? Why had Barnes been there? What did he have to do with it?*

She stomped around on the porch for a bit before sitting down on the bottom step. Her head fell into her hands. I ached to comfort her, but I had lost that right when I left. This was my penance. I watched over my family, yet I could do nothing to actually assist them.

She sat there for a while as I watched, obviously lost in her thoughts.

Suddenly, she jumped up and ran up the stairs. She hit the brakes right as her hand landed on the doorknob. It was agony to watch and not understand the context. *What was going on?* Finally, she turned the doorknob and pulled it open slightly before she stuck her head in. I was too far away to hear the words, but not even seconds after she put her head in, she pulled it out and slammed the door again. *What the hell?*

Suddenly, she turned and took off like a bat out of hell. I followed as she ran through the settlement, peeking in through the boards as I ran to make sure I was keeping up with her.

As I ran along the perimeter, I thought of all the places I had to visit. There wasn't much in the way of good hiding places. Half of the homes had been destroyed by marauders or the remnants of bombs that had torn down buildings. It was a disaster out there. I was glad to be able to check on my family; it was a safe place for them. At least, it had been for the most part. I'd seen the interactions with MB and the guards on multiple occasions. It had angered me so severely that during that one night, I'd gone in and stolen the guard's gun that had gotten so rough with her. At least that way, he couldn't attempt to hurt her if they ran into each other again.

Fuck. I'd lost track of her while lost in my thoughts, and it took me a while to find her cloak floating out behind her. Good. I tried to keep her in my line of sight, but it was proving to be a difficult task today. After a while, I saw her stop outside a different group of houses. *But these houses, these, I knew.*

Yeah, this was the playground area. I wondered what she was doing there. I couldn't see into the playground from where I stood, but I didn't want to move just yet. She was up to something, and I wasn't sure if it would be a good thing or if she would do something reckless.

Was MB being reckless? She did it sometimes, but it usually was with a purpose. I remembered the one time that she had been so irresponsible. It had been when we'd first moved to the settlement. Dad had been talking to someone from the military, trying to find us a place to stay that would be safe for Mom in her condition. Dad had put me in charge of Mary Beth and Nick while he talked to them. Mom had been told to sit down by the military personnel when we entered, so she sat with our stuff near the entrance.

Mary Beth had taken off after a gorgeous girl; she was unique because she looked different from everyone else. The girl had this weird tint to her skin, which both MB and I now suffered from. I think that's what drew MB in. She was always curious. I stopped short, and as I shook my head, I realized it was no good to think about that time now. We couldn't change the past.

After a while, I watched the girls run out of the houses and past my hidden spot toward one of the settlement's different housing districts again. I wondered if I should follow them before Nick and Mary Beth walked out of the houses surrounding the playground and headed toward the school building.

I knew MB had been kicked out of the school a few years ago, so why were they going there? My watch dinged, reminding me I had a place to be; otherwise, the guards would find me skulking around here. I had to be timely, and as much as I was curious, I was also very cautious. I had to be. I had made a vow, and I couldn't break that vow without hurting numerous people.

I sighed again as I walked away. With one last glance at my brother and sister as they entered the school building. I had to come back tonight to figure out what was happening. As I walked away from the settlement, I had to decide on which way to go. I could head downtown, but that's usually where the marauders hung out. They loved to loot everything and anything they could. It was lucky if you could find anything worthwhile without the marauders having been there before you. They were bloodthirsty, too. I mean, I guess I could have joined them back when I came down off the mountain, but I didn't want to leave my family alone. I had been stupid to think that I was saving Elizabeth when we ran away.

I mean, most of the marauders were people like me, like MB, but they had been the unlucky ones. The ones that hadn't been "blessed" by the bombs. They were the ones that were just mutated, singled out because of their deficiencies; the government had taken a lot of them in for experimentation. There were a couple of buildings out by where the highways met that the government had converted into some scientific laboratories. I avoided those like the plague when I was out hunting. The grass had overgrown everything in the last decade. I think that is why the animals moved so far down into the plains. Yet, as I thought back to the place in the mountains where I'd last seen Elizabeth, it wasn't just the government making secret places. She was constantly on my mind, a whisper in the chaos that controlled my every movement, every action, every word. I was a prisoner to the promises that I'd made. I'd wondered when I would be forced to bring MB into it.

I walked further away from the village, and each day, I took a different path. I didn't want the grass or trees to get worn out and broken down, or they would start searching for me. I knew that the guards patrolled more than the settlement. I'd seen them on the outside several times before, but not in conditions I'd want to see them in. They were just as bloodthirsty as the marauders, in my opinion. I'd watched them as they chased down the people they'd willingly let out the gates. The deaths were never pretty; they were more gruesome than anything else. It didn't matter if it was the guns, the bows, or the knives; somehow, someway, they had always made sure that the people were gone. No one to trace back to the settlement.

There was a hole about three miles to the east of the settlement, far enough away that the smells weren't overwhelming if a breeze came in from that side, and that was the place that the bodies were taken to after they had finished hunting them down. I hated it the first time that I found the place; I had gagged so severely on the smells that I hadn't even gotten three feet away before I had thrown up everything I'd eaten. A twig snapped, and my head spun. *Shit.* I needed to focus; I needed to find something to eat. Something to cook so that I could get back and check on them again before it was time for me to bunker down for the night.

V

Mary Beth

Thirteen

After I left the school building, I walked along the street toward home. Growling at the dusty clouds above me, I thought about Mrs. Jamison and her stub at me in class. *Yes, I had work to do, but she didn't have to be so bossy to me about it.* It didn't help the matter that the opaque skies darkened. Reminding me it was going to rain. That didn't help my mood at all. It's just what I needed today!

I thought snidely. *Get a hold of yourself, MB. It doesn't do any good to be negative all the time.*

I tried to think about what had been discussed with Nick instead. Yes, he. agreed to do it, but I was still hoping he would change his mind. That was part of the way I worked. I always tried to be positive, yet I always thought of the negative internally.

I wouldn't have to do this if Mom and Dad had just listened to me when I first tried talking to them. It would have made things a lot easier. We could have celebrated my leaving. Made plans for me to come back and get them. We could have made it all a lot easier. *But no.* Why can't things just work out how I want them to, initially, not after making changes and plans to be sneaky? I pondered.

Now, I needed to figure out how to get everything ready

without my parents noticing that I was running away.

Hmmm... where are they? Are they still at the house, or did they go out? Mom didn't usually leave the house; she wasn't cleared to work in factories or farms around the settlement. I'd have to get her out of the house, but that was resolved. Mom would offer to take the herbs to the marketplace as soon as I offered to take them. I mean, she'd want to take them for two reasons. First, I need to get to work soon, and it would keep me in the good graces of the council. Second, because she can get a better deal with Joaquin than I can, he won't be as nasty with her as he tries to be with me.

My cloak flowed around me. I knew it made me odd, but it was a way to keep myself hidden as much as possible. They didn't remember I was there if they couldn't see me. I darted between the empty and scurried along the dry streets. The air was already humid, but I was praying it would ease up over the rest of the day; even with the rain, the humidity messed with my hair. I didn't need it weighing me down more than it already did.

My feet kicked the dirt as they pounded heavily on the ground, creating a curtain of dust that followed my trail. There was a lot that I still needed to get done before I could leave. I couldn't take everything with me, but there were some things that I could take with me. I couldn't take too long, though; I needed to show up at the factory before long; otherwise, they would contact Mom or Dad to see where I was. That would blow my cover.

I hated the factory; all I did there was put clothes into the military tubs; they didn't trust me to do much else. I'd been working there for over a year now, but that was because of stupid Mrs. Jamison. She contacted someone on the council when the bumps started showing up when I was thirteen, primarily once I couldn't hide them anymore.

The council had the general come to the house to tell us I couldn't return to school. Quoting that I needed skills in the community to be a productive member. Hell, everyone else got to go to school until they were sixteen, and then they could find a position in the community to work. *Not me. I was an abomination*, I deadpanned in my head, *an abomination that was amongst the highest counts of kills for the hunts I've done.* My spot wasn't something I had chosen; it had been assigned to me.

I kicked a wall as I went past it; they just wanted to keep track of my movement. I was sure of it. They wanted to make sure that I wouldn't do something to harm the community. Everyone else I'd ever seen with the bumps ended up "disappearing" or leaving the community. They were almost always young. I think Dad had worked a little magic with the council when I turned fourteen last year. There was a moment when I was sure that General Barnes was coming to take me away, but it never happened.

I slowed down as I got closer to the house. I wrinkled my nose. It would be easier to pack my things before I went to the factory so that I could write a quick note, too. But I had to ensure I got them out of the house before I tried anything.

Taking a calming breath, I walked around the house to the back door. Opening it a slit, I peeked in. Mom and Dad were still sitting at the table; their words were hushed, and I couldn't decide if I needed to wait or go on in. However, before I could decide, it was taken from me.

"Are you coming in or not, Mary Beth?" Dad asked as he stood from the table. "Are your brother and sisters okay?"

"Yes, Dad," I said as I slid in the door. "I forgot that I was the sheep herder and needed to ensure everyone was where they were supposed to be."

"Excuse me?" His voice was steely, and I gulped.

"I mean, yeah, Dad. They were doing fine. I just came to take the herbs in."

He nodded as he turned away from the table. His overalls were faded and stretched tight as he stretched his arms out and over his head. I knelt and started picking up the stray herbs from where they had fallen earlier.

I rolled my eyes; I knew Mom didn't mean to waste the herbs, but having to pick them up was still annoying. I mean, there had only been that one time. It had been right after the girls were born, and they had allowed everyone to go out into the fields to gather what they could to live healthily in this new world. She'd forgotten that the herbs had been in her bag after she got home and started doing the laundry. The herbs had been completely wasted, but we had been more careful since then. I was just glad to have the opportunity to get Mom to leave the house as well; I knew if I waited long enough, she'd offer. It was conniving, but I was willing to be conniving if I needed to be.

"Okay, I'm heading out to the dome. I've got to help with the newest crop layout. But... Mary Beth," he said, grabbing my attention from my collection. "I meant what I said. Don't worry about what's going to happen. We've got it covered, okay?"

I took a deep breath before I nodded, holding my head still as I turned and looked at him. I didn't want him to see that I wasn't completely truthful with him. He was so good at reading my eyes, and it didn't help that my nose twitched when I lied. He looked at me hard, his eyes seeing everything, and I gritted my teeth softly. Anything to get my attention away from the fact that I was telling the biggest lie of them all. He nodded at me once before turning and leaving the room.

After I finished my task, I held the drying plants in my hands as I stood up. I heard his steps fade away as he walked down the hallway. Eventually, the front door closed, and I turned toward Mom, who was still sitting at the table. She had this contemplation on her face that made me wonder what exactly they had come up with.

"Mom, would you want to see if Joaquin will give you a better deal for these?" I asked as I walked to the table where she still sat. "Last time I went to him, well… his offer wasn't like the ones he used to offer me," I said, putting the herbs down in front of her. She turned towards me, and her hand landed on mine as I walked away.

"Did he do something to you?" she asked.

I smiled at her gently and shook my head. "No, he didn't; he's just being weird. I just want us to get the best we can, especially since we will be losing food. Besides, it is almost time for me to be at work."

I slipped my hand out from under hers as I returned and picked up my satchel. Taking the rest of the herbs out, I laid them on the table for her. The silence was oppressive.

"Well, I guess I better get to the factory."

Mom stood up quickly. "I'll walk with you." Her hand reached out for me. It reminded me of how we used to be: friends. It had changed, and I kind of missed it, but at the same time, I had always felt like a parent, like an adult.

"You know that the factory isn't on the way to the village, right?" I cocked my eyebrow at her.

She rolled her eyes. "Of course, silly, but I thought we could at least walk together for part of it."

I sighed—it was not what I intended to do. "Okay, Mom. Let me grab my work shirt, and then I'll be back." I pulled my satchel to show her, and she nodded. I smiled as I ran from the room.

"Hurry, okay. I don't want you to be late." She hollered at me as I raced through the house.

I don't have much time, I thought as I reached my room. Randomly, my hands ran through my drawers quickly, and I grabbed some things I would need for tonight. I looked at the clock; I was running late, but I needed to have this done, so I hollered down to Mom, "I'm still looking for it. I must have put it underneath something."

"Do you need some help?" She yelled back to me, and I heard the step creak under the pressure of her weight.

"No," I panicked. There was so much to get in my bag. Maybe I would have to get back and do some before dinner. I run through the list in my head. I mean, there are some things that I can probably scavenge while I'm on the outside.

Underwear... check

Shirts... check.

Socks... check

There wasn't much need for another pair of pants; these were my best pair anyway. Before leaving the room, I grabbed my hairbrush and stuck it in my satchel. I turned around and returned to my room to grab the shirt from the top of my bed. I walked back out the door and over to the stairs.

"Okay, I'm ready," I said as I walked down the stairs toward the front door where she'd been waiting.

"Okay, kid, let's go." She smiles as she slides her arm

through mine. Linking us together, like we used to walk when I was smaller. I sighed happily, and we opened the door together and walked out.

I smiled. I missed this. It had been so long since we had walked arm in arm anywhere, *low-key*. It felt nice. I was glad to have this moment with her, even though it ruined my plans.

We walked away from the house and towards the center of the village. Taking my other hand from the side of my satchel, I pulled on my hood. I wanted to make sure that it wasn't going to fly away.

"Mary Beth Johnson." My mom chided me.

"What?" I intoned; she hardly ever called me by my full name.

"Why did you bring your bag with you?"

Shit. "I put my work shirt in it; you never know when you might need a bag to carry something in."

"Is there something you're not telling me?"

I blushed. "Mom!"

"What? You're acting differently, darling. You went out for a long time this morning; did you look at the apartments? I thought your dad and I told you…"

I cut her off. "No, Mom. I didn't go to look at the apartments. I met with some friends." It was the worst lie I could ever tell her, and I wondered how badly my nose was twitching. I hoped that it wasn't. I'd made some progress this morning with telling Dad a lie; if I could get this one past Mom, I was rolling in the money.

She gave me a stern look. "Sure." She deadpanned. Well, at least I know who I got my sarcasm from. I smirked and let it fade away. We walked in silence, neither one of us knowing what to say.

Our steps echoed in the empty street as we continued toward the marketplace. About five blocks away, I stopped, pulling her to a stop with me.

"I'd better get to work," I said as I pointed to the factory district that was several blocks down that way. "But I'm sure that Joaquin will give you something great." I smiled.

She smiled faintly in return, "Of course, dear. I love you."

My heart stops. We hardly ever tell each other that we love them. It has always just been something that we assumed. *Was she sus? Did she suspect something? Or was she planning something? I was all kinds of nervous now.*

I cleared my throat and replied, "Love you too, Mom. I'll see you later."

Pulling my arm away from hers, I turned and walked towards the factory. A few steps later, I see her watching me with this look. Sad and reflective, all wrapped up together in one look. I tried to smile and wave back at her. She waved back before she turned and started to walk the rest of the way to the market. I sighed with relief and raced towards the factory. I'd have to see if I could borrow some paper and a pen from Martha when I arrived.

Fourteen

The houses passed in a blur as I raced towards the factory building. It wasn't a factory but more of a workhouse, or what I imagine it used to look like back in the late eighteen hundreds. There were a bunch of women who worked together in the building to make clothing using the materials that had been reused. Once they created something for someone to wear, they would send it down to be sent to another community. It happened this way for many of the settlements that the government created. It was supposed to bring us closer by making us into a working unit for each settlement, but I thought it was just a way to get free work.

Skidding to a stop a couple of yards from the building, I see Martha pacing in front of it. *Son of a bitch!* I swore and slowed my roll.

As I walked towards the building, Martha turned and stared me down.

"Girl," she scathed.

"I know, Martha. I'm sorry I'm late!" I apologized hurriedly. She was the one woman at this place I would not want to make mad. She had been my "boss" since I started working here. Honestly, I thought she was like a second mom. She always tried to make sure that I had enough food during breaks and that the other ladies weren't too rough on me.

"Where have you been? I was about to contact your folks."

"We had a visit from the…" I don't even get to finish.

She didn't even give me a chance to finish. She was hotter than a dash of red pepper. She held her hand up to my face and said, "Honestly, girl, I don't care where you've been. You should always be here on time. You know how those other women get when they think you are getting special treatment."

I knew Martha did nice things for me, but I didn't think the other women had ever noticed.

I smiled sheepishly at her big brown face, "Sorry, Martha."

"Just get yourself in there and start working, girl."

Hours later, I was exhausted and could finally stop for a break. I walked away from the workroom and towards the kitchenette that we had. It was sus. There was never anyone that wasn't in the kitchenette, and I was surprised to see that it was empty. Not that I didn't want anyone to see me. But just to make sure, I looked around to see if the other women had stopped for lunch with me.

Not seeing anyone coming, I went to the pantry and looked through the canned goods we had available. The government supplied each factory with enough food for every worker once a day.

There wasn't much that looked interesting, but I needed something to get me through a couple of days. I didn't want to take anything from home, but I wanted something as a backup if I couldn't find food. So I looked to the back. Several dusty cans were there.

I decided to take a chance and grabbed them. As I turned

away, the cans clutched to my chest, I rushed to my satchel and stuck them in it.

"Got something on your mind, girl?" Martha drawled from somewhere behind me.

Fuck! "Hi, Martha." I chuckled nervously. "It isn't what it looks like..."

"Oh, you mean to tell me you ain't stealing that food from here?"

"Oh, that! About that..."

"Yes?"

"Okay," I paused, thinking of the best option. *Honesty was the best policy.* "Okay, yeah, I was stealing them." I paused and took a deep breath, "but for a good reason. Martha, you knew that I was late today. Well, that's because General Barnes stopped at the house and told everyone that we would start getting rationed again."

"Oh, good Lord, girlie. What are you going to do?" She responded halfway through my explanation.

"Well, he did suggest that one of us could leave."

"Of course, he did." She said with an eye roll. "So, what are you planning, girl? To steal from here for your family? Or something else." There was a knowing gleam in her eyes.

"No, oh no, Martha!" I responded when she suggested that I was stealing for the family. "I was planning on sneaking away and giving them a chance without me. I'm just a burden." I whispered the last part as I looked down.

She stared at me. "You're leaving?" As though she couldn't believe that she had been right when she'd insinuated it.

I nodded, glad she didn't hear my self-negativity there.

"Oh, girl, I'm gonna hafta talk to your folks." Her voice twanged as she put her hand on her hip.

"No! Please, Martha, don't tell them!" I panicked. "I just needed a couple of cans to get me through a few days. I promised I was going to write them a note. If you tell them, then they'll never let me leave. I gotta take care of them. You know how bad it feels when you don't feel like you're protecting your family." I pulled out my ace in the hole.

She sighed and sat down in a chair. Pulling her clipboard from the wall behind her, she grabbed an old paper. The paper was an order that we'd filled a couple of days ago. She turned it around and held it out to me. "Well, if you're going to be so bullheaded, you might as well have someone support you."

I sighed in relief as I reached out and took the paper from her slightly trembling hand.

"Go on, now, write them a note." She said as she pulled out a pen and slid it across the table towards where I stood.

The paper looked daunting, especially when I tried to think of a way to write a justification for going against their orders. I knew it would be hard, and they would hate me if I did it. *Well, maybe not hate.* They'd be disappointed in me, which in many cases was much worse. I had to do it, though. I'd made a promise to Nicky, and now Martha was making sure I fulfilled that promise. As I pulled the chair out and sat down, I tried to place the cans on the table without dropping any. When the last can was down, I picked up the pen.

Mom and Dad,

I'm sorry for not listening to your instructions. I know that by the time you get this, you will be really upset with me, but I had to take action. I understand you think I'm following the same path as Dom, but I'm not. I'm considering both of you, as well as Nicky and the girls. I realize we have only three options at this point that don't involve me leaving, and all of them are terrible:

1 — One of you, or both, cut back on what you eat (which would eventually mean losing one or both of you to death, something none of us could genuinely handle).

2 — We all stick to the portions we've been given, but the girls start to get sick because they need more than what we have.

3 — One of you goes into the Leaving Ceremony, and the only one they would accept is you, Mom. I'm sorry, I just can't. I can't let that happen.

I just couldn't let any of those scenarios unfold. I stepped up when Dom left, and I'm going to step up again and leave tonight. Please don't be mad at Nicky; I never told him what I planned. I did everything independently because I thought it was for the best. I love you both. I'll find a way to let you know when I am somewhere safe, and we can all be together again.

Love,

Mary Beth

I sat there looking at the note. The pen dangled from my fingers after I signed my name. *This was it; I was going to do it.* There was no stepping back now. I'd fulfilled the promise.

Martha sat across from me she had been reading every word I'd written.

"So, this is it, huh, girl?" She questioned.

I nodded, the pen falling to the table. "Yeah, I guess it is. Have you been out there since everything happened?" I asked curiosity plagued me. I knew she did everything she could for her family, but I couldn't exactly remember when I first saw her. I knew she worked such long hours to provide for her kids.

She shook her head. "Nah, I haven't left this place since my kids and I came here back when everyone else was coming..."

she trailed off. A hazy look overcame her eyes.

"I think I remember you when we came in," I said as I looked at her. "Didn't you have two girls and a boy with you?" I could dimly recall her when I was a child by the gate.

"Yeah," the look in her eyes didn't fade away. "It used to be just the four of us."

"Right," I nodded, "I've seen your girls lately, but where is your boy?"

The look on her face was grim.

"My boy," she said with a heavy sigh, "was forced out when he stole some food from his work. We were in some hard times." She said as she looked me in the eyes. I felt terrible; that was why she worked so hard, yet at the same time, I think she was also pointing out some similarities between her son and me. "I wouldn't want any other parent to feel that pain to know their child was being forced out because of bad choices." She continued. "But, you ain't making bad choices, are you?"

"No, ma'am. I'm not. I'm doing this to keep my family safe. That is all I've ever wanted to do."

She nodded and stood up from the table. Turning towards the door, "Ya better grab some more then." She returned the words to me as she stood up and walked out the door. "I want to know that you are safe for a while."

I stared after her. After hearing that she had lost a child to the injustice of this settlement, I was amazed that she was going to help me at all. I went back and grabbed a couple more cans. Sticking them and my note in my satchel, I felt better about leaving. Closing the flap, I walked out of the kitchenette and back to work with a slightly lighter heart.

Fifteen

The day passed swiftly after I went back to work. By the time I was ready to head home, it was already late afternoon. It was almost four in the evening, late but not late enough. As I walked home, my satchel was heavy on my side. The streets were empty, and I couldn't help but think of the group I would join. I got why they got rid of inmates who were taking resources; it was a way to save food for the rest of the people who lived there, but I wondered about the elderly part. *Was there a reason they chose the elderly to be in this group?* It was a complexity that was driving me mad; my head was overrun with ideas, and this was the one that I had finally landed on. I played peek-a-boo with the dome's shadow as it drifted over parts of the ground as I skipped along the road.

When I got to the house, the lights were on, and the girls and Nick were waiting out front.

"Mary Beth," the girls hollered at me in synchronicity.

I smiled. "Hello, Eliza. Hello, Morgana. How was school? Did you have fun with Annabelle this morning?"

They nodded and continued playing hopscotch in front of the house. They were excited to play, and I was happy to see them carefree. Then, as I turned to Nick, I stopped in my tracks. He was sitting on the third step, staring out into space.

"Everything okay, Nicky?" I asked, worry creeping in that he had changed his mind.

"Yea," he replied absentmindedly. "Just thinkin.'"

I nodded as I walked around the girls to join him on the steps. I dropped the heavy satchel to the ground, hoping it didn't make too much noise upon impact. It didn't, and I sighed with relief; I sat down next to him, and we watched the girls for a while as they continued to play. I laughed at their antics as I reached around my brother's shoulder, leaning on him. I squeezed him in a quick hug as I leaned my head against his shoulder. He was so quiet. I couldn't help but look at him from the corner of my eye. His head drifted towards me and landed softly on top of mine. We may have our rocky parts, but he was my little brother, and it was nice to know that our love was still strong despite my declaration from earlier.

I watched him out of the corner of my eye as we stayed outside for a while with the girls. He smiled faintly, and I wished that I could read his mind. We probably sat there for half an hour before Mom called us from inside.

"Come on, guys. It's dinner time." Her voice echoed through the empty rooms and out the opened door.

The girls ran in front of us as Nick and I sat in contemplation. Nick stood up and extended his hand to me. It was a gesture of acceptance from him, and I was glad we had reached that point. I grabbed his hand as I stood up. I smiled at him and watched as he went into the house after the girls, his mood still somber. I withheld the sigh that threatened to leave my lips as I grabbed my bag off the ground.

"I'll be right there," I hollered out as I quickly stuffed my bag under one of the bushes on the side of the house. Before

I stuffed it under, though, I quickly grabbed the letter and stuck it in my pocket. *It was out here*, I thought with relief, *now to make everyone think I'd gone upstairs with it.* So, I walked into the house and up the stairs to my room.

"I've gotta go to the bathroom, okay?" I reminded Mom as I took off my work shirt and threw it on my bed. It wasn't like I'd need it where I was going. I grabbed one of my old rock band t-shirts; it was filled with holes but was comfy. I pulled it over my head and left it around my neck. Pulling my arms through it quickly, Metallica floated down over me as I adjusted my cami. I hated having my bare skin show.

I ran into the bathroom, splashed some water onto my face, and stared at myself in the mirror. As I leaned my hands against the counter, I tried to soak in the last time I might ever see myself in the mirror. My eyes were the most noticeable feature. They were a brilliant teal color. It almost matched the mutation bumps that trailed over my arms and stood out on my face. I didn't hate myself, but my mutations had made life complicated, or maybe I was making life hard, the devil on my shoulder countered. I laughed internally; it was a debate I'd had before, and I still couldn't decide.

A chill raced through me, reminding me that there were many cold nights in Colorado. I was going to be out walking in an unknown world, and I needed to be more prepared.

I turned and walked back into my room. I looked around before seeing an older blanket and grabbed it off the chair where I'd thrown it the last time we had done laundry. I'd almost forgotten to grab something to keep me warm at night. Then I looked over at my dresser. My journal was lying on top of it, and I fingered the necklace mom had given to me last year for my birthday. I was indecisive.

I turned from the bed, walked over to the window, and cracked it open. I quickly looked outside, stuck out, and double-checked my surroundings. No one was there. *Good.* I bundled up the blanket and dropped it into the bush under my window. It wasn't the same one that I'd thrown my satchel under, but it would work. The bush was almost dead, but it never read did die. It was something that I never understood. I mean, how could it have lived so long without direct sunlight? But it got some water and light fragments, so was it possible?

Now that I finished the essential pieces, it was time to figure out what I would leave behind. The letter burned a hole in my pocket, but that didn't seem nearly enough now that I was home. I fingered the necklace again before I reached around and opened the clasp. As the necklace fell into my waiting hand, I looked at the carefully constructed charm built for generations. I looked at all the charms before deciding to leave the one that would mean the most. After taking the charm off, I knew it would have to be hidden if I went downstairs. Mom would notice if something were missing from the necklace; she had worn it for almost thirty years. In my pocket, it went. My hand brushed against the paper of the note, and I pulled it out. *Okay,* I reassured myself, *this was the moment.* I opened my journal on the dresser and turned to my last entry. My journal was not enjoyable, but I'd been completely honest. *I knew Mom checked on it; Nick and I had to get our nosiness from somewhere.* I rolled my eyes as I imagined her coming into my room, day after day, reading it. I placed the letter into the journal, leaving it where it stuck out a little, and then closed it. I put the charm on top of it all, something for them to remember me by until I return home. *Which I was going to, or they would come to me... One way or another.*

I quickly left the room and went to wash my hands. The water sometimes appeared dirty, like it had not been filtered enough, but it worked.

I jogged down the stairs and into the kitchen. Everyone was already sitting at the table. It wasn't a large meal—it never really was—but it would be enough to fill our stomachs. A fresh loaf of bread was on the table, and I smiled. Mom had managed to get something from Joaquin. I wondered how much flour and yeast she had been able to haggle out of him.

As I took my place at the table, I watched Eliza and Morgana hit each other on the sly. Make sure that Mom or Dad never saw them. My chuckle rang out around the room as everyone's head swiveled towards me. Nick rolled his eyes at my wide-eyed expression while Mom and Dad gave me a look of confusion. Eliza and Morgana's stink eyes were enough to keep me from saying anything to get them into trouble. I wanted tonight to be the best night. *It was my last night for a while.* I shrugged my shoulders. Mom sighed as she reached for my hand. We all joined hands to say thanks. Although, I never understood why we gave thanks. *I mean, if there was a God, wouldn't He have saved us from the bombs? Wouldn't there be enough food for everyone? Why was there such a chemical, or whatever, that caused the disaster of my mutations?* Mom continued to pray and ask Him for the forgiveness of our sins as we strived to be in His image.

Yay, I thought. *This is another way for me to feel bad about myself because I'm not "the image of God" and believe in His Holiness.* The prayer ended, and everyone picked up their forks. Then, we started to eat.

I took in the sights and sounds of everyone as we ate.

Mom and Dad peppered the girls with questions about school. Every once in a while, Nick and I would chime in. Mom watched us with this sad look that made me wonder exactly what was going through her mind, but I was too preoccupied with my plans to worry too much about what she was thinking. Nick and I would exchange these glances as we watched the skies darken outside the kitchen window. Finally, the bells rang from the old grandfather clock in the hallway at five forty-five.

I stood up from the table, my mind already working overtime, as my plate of half-eaten food was pushed in by my movement. The lullaby whispered through my mind as I passed the plate to the girls. I pushed the chair in, the legs squeaking against the ground.

"Well, it's time to go hunting," I said, nervous energy running through me. Nick stood up slowly.

"Oh," Mom gasped. "This is the slot you got?" Her eyes were wide, and again, I wondered what she was doing.

"Oh, nope. I just thought I'd get up and stretch out," I quipped. Nick elbowed me in the ribs, and I nodded. "Yeah, Mom, this is the time slot. I got notice at work that they moved my spot up." I felt terrible about the lie, but it was so small compared to the bigger idea that it was easier to say it without my twitchy nose giveaway.

Nick pushed the rest of his food to Morgana as Eliza chowed down on my remains. I gestured to Nick to grab his rifle as I replied to Mom. He nodded and walked out of the room.

"Since they only give out three slots a week, I was surprised they moved this one up. I had that one earlier this week and this morning's; I thought it would be later tonight, but nope."

I avoided mentioning that they gave out slots to minimize how much I caught. I knew of several other hunters who would go five to six times a week and catch smaller items. I was usually the one that caught the larger animals. Nick was good at the small animals, so I knew they would let him go several times more than me; that was their way of keeping me in check.

What pigs, I thought. *It wasn't like I intended to catch the more prominent animals; it just happened.*

Dad stood up. His chair scraped across the dirty-looking, brown linoleum floor. He stood behind Mom's chair, rubbing circles into her shoulders as Nick walked back into the room.

"You both be careful now, you hear?" he insisted, hazel eyes sweeping us both. We nodded and headed out. Mom grabbed both of our hands, giving them a quick squeeze before letting us continue. *It was so weird.* Yet, I couldn't focus on it as my nervous energy was ready to burst inside me. The lullaby continued as a steady beat inside me as I grabbed my bow and arrows. Mom must have moved them out here after she got home from the market this afternoon.

"We will be." My voice echoed in the house; Nick trailed behind me, trying to arrange his bag to accompany him on his soon-to-be first solo hunt. I placed my bow and quiver over my shoulder before returning to the hallway.

Leaning in the doorway, I peeked back into the kitchen as I looked in from the hall. This was the last time I'd seen them for a long time. Dad was still standing behind Mom, his hands working at the knots in her shoulders. The girls were probably still pigging on the extra food we'd given them. I smiled faintly. This was a good way to remember them. I'd see them again soon.

"We're heading out now. See you soon." I hollered from my spot at the doorway. There was a chorus of sounds, and I backed away slowly from the scene. It was something that I wanted to imprint into my brain. An easy way to recall everyone when I was feeling lonely.

When I couldn't walk backward anymore, I turned towards the front door and opened it. The door opening and closing echoed through the house as we walked away.

In the night's open air, I ran to my bedroom window. The blanket was tossed all over the bush. My satchel was still hidden where I'd left it earlier, and I reached under and grabbed it first before I grabbed the blanket to stuff inside.

Nick followed me, stealthy-like, but his pace was slower and almost strained.

"Are you sure you still want to do this?" His voice trembled.

I sighed internally but gave steel to my voice as I responded.

"I have to, Nicky." I asserted, "What would happen if," I spat the word out, "our portions get decreased again? It's bound to happen."

"You don't know that for certain," he tried to argue with me as we walked away from the house towards the marketplace, leading to his solo hunt.

"Maybe," I speculated, "but who says they won't?"

He stopped and looked hard at me as I continued past him. I didn't stop until I'd gotten several steps ahead. Then, as I turned around, I looked at him. Yes, he was a tall boy, but so were the other men in our family. The deficiencies didn't make us shorter. They just made us bitter. His eyes were lightning bugs, bright against the darkness of the night. I smirked, he may not like it, but I was older; therefore, wiser...

I walked back to where he stood rooted and brushed his

hair out of the way of his glasses. I looked him in the eyes.

There were so many things that I wanted to say. As I searched for the words, I realized something. *There was nothing that would make things easier for him.* There was nothing adequate to convey my love for him and our family. Words failed me, and I went simplistic.

"I love you, Nicholas. I'm doing this for us, okay?"

He nodded his head, and a sad smile played on his lips. "Please," he paused, his voice trembling. A tear rolled down his cheek. "Please, promise me that you'll be safe out there. Promise me that you'll come back." The words were drenched in sorrow.

I smiled half-heartedly for him, I preferred not to make a promise I wasn't confident I could keep. "I'll sure try."

A tear fell down my cheek. The wetness splashed against my cheek, and I quickly rubbed it away.

He nodded and pulled away from me. "Just be careful, okay?"

"I will." I wanted to reach out and hug him, but his watch beeps at him. Reminding me that time was running short.

"Got your bow and arrow?" he verified.

I laughed; of course, he would try to take control now. "Of course," I replied, shouldering them for his benefit.

"A knife?" He inquired.

I'd forgotten that one, but I was sure I'd find something if needed. "'Course," I lied.

"What about water," he asked, turning towards me. "You got something in case it's more acidic than what we're used to?"

"They give you something for it at the gate," I said, remembering that it was a requirement the government gave the council. If someone had to leave the settlement, they needed a sporting chance at survival, so they could give some materials as provided. "Besides, when did you turn into Mom?"

He laughed quietly, "No, I'm not." He looked affronted, "But I'm the closest thing to her right now."

I laughed. At least we were still being nice to each other. We walked through the marketplace quickly, but no one was out at that time of the night. Now, the fence for the hunting entrance started to loom in front of us. "Guess this is where we part, huh? Wow, it's so quiet. I wonder where everyone is." I babbled as we stopped.

"Yeah, I guess so." He agreed as he turned towards me. "I love you, sis. Be careful." His look conveys so much. He gave me a quick squeeze before he ran off towards the opening.

"Nick," I yelled at him after a couple of steps. "Wait!"

He stopped, turned, and looked at me. "What?"

"My note… You asked for a note. It's on my dresser," I said, my words faltering as they came out. "Please ensure that they get it."

He nodded before he continued on his way to the entrance.

I watched him finish the journey, disappearing into his first solo hunt.

I take a deep breath and hold it. I got this. *Twinkle, twinkle, little star. How I wonder what you are...* The melody washed over me as I released my breath and moved away.

Sixteen

My walk to the next gate wasn't too far from the hunting entrance; however, it was far enough away that you couldn't get confused about which entrance you were going to. I forced myself to walk away without looking, away from the only family I had at the moment. I knew I needed to be strong to get through the upcoming weeks or months of being alone. If I looked back now, there is a good possibility that I would change my mind, and I felt it would be better not to do that. I couldn't.

As I reached the gate, I finally turned around to look. I knew he wouldn't be there, but a tiny part of me had hoped he would. I swallowed back the sigh of disappointment. Not only that, but I was in a conundrum of feelings and just needed to get out of there before I did something stupid and returned home.

When I got there, the area in front of the gate wasn't full. As I neared the entrance, they were just starting to bring prisoners and the elderly out. People huddled as guards passed by, passing out water filters, cheap little things that would last for a while if you knew how to use them right. Then, I watched as some prisoners grabbed knives from a passing guard, and I wondered if they were passing out weapons.

Why would they do that? Were they trying to start a fight? Did they do this every time? I wondered. There weren't that many prisoners, but I recognized several elderly citizens. I gravitated toward an old man who stared off into the deadly skies.

"Mr. Cortez," I called out. The man jumped at my voice, turning towards me.

"Mary Beth Johnson," he admonished me. "What in the world are you doing here?"

He was gripping something tightly in his hands as I neared him cautiously. "I don't have a choice, sir. It was me or the girls."

"What do you mean, you or the girls? Did someone threaten you?" His own demeanor changed.

"No, sir. Not in the way you mean. You know how they are always rationing food?" He nodded, "Well, our rations have decreased again. I couldn't let Mom or Dad take my place."

He nodded in understanding, even though I could see the confusion in his eyes. Silence reigned over us as the groups continued to build around us. I wondered why he was here, but it was not my place to question an elder. My mom would have me hide if I were ever that disrespectful. We were supposed to be thoughtful and kind to anyone over a certain age.

The crowds continued to grow. There had to be at least thirty or forty people here. I didn't know that so many people had gotten into trouble or were "unwanted".

The "unwanted" status was implemented a couple of years ago when one elderly got sick. I think my mom said that they had Alzheimer's or something like that. The person had gotten hurt trying to get away from their safe house. The council decided to send the elderly out before they got too bad. It was a sad practice, and I couldn't believe they had just gotten rid of people like that. It made me wonder if Mr. Cortez had gained that status.

Finally, one of the guards approached where Mr. Cortez and I stood. He handed Mr. Cortez a water filter and then turned to me.

"What are you doing here, freak?" It was Sir Thick-a-Lot. *Didn't this man have anything to do with his time but harass me?* "Finally, learned your place, huh?" He smirked as he tossed the water filter at me.

"What the hell?" I growled at him as I caught the filter mid-air.

He smirked at my obvious displeasure. Another guard was handing out filters at a nearby group that caught Sir Thick-a-Lot's eye.

"Look, dude, it's the freak!" He hollered at his friend. "We're finally going to be rid of her."

My spine stiffened. *What a jerk!* I bit my lip to hold the words I wanted to spill out and bring him down to size. I'd been doing it for so long now that I automatically reacted.

Wait, I don't have to hold back anymore! I realized and smiled wickedly. I felt like rubbing my hands together with everything I wanted to do. Now I could finally let loose and give this asshole what he deserved.

His attention was on the other guard, so I kicked at his kneecap, swiping his leg out from under him. The filters flew through the air as his body thudded against the ground. I grabbed the container of filters and stared down at him.

Mr. Cortez came in closer to me, his hands still gripped

something fierce. I could see the whites of his knuckles even in the lowly lit area.

"Why you…" The big-boneheaded jerk fumed as he pushed himself up.

"Is there a problem here?" The Yankee brogue sent shivers up my spine as Barnes walked behind me. I stood still. Here was my chance to ensure that I would get out of the fence.

"Oh, no, sir!" I goaded the guard as I turned around and saluted the General, killing two birds with one stone. I could be a smart-ass with both of them, and I would never have to see them again. "We're all fine here. I was just showing this dumb-ass that he needs to stop fucking with me. He almost threw my filter on the ground."

My ego was getting big, but it felt so good to let go finally!

"You're a dead bitch," Sir Thick-a-Lot grumbled, turning towards where I stood at attention in front of General Barnes. "I'm going to kill you now; there's no need to…" I could see his face out of the corner of my eye. It was all red and blotchy. My inner devil smiled in satisfaction.

"Excuse me, Officer McLaggen," Barnes looked hard at the guard, "What is there no need for?"

He realized the General's attention was on him, so he stopped and stood straight. "Sir, my apologies. I was just giving out the water filters when this mutant attacked me." The spittle flew across the space between us, landing on my cheek. *Yuck.*

I wiped my cheek subtly before turning on McLaggen, my bow and arrow already notched and ready to go, aimed at his head. "Excuse me," I demanded, "You have done nothing but harass me for months. It was little things, but it's gotten worse. You deserve so much more than what I just did. Would you like me to demonstrate?" My trigger finger itched to let the arrow go. I'd never killed a man before, but I was tempted to with him.

"You better give her an extra one," Barnes stated, surprising me. "Considering that you almost destroyed her first one with your carelessness."

"Sir?" McLaggen stared at him, Barnes' eyes were dark and stormy. "Yes, sir." He said a moment later as he grabbed the box from my hand. I smiled sweetly at him as he handed me another water filter. I grabbed it and pushed both into my satchel before turning towards the General.

"You're dismissed," Barnes intoned, and Sir Thick-a-Lot took off like a bandit, heading as far away from me as possible. I was gloating too much to notice that he had an evil gleam in his eyes as he walked away.

"Thank you, sir," I stated, looking into his eyes.

"Hello, Mary Beth." Barnes paused, "I thought your parents said that no one was going to leave?" The question floated between us.

I swallowed hard. Damn. I severely hoped that Nicky would get home and tell our parents before this jerk could tell them about my fantastic escape into the wilderness. They don't need to hear another loss from him, although he would be a first-account witness of my departure this time. "That's right, sir." I affirmed, "They didn't want anyone to leave."

"Then," he paused for good effect, I'm sure, "you are leaving of your own accord?"

Nodding, I turned away from him and looked at the gate. "How much longer until we can leave?"

"Any minute now, I'm doing a last run-through to see if everyone has what the council has sanctioned for their departure."

I nodded again, my lips tight. *Twinkle, twinkle, little star. How I wonder what you are...* The melody drifted through my head again, and I took a deep breath. We didn't exchange another word, and after a few moments of silence, I watched him walk away. His footsteps were in a steady rhythm as he headed away.

Mr. Cortez clears his throat. "That was awkward. Do you not like General Barnes?"

"No." I answered honestly, "I don't trust him. He seems rotten, like something is eating his insides, ya know?"

Mr. Cortez nodded as he looked around at the crowd. "Are you prepared, girl?"

"As can be," I said, putting my bow and arrow back where they belonged. My hood was down for the first time in a long time in a public setting. It was liberating.

Suddenly, the gates creaked open. A stream of people rushed to the gate. *What was I missing?* I didn't think anyone besides the prisoners would be excited to leave the settlement. Mr. Cortez pressed something into my hands as he whispered in my ear. "Look up. See all the guards?" I looked up. Confusion was evident on my face. There were indeed guards stationed all around the fence in this area; some milled near the bottom, and some had climbed ladders and were sitting on the top. Their eyes roamed the crowds almost hungrily. There were more guards than I would typically see at this gate. Anxiety grew.

"We don't get away, we die here tonight." He stated calmly as he gave me a quick hug goodbye.

Fear crept into my soul. *No, I had to get out!* "What the..."

He pressed the item into my hands harder. "You need to

run. Run fast. I'll help you as much as I can." He pushed me forward as he started falling into other groups.

I watched as a woman guard started to draw back on her bow, and another guard put the rifle up to his eye, the scoop clearing the view for him in the pandemonium as groups blurred together. I let loose, my feet flying off the floor. I pushed through people, not caring who I was taking down, I just ran. I made a promise to Nick, which wasn't what I had promised.

Getting through the gates wasn't easy as people started falling, pushing their way through, panic building around me. I ran over bodies, tripping over feet as I plowed ahead. My feet pound against the earth. Out of the corner of my eye, I watched as several prisoners took on guards who were on the ground. The earth blurred around me as my feet carried me through the haze. As I slipped out of the gate into the unknown terrain, my heart pounded, fear and adrenaline pushing me farther and farther.

I ran around trees and jumped over stumps. The sounds of screams filled my ears as I pushed one of the prisoners out of my way. It was still too close. Everything was a blur around me. I couldn't stop, not even for a moment. I ran as I had never run before. Out of the corner of my eye, I saw a girl fall over a brick or something. Her head hit the ground hard. I could hear the crack as she landed. *Fuck.* Everyone was scattered, I could see several people as they took off in different directions. I heaved as I pushed myself further.

I'd made it about twenty or thirty feet before I heard the sounds of gunshots. Were they fighting back? The object Mr. Cortez pushed at me was heavy in my hands. At one point, it almost slipped out of my grip, but I knew it was necessary;

otherwise, he wouldn't have given it to me, so I held on even tighter.

I was still too close. I could hear the falling of bodies as they fell around me. The dead thud of the lifeless bodies echoed in my ears as I traveled over the rocky terrain. Dirt spread through the air, and dead grass crinkled as I ran harder. The farther I moved away, the more the grounds changed under my feet and around me. Buildings came into sight as I continued to run. I zig-zagged through the empty lots as though the hounds of hell were nipping at my heels. I lost track of how long I ran. My satchel knocked into my sides, a heavy beating to remind me that there was a point to my running.

Finally, when my feet could take no more, I collapsed to the ground. I fell flat on my side, avoiding my bow getting bent by the impact. My hands lost their grip on the objects as they slipped out. The sound of them hitting the harsh ground was the only sound around. Otherwise, the air was silent around me as the sky darkened further.

My thoughts were erratic. The lullaby had continued to play the entire time I had been running, pushing all other thoughts away, but as it faded, I realized there was so much to do.

I had to make sure that I wasn't followed. I had to find shelter.

I struggled to catch my breath as I sat up, pulling the bow off me. With my trusted weapon in hand, I turned and looked behind me. The area was empty, the settlement far behind me. How far did I go?

I sat there and stared at the space from which I had come, making sure it remained empty, while I thought of what to do for shelter. I needed something for the night, a place to recuperate and figure things out. I had no clue where I was or how even to find my way to where I was going, if I was going anywhere, now. After several minutes of not seeing anything, I finally relaxed a little. I let my hands release the bow, putting it on my side before it rested on the dusty ground.

I glanced around me. There were some broken and demolished houses. It appeared to be an old neighborhood of some kind. There was nothing high up, no apartment complexes, so I would have to find something for the night. Even though it wasn't ideal for me to be on the same level as possible pursuers, I would make it work. I pushed myself up and off the ground before I rubbed my hands together to shake their dust residue. I glanced down at the ground, Where I saw what I'd been carrying so protectively… a knife, not just any knife though, this was an actual hunting knife. I just knew it in my bones. His water filter had been put together with it as he had handed it to me.

Well, I picked them up gingerly, damn… How'd he know what was going to happen? Where did he get the knowledge of what was going to happen? Why did he give these to me? Why would they give us water filters and weapons if they were just going to kill us? There were too many questions, and my head hurt.

The thoughts circled as I added the two items to my ever-growing satchel. I took a deep breath before putting my bow back on my shoulder and walking towards the house. There had to be one that was habitable. Habitable and safe, that was my goal.

VI

Dom

Seventeen

It was already dusk by the time I got back to the settlement. I had spent the day tracking and looking for any animal, but it was like they were all hiding. I hoped that wasn't an omen. I worked my way around the walls as I came close to the house, only to be confused by the most unusual sight in front of the house.

I watched Nick and Mary Beth walk around the house, carrying their hunting gear—not unusual. Yet, as soon as MB started stuffing a blanket into her satchel, I knew something was up. I was intrigued and scared simultaneously. *Exactly what's going on?*

I trailed behind them as they walked towards the hunting grounds, peeking in every chance I got to ensure I didn't lose them, almost running to keep up, when suddenly they stopped. I couldn't figure out what they were doing before Nick started towards the hunting gate, and MB stood where they had stopped.

Then, she turned and headed in a different direction. I paused, my heart pounding in my chest. I knew the way she was heading, and it wasn't a good sign at all. The animals in hiding must have been a sign; I had to think about my day to see if I missed any signs. I listened for any other noises as I watched. If she was going that way, I'd have to go around the other way. I looked up to see if any guards were posted, and it was almost empty. That was not a good sign. The entire settlement is at least five miles wide, and to go the other way around, I had almost an hour hike ahead of me. Yet, in my bones, I knew that when I got where I was heading, I'd see MB there, which filled me with dread. Did Mom and Dad know? *Probably not.* She was hard-headed, we all were really, but she was so damn stubborn that it was almost admirable.

I ran, turned, and hid from guards as I went. The guards were sparse, and it made me even more on edge. There were few times a year when there weren't many guards, and it was never a good time. I ran until I got where I needed to be or where I assumed that I needed to be.

There is no way I can get any closer. The guards milled around. The top of the walls was littered with guards that sat on top as they stared downward.

I waited, praying above all that I was wrong and she wouldn't be this stupid. This would be the worst time for her to go out those gates. It wasn't a celebration where people were picked up by other settlements and taken there because those settlements were losing too many people or something more sinister. Oh no, I'd watched those ceremonies. There were always at least three government vehicles in the streets when the gates opened during those days. I'd followed one of the vehicles once; it had taken some younger kids downtown to a tall building with always lights on, even at night. That was the other place. I could still hear screams sometimes in my nightmares. I swore that I would never go to that place again.

I'm so lost in my thoughts that I never saw when the gate

popped open. Shit! Just as the silent assassins of arrows flew through the air toward the mostly unsuspecting group, my heart plummeted. *Why did she come this way?* I could feel the blood as it pounded through my veins. I pulled out my pistol, which was held tightly in my hand as I watched from my hiding spot. I had traversed the bones of those they did this to, not even hours ago. This was the next patch of remains to go into the pit. I watched, my heart in my hands, as people pushed and prodded against each other, falling to the sounds of bullets and the swishing of the deadly arrows.

I saw her as she reached the front of the gates. Her shadow flew past me as she ran. I sighed with relief and anxiety, I didn't know, but I knew that they would be following her. They never let anyone who went with this group go. I turned in the direction she headed, racing after her. I constantly kept my eyes on our tails. There would be someone coming. I just knew it.

She ran zig-zagged through the empty streets. She didn't stop at any empty retail stores, which was good because I could hear the sounds of engines behind us. I ensured she continued one way before I stopped, catching my breath as I waited. The vehicle was coming. I would have to throw them off course. It wasn't long before I saw it. The green camo paint of the Army Jeep was bright in the empty streets, even with no light to guide it. They kept the lights off, probably because they wanted to get the drop on her. It was still a couple of blocks away before it spotted me and started heading towards where I stood.

Good. I decided. Let them follow me. I'd lead them right into a river or off the bridge into the highway if I was fortunate. I fired a warning shot at the vehicle, letting them know I meant business if they followed. Apparently, they didn't care, and I smirked. Fantastic, I wanted to give them a reason to hate mutants since they were so gung-ho about us being the evil ones.

I took off. My footsteps fell quickly and lightly. I'd been doing this for a long time now. I ran, always a little faster than what the vehicle was doing. It wasn't speeding, that was for sure, but it wasn't going residential either. I'd shoot at the windows whenever it got too close for comfort. My breath was coming hard and fast; I needed to stop; I was slowing down, and I wasn't even close to the highway yet.

The vehicle was creeping closer again, and I knew I couldn't take much more, so I stopped. It was time to stand my ground. The car stopped, maybe fifty or a hundred feet away, before two guards emerged. They must not have considered her much of a threat. There was one colossal guy who came out on the passenger side. It wasn't that he was bulky in muscle; it was like he just had too much to eat. The other was some skinny twerp. He had to be a newbie because he carried himself so unsure. He was just doing it because he had no other option. I had no idea why a newbie would be driving, but then again, it wasn't any of my business what the government did in there.

"Well, look what we have here. Whatcha say, Conrad? Should we kill him or take him back for the experimentations?" The chunky one said. He itched his belly as his gun hung off his side.

The skinny one shrugged his shoulders, clearly uncomfortable but unable to stand up for himself. Well, he got himself into this situation. Not anyone else. I shook my head sadly.

"What do you mean?" I antagonized him, "You ain't doin'

shit! I'm gonna take your ass out, you lard ass!"

The heavy one pulled on his pants as he took a step forward. I pulled my gun up, aiming it at his head. "I'd suggest that you stop right there." He looked at me, hatred burning in his eyes, and stopped mid-step.

"What do you think you're going to do? Shoot me? You're not going to, or you would have done it already." He jeered.

"You haven't given me enough reason yet. Why were you following me?" I needed to make sure that they were after Mary Beth. I wanted to avoid killing an innocent unless I had to.

"We weren't attempting to follow you," the thin one, Conrad, said. There was someone we missed and had to get back to the settlement with." He sounded so truthful that I almost believed him. "Have you seen a girl with long black hair? Carrying a bow?"

The hefty one laughed, "Don't lie to the mutant. We're looking for her because she deserves to die." He smiled eerily. "I can't wait to kill the bitch."

Oh, my big brother's radar went off the scale. No one, and I mean no one, messes with my sister. I closed one eye as I let out a menacing smile and gently pulled the trigger. The bullet punched its way through the man's eye, causing a gaping hole in its wake that quickly filled with blood and gushed out. Hefty fell backward to the ground, a pool of blood forming around him and soaking into his uniform as the light went out from his soul, if you swant to say that the asshole had a soul. The gun kicked like a sunnabitch in my hand, and my ears rang for a moment as I watched him fall.

Conrad let out a scream as he turned tail and ran away. I felt like laughing. It was an insane response. This was only the second time that I had killed a living person, and both times, it had been for the protection of my sister. There wasn't anything I wouldn't do to take care of her. I must have stood there for over an hour staring into the dead air above the man, my hands slowly falling to my side. I must have been in shock because the light was starting to fade in slowly over the horizon before I realized that the vehicle was still running.

Shit, I needed to take care of it. They could see her quicker if it were still in working order when they found it. And me. They would be looking for me now. I'd let that other guy get away. I couldn't believe it. Fuck, he was probably already halfway back to the settlement.

I looked around me. There were chunks of houses and buildings, rocks, and miscellaneous things. I had to find something that would make a dent in this vehicle. Something to make it inoperable. I tucked the gun back into its holster before walking to the nearest chunk of cement. It had to be as big as my head. It was perfect.

I sat on my haunches as I tested the weight in my hands. It wasn't too bad. Picking it up, I stood and heaved it over to the vehicle. One, two, three... I pumped myself up before launching it at the front windshield.

The sound of crunching glass was like music to my ears. There was still so much to do, so I walked around and popped open the driver's door. The inside of the vehicle was so cold, like an icebox. How the hell did they manage to have something so lovely still when the rest of us had shit? It was ridiculous. I pulled the keys out and walked away. I took a couple of hundred steps away from the vehicle before I threw the keys into the abyss of the land.

I returned to the Jeep and looked through the doors for

something I could use to damage it. I avoided the passenger side like the plague, though. Just because I killed the man didn't mean that I wanted to look it in the face. I wasn't a sociopath. I did it for the survival and protection of my family. That was all. Finding a crowbar in the back end, I took it to all the windows I could. The sound of metal hitting glass was sweet in the most agonizing way. I just wanted to get out of here and go and find MB, yet I had to make this something that would deter them for a while. The last windows were on the passenger side, and I tried to make it quick. I avoided looking at the ground as I smashed out the back window, stepping towards the front through my foot landed in the puddle of blood. I shuddered. Now, I would be carrying a part of that man with me forever, not just the stain on my soul but his blood now soaked me.

I threw the crowbar through the window and returned the way I came. I knew which way she had headed; it was the same way I had gone with Elizabeth all those years ago. Once I found her, I would worry about the guards and anyone else coming after her. I needed to make sure that she was safe.

I traveled until the light of the sun was almost at my back. I needed to rest, I needed to do many things, but I couldn't do that until I saw MB and made sure that she was heading to safety, even though I was pissed that she had taken off like that. What in the world was she thinking? I also had to figure out about everyone else. I wouldn't be back for a while to protect the family if she was heading where I thought she was heading. If she were going there, I would need to ensure she made it out and through the wastelands as safely as possible. But I couldn't let her see me. It would break the promise I'd made when I'd left sanctum. They would kill me on sight if I were with her, so I'd have to watch over her until then. That's when I could come back and ensure they were okay. Meanwhile, I had to trust that the devil wouldn't take them all to hell.

VII

Mary Beth

Act II – Colorado: Broken Peaks, Dark Skies

Eighteen

God, it was a wasteland. The buildings crumbled with the lightest winds, chunks, and boulders falling off everywhere. It was a complete disaster, worse than even the most depleted home in the settlement. I thought as I tried to pick through some remains of homes. *Was there anywhere safe to stay?* I had to question myself as my search continued. I was still anxious. Would they come after me? No wonder they had that exist so close to the hunting grounds. It was used for genocide. But where did all the bodies go? Who else knew about this? Did my parents know? There were so many questions.

It was still dark out, but I was unsure how long it would last. I must have been running and hiding for hours now. At one point, I could barely see my hands in front of me, and I wondered what time it was. I wished I had liked wearing watches, but I had always gone by the sun's light to give me ideas of when I needed to be somewhere. I was generally on the mark when telling time that way. I was like a sundial. However, sundials don't work at night, so apparently, neither did I. Time got me thinking of Nicky and his watch, and then it spiraled from there.

I couldn't help but wonder what had happened when Nicky

got home. *Were they mad at him?* I knew they would be angry at me, but whatever. I tripped over a large chunk of a wall, falling flat on my face. I could feel the marks of scuffed skin as I pushed myself up. Damnit. I was so lost in my thoughts that I hadn't been paying the best attention to my surroundings. I pulled myself off the ground and wiped off the debris. That was the worst thing I could do; it was an amateur move, and I wasn't an amateur. *At least, when hunting, I was almost an expert.* I thought cockily as I stopped and looked around at the surrounding houses.

What the hell was I supposed to do? I mean, there was so much debris around. What would be the safest thing for me to do? I couldn't just stand in the middle of the street anymore. It wasn't as dark now. It was lightening up, and exhaustion was starting to set in. I didn't know what was safe and how long I had until someone would be looking for me. I couldn't be picky anymore.

I started to look at the surrounding buildings. There had to be something that was somewhat habitable. There it was. It caught my eye. The perfect place. There was a house that wasn't destroyed. It looked like at least a couple of walls were still fully intact. I searched around the building to ensure it was somewhat safe and inhabitable before climbing into the ruins that led to where the intact walls stood. I dodged under broken beams and over half-shattered walls and tumbled through the messy rooms until I found a room.

It was a disaster, but what did I expect? The entire world was a disaster. Someone had already been here at some time in the recent past, I decided, as I looked around. There were little signs all over the place. There was an old and ratty mattress up against the wall, with a pile of clothes or something like it sitting at the end of the mattress. There was debris facing toward what I would have considered the street would be. I sighed; at least it was something to protect me for a while; I could already see the light peeking through the rocks and rubble. It would make do. I walked over to the mattress and flopped down on it. It wasn't the most comfortable, but when had I ever really cared about comfort?

I wasn't sure how long this would be safe, obviously because someone else had been here before. I needed to figure out how long I had to get out of there. I mean, someone could have been here just hours ago. But the bed was cold, like an ice bucket, so that much was comforting as I estimated that it had been longer than hours since the last inhabitants. Sighing, I removed my bow and quiver and placed them by the wall. They were still close enough that I could grab them but far enough away that someone couldn't pull them on me either. Then, I pulled my satchel over my head; it was heavy; how I had carried it this far without complaint was beyond me. It must have been the adrenaline. I placed it between my legs before I opened it.

There was a treasure trove inside my satchel. I marveled at how much I had managed to fit in there! I carefully placed the blanket next to me and began to sort through the bag. Eight cans of food, three pairs of underwear, a couple of shirts, and socks. The necklace in my pocket poked me in the side of my thigh, a gentle reminder that it was still there and that I should probably put it back on. Leaning to my right, I reached into my pocket and pulled it out.

I sat up straight, and the necklace slid down between my fingers. The thick golden links were taut as the pendant pulled it down. It was a beautiful necklace, a symbol of our family's legacy. It had been my mom's when she graduated. She'd gotten it from her mom, who had gotten it from her mom for quite a few generations. As mom told me, each generation would add a little to it before giving it to the next girl in the family line. I guess I was the last to have it because there was nothing I could add. I thought sarcastically as I went through each piece in my mind.

The most significant piece, and what was the original piece according to Mom, was a woman's silhouette. She was white in the blue background, her head held regally with a golden twisted frame surrounding her. It was made of marble, which I didn't know about, but it made it extremely heavy. Surrounding her on a more prominent link that held all the pieces together were several kinds of stones. Some mothers in my family line had added birthstones of the child that they were giving it to to make it more uniquely theirs. It had been a tradition for many years.

There was a garnet, which mom told me was thought to keep the wearer safe during travel. My great-great-grandmother put the stone on the necklace when she gave it to my great-grandmother because she would travel across the ocean to America when she got the necklace. When she had given it to my grandmother, she had added my grandmother's birthstone of a ruby. Mom had enjoyed talking to me about the necklace; it was 'our legacy,' she said, and it was vital for us to know the meaning so that our children could also see the story. When she asked her mother about the ruby, she told her it was believed to protect its wearer from evil. When her mom had given it to her, she had added my mom's birthstone... a turquoise gem.

I'd once asked her what her birthstone meant because she

never told me. I guess I was still a little too young when she gave it to me. Or maybe it was because I was already itching to go outside and play when I had gotten it. Yet, when I got older, at least a little older, enough to understand that it was a unique necklace. I realized that it did have a lot of meaning for my family. *It was special.* She told me that it meant good fortune and success. She had a lot of good fortune and success because she had all of us. The last two pieces caught my eye as they twinkled in the darkness. Two letters…

My mom had added two letters to it right after discovering she was pregnant with me. She said a letter for her name, a K for Karen, and an M for me. She was optimistic about my name and wanted it to be remarkable. I smiled. I know she wanted it to be uniquely me, but I left my letter for her on the dresser when I left so that she knew I was still there and loved her and the rest of them immensely. I still had her with me. I hoped we could repair our relationship when I came back for them. I loved her, even with all her flaws, because I was just as flawed as anyone else. *She was my mom.* She made me into who I was by being who she was.

I was glad I'd brought the necklace when I left. As I unclasped it and put it around my neck, I felt her arms wrapped around me, hugging me like she used to when I was a small child. I pulled my long hair to the side as one hand held the necklace pieces together until my hair was out of the way, and then I put it on. I smiled dimly as it rested on my heart.

I returned to my bag and rearranged things around in the dark until I felt like the food wouldn't clank too much together because it had my clothes separating them. I knew the more noise I made, the more attention I would get. I didn't know if I would be chased, but I would be careful. My eyes closed slightly as an ache rose out of my chest, causing me to yawn. The exhaustion was hard to beat, but I needed to make sure I was ready to go at a moment's notice.

The hunting knife and several water filters were in the front pocket of my satchel. That wouldn't work; I needed it to be easy, so I just reached in and grabbed the knife if I needed it. The water filters had to be moved. Hmmm. They could go in the side pockets so I could quickly reach them when I needed to get some water. Thinking of the water, I realized I'd forgotten to grab something to put water into. I slapped my head in frustration. I felt like an idgit. Now, I had to scavenge even more tomorrow before leaving my neighborhood. There was no way in hell that I wouldn't make it far without water.

I shook my head in disgust. I was better than that. I felt like rolling my eyes at myself. I put my satchel at the top of the mattress. Hopefully, I could use it as a pillow as long as the cans didn't hurt my head. I had a couple of hours this morning to deal with it. This way, I could ensure that everything was safe while I slept. I shook out my blanket and curled up on the mattress. I pulled it over my legs and around my shoulders, suddenly blinking hard.

Why did I do this? I thought. *Did it make a difference? What if they punish Nick for helping me? What if they force them out, too? What if Martha turns me in for stealing the cans? Would she? Her son was out here. Maybe I could find him. What if I couldn't? What if he was dead?*

There was no way to stop the thoughts pounded in my head now. I had stopped long enough to gather myself, and now it was time for everything to crumble. Tears fell from my eyes as I thought of my family. I wish I'd had a picture of them. The necklace and everything else were lovely, but it wasn't them. I missed them. I missed them a lot. The tears slid down my face, burning against the harsh reminders of my slip-up outside. The salty tears reminded me this was my choice, and now I had to live with the consequences.

I held in the sobs that wanted to escape. I cried quietly on a dirty, tattered mattress in the dark room. I was truly alone for the first time in my life. I didn't know how to handle it. I didn't know what to do. But I would have to.

Eventually, the tears subsided, and I succumbed to the silence.

Nineteen

The hazy light from the mid-morning sun drifted through the broken walls as I became aware of my surroundings. *Had I slept that long?* My throat felt parched, my head was lying on the mattress, and there were aches and pains all over it that I'd never experienced before. *So, sleeping on my satchel with cans was not a good idea.* I thought to myself as I sat up.

I groaned as I stretched out. As I rolled my neck, I heard the cracks as they popped. Wow, that was a first. It had been a rough night. I don't think I'd ever run that hard or fast. My arms rested lightly on the mattress, and I twisted around to check my surroundings; everything seemed still in place, my right hand on my bow. It was a comfort to me to know that it was still there. The lullaby played softly in my head as my heart started to race and the realization set in. I couldn't stay here long, I'd realized, and no matter what, I'd slept way too long now. Anyone could be outside looking for me.

I pushed myself off the bed. My body ached, but there was no more time to stretch my muscles; my heart was still pounding. Even as I stood, my body betrayed my thoughts as they automatically started to stretch out. It was an everyday routine, and I forced myself to go through it quickly. I looked around, doing another inventory of my surroundings and the ruins as I stretched. The first time had been a quick look. This was more of my hunter instincts, making sure of my surroundings. It would be my luck to be in the middle of a stretch, and someone come upon me and take everything I own or down. The thought was like an icy cold bucket of water dumped over my head. I watched vigilantly as I finished off my stretches.

I still felt like I was about to die, but at least it wasn't as back. What I needed to do was figure out how I was going to pee. It was like a weight that was pushing down on my bladder. I needed to go *and bad*. It felt wrong to pee in the shelter that had kept me safe all night long. So, I grabbed my blanket off the bed and folded it up again. Sticking it in my satchel, I pulled the satchel over my head and looked down at my bow. I needed to defend myself if someone came upon me while walking. *What could I do?*

I stared at my bow for a while while my bladder continued to scream at me that I needed to go to the bathroom. Finally, taking an arrow out of my quiver, I placed it in my satchel where I could quickly grab it.

I thought I might not be able to do a quick draw on someone coming up, but I could stab them with the arrow if necessary.

Drifting through the broken rooms back to the grassy, dry landing at the back of the building, I scanned the horizon. Nothing seemed out of place; I couldn't see anyone around. Thank the Powers that Be. Whatever They are. There had to be something, even if it was God; I just didn't believe in Him specifically.

I looked for an area that would provide me with some protection to pee. Finding a hidden but unmistakable area,

I could see from my destination, I put everything down, carrying the arrow with me as I went over and quickly did my business. I walked back towards my belongings, scanning the area again. I looked over the house that had kept me safe during my rest and was thankful. At least something had worked in my favor so far. The melody picked up in intensity as it played in my head. I had to keep moving. This was still too close to the settlement and wouldn't offer enough protection.

Hauntingly, the words to the song started to play in my mind. *Twinkle, twinkle, little star. How I wonder what you are. Up above the world so high.* The tone was deep, almost a baritone, and chilled me. That voice wasn't mine; I was sure of that, but it felt so familiar. Yet, it wasn't my dad's or Nick's. I couldn't remember Dom's voice too clearly, so it continued to be a mystery.

Like a diamond in the sky. Twinkle, twinkle, little star. How I wonder where you are.

The sky! That was it! It was a eureka moment. I knew exactly where I needed to go to find a spot that would work for our family. *I needed to go higher, up into the mountains.* Most of the bombs had hit the flat lands of Colorado. Not many landed in the hills; I knew some did, but there had to be someplace I could find that would be safe for everyone. The song faded as I realized that once I found a spot and marked it as mine, I could return and get my family, even if it took a while. It would be better than being down here. There were too many people still hiding around here. Considering what happened last night, I didn't want to take any chances of being this close to any settlement down here.

The mountains had been running through after the bombs.

People killing people. I remember hearing Mom and Dad talking about it when I was younger. There couldn't be that many people up there.

I didn't want to go somewhere that had a lot of people. That could be disastrous. I'd just have to keep searching once I got up there until it felt like the perfect spot.

My mind was made up, and I turned towards the hazy, tall shapes in the distance. I had quite a way to go, but if I was safe and aware of my surroundings, I bet I could get there without much trouble. I adjusted my bow on my shoulder. I popped my neck again, side to side, hearing the little bings of bones moving against each other before I squared my shoulders and walked away.

The streets were uneven and hard on my feet as I moved. I wore a ratty pair of old sneakers, but they were comfy. A reminder of home. I headed towards the mountains, keeping the tall hills in sight as I walked. The sun wasn't too bright today; I assumed it wasn't because I didn't feel like I was dying of heat while I walked. My throat was still parched, and I hit myself in the head as I realized I'd forgotten to grab water before I left. I scanned the area as I walked. I needed to get some water ASAP.

Every good hunter knows that you have to stay hydrated if you want to stay alive. Dad had always told me that. Walking, I would stop at the houses and old businesses looking for something salvageable. I must have been walking for several hours before I found myself getting tired. Everything that I saw was crap. Holes that ran straight through the bottles. Not to mention the many containers with no lids, I was starting to feel like this would be a hopeless endeavor. Then I heard it. The tinkling of water. I stopped and turned around in a circle as I tried to locate where the water was coming from. It was so faint. Yet, I knew I had heard it.

Why was this so hard? I was getting frustrated.

Finally, I just stopped and stood there with my eyes closed. I took some deep breaths as I focused on the sound of water. It was moving like it was moving through a stream or river. This wasn't like the sounds of the faucet running at home. No, this was natural. Finally, I started moving. I didn't open my eyes, trusting my instincts and hoping the environment would work with me; I moved towards the noise. I stumbled over rocks and dirt, but I kept going, hands outstretched until I could hear the whishing of the water as it tumbled nearby.

I kept going toward it, knowing I was in the water because I almost landed flat in there. My feet were completely soaked, and the water lapped at my shoes.

I stopped and opened my eyes. *It was wondrous!* We didn't have any free-flowing water in the settlement; seeing it flowing freely in front of me was impressive. Yet, at the same time, I realized that it could be acidic. I pulled my feet away from the water quickly, hoping against hope that it wouldn't eat through my only pair of shoes. I shook my feet out as I looked over my shoes. It didn't look like it was eating through my shoes, which was a good sign, but I needed to ensure it was drinkable.

I pulled my bow off and laid it gently on the ground before I swung my satchel around, pushing the arrow to the side as I pulled out a water filter. Looking it over, I saw two parts to each filter. The first part was a little tester strip, but only eight test strips were used for each filter. I would need to be careful and not go too crazy each time I checked the water out. I didn't know how long I would be out here without a good source of clean water, so it was better to be cautious. I looked over the colors that it showed on the side, determined to make sure that I knew the right color for water that would be drinkable. After reading it, I knew that I didn't want anything that was either too red or too purple. Red would be acidic and would eat my intestines up. Purple was harder and could do the same thing; at least, that was what I'd assumed. I wanted something in the yellowish-orange-green area.

Satisfied with the information, I pulled my satchel off and placed it next to the bow before kneeling to test the water. I barely stuck the strip in the running stream so it wouldn't take off on me, but I could get enough water on it. I pulled it out and watched it change colors. I stood there for minutes before I determined that it wasn't changing colors anymore, and I checked against the instructions. It was a yellowish-orange color, which wasn't too acidic, thankfully. I wondered if all water was the same or if this was just skipped because it was down in a valley.

I smiled as I realized I didn't need to use the filter, so I put it up. Stuffing it back into the pocket of my satchel, I rocked back on my heels before I sat down better on the ground. It was safe, so I sat down, knowing the radioactive waste wasn't still soaked in this area. *Maybe it had never been.* I felt so tired, so I was happy to stop for a while. As I scooted away from my bag and bow headed towards the water, putting my hands in the water was pretty refreshing. Cupping them together, I brought forth a handful of water.

I gulped it down as I had never tasted anything so refreshing, and maybe I hadn't, but it slid down my throat like the sweetest treat. Excitedly, I drank more water until my stomach ached and was full. I sighed with contentment and leaned back. I pulled my bow to my side and breathed deeply.

I felt like I'd been walking forever since leaving the settlement. I leaned back and took another deep breath. Intellectually, I knew it hadn't been that long. The sun wasn't even wholly overhead. Yet, I was so weary. I missed my family. I missed the look on the girl's faces when they were playing outside together, the pure joy they gave each other. How Nicky would try to take over, and I'd have to knock him down a few pegs. I even missed my mom's arguments, and disapproving looks when I got into trouble. Hell, even Dad's humor was sorely missed. They weren't here, yet they were in my heart, which kept me going.

I looked around the brook, and there wasn't much that suggested that it was often used; it was kinda plain.

The sidewalk was cracked and broken into many pieces. The trees were a little greener down here but still looked half-dead. There were a couple of deteriorated boxes several feet down from where I sat. The grass was even somewhat greener than everywhere else. Maybe it was because there was some water nearby.

I adjusted to the feeling of water in my stomach before pulling the arrow from my satchel. I needed to ensure I could defend myself in a minute, but I also needed to eat.

And this was a good enough spot to eat something before I continued. I placed it gently on the ground next to me before pulling my satchel over. After I opened the bag, I started moving stuff around. Finding one, I pulled it out and placed it next to me before putting my blanket back in the bag and closing it. Before moving my bag away again, I grabbed the knife from it and placed it next to the can.

Now that everything was in place, I felt more focused. As I

grabbed the can and the knife, I placed the car in between my legs and sat Indian style. Holding the knife tightly, I grabbed the side of the can with the other, ensuring it wouldn't move. I punched the knife tip through the lid of the can and started to wiggle it as I began to pull it out. Continuing this fashion, I went around the whole can before the lid sank into the food. Smiling, I wiped the knife on my jeans before opening my bag and returning it. I had only done that once or twice before, but it was always with Dad there to help me if I needed it. I felt accomplished.

I didn't bring anything to eat; it was another dumb move, but I had no problem using my hands to eat. As long as I had something to eat, I'd be fine; it wasn't like I couldn't scavenge and find some utensils later. I rocked myself forward again and stuck my hands in the running water. I pulled them out and rubbed them together. I did this several times before deciding that they were clean enough to be used to eat. I didn't need to get sick from everything I've touched since last night.

As I sat back and looked down at the opened can, the lid remained. There was no label on the outside; it was just that metallic color. This made it harder for me to determine what to look forward to because I had no idea what it was. But that was precisely what the government did for canned goods when they gave them to the villages and settlements they had.

At least, that's what I'd heard over the years. I guess there had been numerous fights when the settlements were first created when they handed out food to people. People had been fighting over fruits and beans, saying that someone else got more of one thing than they did. I didn't see any point in fighting about any of it. It was food. I guess if you had just survived the bombings, you would have been easily agitated.

I removed the lid from the can and put it on my jeans to cover the food. I knew I couldn't drain a single can in a sitting; otherwise, I'd run out of food sooner than I intended.

Oooh, I thought as I glanced down into the container. *What a lucky start to my day.* The can was filled with peach slices. We hardly ever got them when I was home; when we did, Mom split them among us kids. A quick tear ran down my face, salty and fast, ending at my chin.

I gotta stop thinking about them. Every time I think of them, I get emotional. Being emotional won't help me when I'm out here. Again, the lullaby drifts through my mind, that deep baritone voice echoing it through my mind.

I shook my head and wiped the tear away before pulling out a couple of slices of peaches. There was no need for utensils with this. This was pure finger food!

Tilting my head back, I put the peaches to my lips, my fingertips holding them by the tip. I take the first bite, the juices sliding down the corners of my mouth. I closed my eyes and savored the taste of the sweet fruit as my teeth tore through the piece. The following piece is devoured without ever opening my eyes. This went on for a couple more slices before I forced myself to put the lid back on the can. As I dropped my hands behind me, supporting my body, I enjoyed the flavors and peacefulness of this place. As the peaches burst across my taste buds, I just wanted it. I leaned up, my stomach still growling, as I wiped my hands across my pants before I opened the can again and grabbed another slice.

This has to be it, I reminded myself before eating it. I hoped that I'd be able to find some more canned goods as I continued eating.

After gobbling the next slice, I tilted the can and drank juice. Before I stopped again, I made sure to leave enough juice in the can to keep the other pieces juicy and delicious. For the second time, I put the lid back on the can and pushed it in on the sides of the top to keep it steady inside.

Suddenly, it dawns on me. How could I keep the can from spilling all over my stuff? *Stupid.* I called myself as I stared down at what had become my nemesis in this new journey.

"Hmmm..." I raised an eyebrow. I could stick it towards the edge of my bag with a couple of cans next to it to keep it steady, but that could also spill. If something happens, I could carry it, but I can't be as quick with my drawing. All I can do is see and try.

I put the can down, dragged my bag back over, and opened it again. I moved the blanket out as I rearranged the bag, placing several cans in one area before I put the opened one in there, with several more standing upright next to it. I put several layers of clothes on the opposite side of the cans, trying to make it compact. After a while, I figured it was as good as possible. I put the blanket back over everything and closed it up before putting the arrow back in and looking around again.

Twenty

My hunting instincts kicked in, and I felt the slight buzz of being watched. I'm surprised I'd been in this area as long as I had without anyone coming upon me. But my survival skills, honed through years of living in the settlement, have kept me safe so far.

I thought that there were rebels, scavengers, mutants… because that's the reasoning that the government gave us when they put up the wall around the settlement. *So, why haven't I seen anybody yet?* With my hair pricked and my nerves on end, everything felt surreal. The lullaby drifted through my head again, a bittersweet reminder of the life I left behind and a comfort in this desolate place.

I started to stand up before remembering that I had no clue when I would see water again. *Well crap!* I had no luck finding a container during my walk here; maybe something would be around here. I hoped anyway. I glanced around my surroundings again, my nerves still on end, before I decided to check out the deteriorated boxes. Maybe there was something in one of them.

As I walked up the riverbed, I spotted the straps of cardboard. I prayed as I looked underneath them, hoping for a miracle. It seemed like a hopeless endeavor. Yet, just when I was about to give up, a glint of something shiny caught my eye in the afternoon glare. I walked towards it and pulled it out from under a part of cardboard that I hadn't looked at yet, and dirt came up with it. It had been partially buried in the ground, so I didn't notice it immediately. It was an old metal bottle. I struggled to remember its name.

It wasn't a Coke bottle because I remembered Mom and Dad would always get us a 6-pack of Coke as a reward since we didn't always drink soda. *What was it called?* I know Dom used to have one for when he wrestled. *Handy bottle? Flashy cup? Hydro bottle?* Thinking of the elemental name for water. It sounded better, but not quite yet. *Hydro flask?* It was like a bell went off. That was what it was called.

As I held it in my hands, I started wiping it down. I tried to clean as much of the dirt off the side as I could before turning back towards the stream. I pushed it under the flowing water and watched as it cleaned the outside and filled the inside. At least I would keep it clean before taking water with me. Pulling it out from the water, I emptied it and put it back in again. This way, there would be no dirt residue in the first bottle. I watched as it filled up again. *Twinkle, twinkle, little star. How I wonder what you are? Up above the sky so high, like a diamond in the sky.* The lullaby picks up again in volume, the voice deep and comforting with my raw nerves. I never understood why the song was so important, but it had always stayed with me, even when I outgrew mom singing it to me at night.

Once the bottle was filled, I pulled it out of the river and returned to my belongings.

My nerves were still raw, my senses on high alert for any noises, but I needed to appear normal. That's the only way

I would catch someone. If they didn't know I was aware of them, then it could be a surprise attack. I just knew that there was someone, but where?

With that thought in mind, I looked down at the bottle and my satchel. *Now, what was I going to do?* I pursued my lips. There was no way that I could carry the bottle in my hands and be prepared to fight someone if I had to pull my bow.

I plopped onto the ground, placing the hydro flask beside my bow. There had to be a way. There was a notch on the lid for the hydro flash, but my satchel didn't have a strap that connected through a lock. It was sewn together. That wouldn't work. I could put it inside, but then I would have to rearrange everything. That would be stupid.

Thickets and broken branches lay around me, and the tall semi-green grass swayed gently in the soft breeze. A surprise for me. I hadn't felt a breeze for years.

A lightbulb went off.

That's it! I got it... I could see which branches or blades of grass bent the best and which ones would not break when I used them to tie the bottle to the bag. I messed around for a while with this, making it so that the bottle could rest on the side of the satchel while I walked. After feeling somewhat accomplished with this task, I thought of another.

There were branches, rocks in the riverbed, grass, and everything the natives used to make their hunting apparel. Now I could make some to be safe. Dad had always told me hunters used to hunt with spears and bows in the old days.

Getting up from my spot, I started surveying the surrounding branches. I wanted something thick but not too dense, long enough to reach the ground as a walking stick.

It took a while, but eventually, I found a perfect one. The

branch was a little thicker than one of my fingers and taller than me. At some point, it had to have been one of the main branches of one of the trees, but it had fallen off and died some time ago. It was intense as I tapped it against the sides of trees and the ground.

I sat beside everything and pulled my knife from the bag again. I probably should carry it closer to me than that, but oh well. That wasn't my focus now. I put the stick between my legs, turning so that I could still work without breaking it. The branch dipped into the water, just a little, as I adjusted to a better spot. I held the branch with one hand while I used my left hand to pull the bark off, occasionally using the knife to help pull it off when it was stuck. It would just rub my hands raw if I didn't.

Once all the bark was off, I sharpened the end in front of me. I thought this would take some time as I continued to work on it. I wanted it to be perfect, sharp enough to cut through something or someone's skin if I threw it at them. It took so much time! I swore I must have taken four or five breaks to rehydrate before finally finishing it.

I touched the tip. "Ow!" That was almost as sharp as my knife. My nerves weren't as on edge as they had been hours before, even though they reminded me that something was out there. I had moved while sharpening towards the wall, hidden under several trees that were still partially full. I thought I should do a couple more, but how would I carry them? I rolled my eyes. I was being too demanding of my abilities and needed to relax. I leaned back against the wall, it was cool against my back, and took a couple of deep breaths.

I smiled, really, truly smiled, for the first time in what felt like a long time. I felt more confident about moving forward.

More than I had before. I touched my necklace, thinking of how the stones had strong properties, and stood up. I could do this. I dropped the newly made spear and knife down before I looked around one last time. My nerves weren't on edge now, and I felt confident in myself and my actions. More than I had ever felt when I had talked with Nick before leaving.

"I can do this!" I shouted out, needing the affirmation out loud. I believed in myself as much as I tried to project to Nicky when I first suggested doing this. It was a landmark moment.

I felt stronger. I reached down, picked up my bow, and placed it around my shoulder again. The arrow went right back into my bag, still sticking out, so I had something if I needed it for shorthand reach. Again, I thought about how I probably should have the knife on me somewhere, but I just didn't know where to put it. I can make do with the spear and arrow for now. I opened the pocket of my satchel and put the knife away. Lastly, I reached down and grabbed the bottle and the spear.

I looked longingly at the river again before returning the way I came. I would find somewhere safe for my family and then return to this spot and enjoy it fully.

Twenty-One

I spent the rest of the day scavenging through the buildings in the area. I knew the water nearby was clean enough to drink, so I prioritized finding more food and shelter for the night. I had to be about five miles from the settlement, so I hoped they wouldn't be trailing after me now. It didn't mean that my nerves were going haywire with every bit of noise, every crash, the whistle of the wind that happened.

It had already been midday by the time that I finished the spear, and I wasn't about to travel during the night again. It got dark and fast, and there was no way that I would attempt to travel in that without some kind of light to guide me.

As I walked, I saw the crumbling towers of apartment complexes and fallen buildings. I held on tighter to the spear. I had no clue where anything was in this new environment, which made me nervous. I walked deeper and deeper into the wreckage of buildings as I moved rocks and found cabinets, broken furniture, and ran-through businesses. I remembered Denver as this great city, filled to the brim with interesting sights and sounds; there was nothing like that now, and it was depressing.

Some areas were so overrun by nature that it was terrific, it was an amazing view of nature and disaster. There were open gardens that used to be bedrooms and living rooms. Some bathrooms had tree stumps growing through the floors. After going through so many buildings, I stopped when I found an old sporting goods business. *This had to be a good place to rest for the night.* I thought as I peeked through the windows. The building wasn't destroyed; the door still looked steady, so I pulled on it until it opened.

Wow. I hit the jackpot!

The room was filled with sporting goods. It looked like nothing had been touched in the years since the day our lives changed. I was practically skipping as I walked into the building. Tents, sleeping bags, and even backpacks better equipped for a long journey than my little satchel were there. I was ecstatic!

I grabbed everything that my little heart could desire. I found containers for food, even dry foods, and as I took my satchel and bow off, I wondered about my luck. I had some stupid lucky luck. There was no way a place like this would have stayed as complete as this with everything that happened.

I found a mini-camping stove and some butane tanks to go with it. It would be great if I could figure out some of the cans meant to be eaten hot. My stomach growled loudly, reminding me it had been hours since I had last eaten. I grabbed a sleeping bag and one of the backpacks that could carry my bow and brought them over to where everything else lay.

I grabbed the can of peaches from my bag and started to eat them, using the utensils I found as I moved everything from the satchel to the backpack. The sleeping bag could be carried on the bottom of it while my bow was firmly held in place by the straps on the back with several of my arrows right behind it. It was ideal, and while I was still in shock about my stupid lucky luck, not to mention that I wasn't ready to give up my satchel. I could carry both and quickly make my satchel into my go-to bag for anything I might need.

I noticed that the sun was starting to set. It was visible from my spot as I looked out the store door. It reminded me that I needed to bunker down for the night. There had to be a spot in here that I could hide in case anyone came looking. A couple of tents were up for display with the bags inside them. I found one closer to the store's back end, and no one would go looking that far if they wanted someplace safe for the night. I carried everything to it. Checking the store out again, I felt comfortable staying there for the night. As I shut myself in the tent, I thought of my parents and family and hoped they were all safe and well-fed.

As I lay down in my sleeping bag, I could feel the warm wetness of tears in the corners of my eyes. That night was the only time I had decided to allow myself to be weak, to feel those sad, overwhelming feelings of loneliness and stupidity. I had left the safety of the settlement for the unknown, and now I had to prove to them and myself that I had made the right decision.

Twenty-Two

The next few days passed in a blur as I continued my relentless journey towards the mountains. Even shrouded in hazy uncertainty, I was resolute in my belief that they held the promise of safety for my family.

I came across what had to be the center of Denver. I had walked probably fifteen or twenty miles from the settlement, and each day, I felt more secure in my abilities. The buildings in this area were complete rubble. Only one shredded-up building lay partially on a hill, or what I assumed was a hill. It dipped down heavily on one side. I walked up to the building and looked down, and it went down. A bomb had to have gone off near here. There was nothing but this crater that expanded for what seemed like miles but was probably only twenty or so street blocks wide, total in both directions.

I swore I could see many high-rise buildings in the distance, but something told me to stay away from them. I turned and looked closer at the building. It had to have been beautiful at one time, I determined. A bit of shiny color was all around it, including down in the crater. I wondered what was glossy, so I grabbed a piece that called out to me. As I looked at the piece, I realized that it was made of gold. I had gold in my hand, but I didn't remember any building with gold on it.

Hmmm. It was tarnished and turning green in parts, but it was huge. It kind of looked like the shingles that were on the roof of my family's home. I put it into my satchel after I finished looking at it. I didn't know what it belonged to, but who knew if it wouldn't be worth something if I ran into someone who wanted to barter?

I was lucky that it didn't look too nasty.

Speaking of nasty, I wondered why I was having so much luck. I hadn't seen another soul during my travels at all. Even though there had been times when I was sure that someone had been there. I'd refilled my water bottle twice at the same river before I had journeyed further.

It was like there was nothing left of anyone or anything. Yet, I knew it couldn't last long though. I turned away from the dipping land and started heading south, or what I assumed was south. I'd been heading west for so long that there was no way that I would travel into that crater.

The first night in that sporting goods store had been tolerable, but I was unwilling to take risks. I spent the next several nights in what I believed to be abandoned homes, always on high alert.

Shaking my head, I tried to focus on what I was doing. I used my spear's blunt end to move objects around when I came upon broken slabs of concrete and bricks to see if there was anything useful in them. Although I was careful with the spear, I didn't want it to break before I used it. My resourcefulness was my key to survival.

Frankly, the thought of stumbling upon a lifeless body terrified me. Despite the chaos that ensued when I fled the settlement, I had never encountered one. The dread of facing such a sight alone in this unfamiliar territory was a constant companion.

I was running out of food, too. Only one can be left, and it would be gone when I settled for the night. I had to find somewhere safe; even better, it would have food. But I was starting to doubt that I would ever see something like that. There weren't even any animals moving around in this area. I'd searched for them every morning after that first morning.

As I walked, I couldn't help but marvel at the destruction around me. The bright red of the brick rubble stood out against the hazy light, and the occasional page fluttering in the wind hinted at a past life, perhaps a library. But I quickly pushed these thoughts aside, focusing on the present and the need to survive.

Hmmm, it must have been a library before... but my thought trailed off as I turned away. On my left side, a little further up, was another remain of the building, and something metal caught my eye as I paused in the middle of the street. *What is that?* My curiosity peaked, and I started to walk toward it.

There were stairs, although not the best by any means, and as I climbed them, I tried to be careful. I could hear and feel them as they broke under my weight. Eventually, I reached the top, where the metal glistened in the hazy light of day. The curve of a C stood up from the rock that held the rest of what I assumed was a sign. Reaching the top, I put down my spear and knelt near the pile.

I picked up rock after rock. I moved them away from the curvy C until I uncovered the rest of the word they covered. The word Colorado stood out in the rocky bed before me when I finally finished uncovering it. It was curvy and pretty. It reminded me of Mom's writing when she would help me with my homework at the settlement. I smiled in remembrance. I was improving at thinking of them without breaking them down, although I still tried to limit the time spent thinking of them.

I stared at the sign for some time before a sound echoed. A loud, harsh pop was followed by the squeal of tires. *What the hell?* I fell, completely taken off guard. *Why were there tire squeals? Were they after me again?*

I grabbed my spear and tried to roll around the rocky bed to be behind it, thinking it would offer me some coverage. I monitored the street below me as I watched a vehicle, the one I assumed I heard the squealing of tires from, swerve and zigzag across the street and around the building I was covering, not wanting them to see me. There were only certain people who had vehicles, and it was not someone that I wanted to see.

Oh God, I'm going to die. The thought crossed my mind as the vehicle crossed before me and zoomed off in a different direction.

My brow furrowed. *What the... that was weird.*

I pushed myself up slowly, still listening for the sound. I felt comfortable being up and exposed when I heard nothing but silence. I picked up my spear as I looked around me.

What did they just shoot at?

I walked down the crumbling steps and looked in the direction from where the car had driven off.

THERE!

Something caught my eye; it had to be thousands of feet away from where I stood. Maybe even half a mile.

It was a heap. A heap of something. I was sure that I hadn't seen it there before.

Well, crap.

I couldn't just leave it there.

What if someone was hurt? The angel on my shoulder asked me.

Yeah, but if it is a person, then what did they do to get shot at? The devil countered as I stood there, debating whether to go and check.

What would your mother say? The angel inquired, and I sighed as I headed toward the blob.

I moved stealthily as I checked everything around me. I walked or ran towards the pile, making sure that it was safe to check whatever was out.

When I saw nothing, I quickened my steps until I was flat-out running to the thing. As I got closer, I could see that it was a person. My heart rate quickened as I saw that they were sprawled out on the ground with a puddle of red starting to grow around them. *Fuck! What do I do?*

I can't tell if it's a boy or girl at this point, only that the popping noise had been a gunshot and it had hit the person.

Twenty-Three

As I reached the person, I noticed that it wasn't a boy or girl but a man. He had been shot. But it didn't look good. It looked like it hit him right between the shoulder and his chest. I prayed that it didn't hit his heart, I mean, I didn't want to see a dead guy.

I knelt as close to the ground as I could without soaking my clothes with his blood. What I assumed was a fedora cap or something similar to his lay a ways away from his head, and his blue-black hair covered his eyes. He groaned in pain, and I sighed. He's still alive.

He was in dark fatigues, probably stolen from some army soldier, but I knew he wasn't a soldier. Jade green mutations mark him as an outcast… like me.

"Sir," I called out to him, "Sir, I'm right here. I'm going to try to help you. I'm going to turn you to see if the bullet went through."

Gingerly, I started to turn him onto his side, pulling him towards me by the arm closest to the wound. He groaned loudly, but not a single sound escaped his lips after that.

When I finally got him to his side, I leaned him against me, not worried about the blood at this point, to keep him upright while I looked at the wound. There was an apparent exit wound on his back, and I sighed in relief. At least I wouldn't have to go searching for it. I moved his body slowly back down as I moved away from him. But he didn't make a sound, and the blood started pounding in my ears. *That wasn't good.* I pulled a shirt from my satchel, thinking of the first aid kit in my backpack. I've got to make bandages quickly. There is no time to lose. I pulled at the shirt, trying to rip it into strips, frustrated that it wasn't working.

Stupid, I called myself, realizing that I needed the knife.

Opening the pocket of my satchel, I grabbed the knife from the top and got to work on tearing up my shirt. I needed bandages, but the rags would do till I could stop the blood flow. Then, I needed to wrap his wound and seal it.

I wished that the lighter was closer than I had it currently. Then, I could seal the wound, stopping the blood flow.

I wondered if he had one on him. I'd hate to have to move him again, but if I could seal the wound closed, then he would have a better chance; at least, I think he would.

I started searching his pants to see if he had anything on him that I could use to help him out. He wasn't carrying much on him, that I could tell, besides a small bag that fell when he did. It was still in the pool of his blood that was building. When I found nothing in his pants, I grabbed the bag and started rifling through it. *Yes!* I exclaimed internally when I saw a box of matches at the bottom of the bag. At least he was prepared. I pulled them out and lit one up.

Putting the flame under my knife, I watched him as I tried to make the knife as hot as I could. It took several matches before I thought it was hot enough to try, and I knew I was pushing my luck as his breath got shallower. I pulled him to his side again, yet there wasn't a single sound from him, which worried me. I tore his shirt open, in the back, by the exit wound to get a clearer view of it. Once cleared, I placed the scolding hot knife flat against his skin.

The smell of burning flesh burnt my nose as the knife worked to put his skin together. I counted to thirty before I removed it, checking the skin underneath. It still looks raw, so I put it back on again.

After I pulled the knife off a second time, I could see that his skin was a blur of pink, red, and tan. I prayed that the wound was shut as much as it looked like it was.

I felt lucky that my dad was such an outdoorsy type. He had always talked about hunting and how I needed to be prepared for it, both when I started hunting and in case of emergencies.

I put him back on the ground, took out another match, and heated my knife again.

I had to close the front, too, I thought. Otherwise, he might bleed to death from there. It took another set of matches to ignite the knife again to the scolding hot range. I stopped occasionally to check for his pulse since his breathing continued to be so shallow.

It's there, but it wasn't strong.

When the knife was finally hot again, I pulled his shirt down in the front from where I ripped it in the back, pulling the sleeve entirely off.

I laid the knife on the wound again. The sounds of sizzling skin ate at me as his skin burned together. The smell clogged up my nose, making my gag reflex choke. I felt like I was going to die from the smell, but I kept going, pushing the thoughts of throwing up away. My parents would have expected me to help someone if I could, and I could now, so I did. I counted to sixty this time before I pulled the knife off. The wound on this side looks just as nasty and blended as the other side.

Well, at least it's closed. I thought as I stared down at it.

I grabbed the long strips of my torn-up shirt and started wrapping his shoulder. I tried to make sure that I covered as much of the wound as humanly possible as I pushed and pulled him around to get it all the way covered. I was able to put several long strands that I could around his shoulder completely, tying them together as tightly as possible. Finally, I reached the point where I had nothing to wrap it with.

I sighed as I checked his pulse one more time. The lullaby had been playing in my mind the entire time, and I realized how exhausted I was as I took his pulse. Seeing that he was still breathing, even if it was still a little shallow, and that his pulse was steady and not completely strong, I finally stopped and fell back onto my butt.

My gag reflex reminded me of the stench as I quickly doubled over to my side and threw up. As I wiped the puke from my lips, I checked the surroundings to see if we were still visible.

I had been so focused on him while I was taking care of his wound, but now that he was taken care of, I needed to make sure that we were safe. Being out in the open like this wasn't ideal, and I thought about our surroundings again.

The remains of the library were nearby; maybe I could drag him there. I thought as I bit my lip. But what if I hurt him more? There were no sturdy walls around us in any of the buildings. I looked again to make sure. We needed walls for protection.

There was no real choice. If I wanted to do the right thing, I needed to get him to safety first.

I pushed my satchel under my backpack's strap before

putting his bag around my neck and under the belt on the other side. My spear would have to wait a minute. I could come back for it.

I stood up and put my hands under his shoulders, carefully with the side that was wounded, and started pulling his body towards the building. I grimaced every time his body ran over a large chunk of brick or concrete.

It couldn't be helped.

As I pulled him over the edge of the building, I pulled my lips back as his feet hit the ground hard. That was the worst. I swore I was frowning the entire time as I pushed things away with my feet and tried to find a good solid wall where I could put him.

After a couple of minutes, I paused and held him as I located a viable wall. I started up again and dragged him towards it. In front of it, there was a pile of paper that I could put him on to be safe.

As I finally reached it, I placed him on the pile before I pulled his bag off and put it by his side. I raced back to where he had been and grabbed my spear. His hat lay on the ground, a black mark on the broken earth, and I grabbed it as a last-minute thought. The blood trail wasn't as bad as I thought it would be, and I threw water out over it as I went, hoping to dilute it enough that no one would go looking for us.

I returned to where I had put him in the building and prayed that I had made the right choice and that this guy, whoever he was, would be okay.

VIII

Dom

Twenty-Four

I t took a while for me to catch up with her, but I had been able to see her as she reached the stream. *I couldn't believe it. How the hell did she find these places?* It was like she had an internal compass that, with every pivot, every swerve, she managed to go to the same places. I watched as she went from the river to the sporting goods store, where she slept for the night. I stood guard over her for several hours as I waited outside the front door before my eyes started to droop. She was more than just a girl I was following. She was my responsibility, my sister. I headed away, far enough that she couldn't see me but close enough that I was still near. I wasn't ready to see her yet. I would have a lot of explanations to do, and honestly, I couldn't give her the ones she needed. If I refused to tell her, it would cost me more than just her love and trust. It could be my death if I did.

The light drifted across my face as the opaque skies lit up. I was running on fumes and needed to get some rest. She should be okay during the day for a little while. At least a couple of hours so that I could get some sleep. From what I remember Dad teaching us about hunting, she should have been pretty well-off before she needed any kind of backup... That is if she stayed away from downtown. If she went downtown, she would likely be okay if she stayed away. If she got close, well then, she'd be in trouble, and I'd failed at the only job given to me when I left Sanctum.

I found a nearby spot and set myself up for a quick rest. I needed at least a couple of hours before I followed her anymore—not that she needed me to follow her. It was like she had followed my tracks from when I came through years ago. The thought of facing her, of the questions she might ask, filled me with dread and uncertainty.

She had been to each place so far, and it reminded me of my travels. I shook my head as I leaned against the wall, my gun palmed in my hands as I faced the only entrance to my hideaway. I lowered my Gatsby newsboy cap down over my eyes. It was the one thing I had left from Lizzy and our time together. It was my treasure, something I would happily fight over if anyone ever tried to take it from me. But it also reminded me of the loss, the pain of our separation. I sat there and let my mind wander before drifting into an uneasy sleep.

I woke up at almost noon, according to my watch. After adding water, I grabbed one of my dry ration packs and chowed down on it. It was stale and tasteless, but it was food in my stomach. I had about 20 that I kept in my bag so that if I couldn't catch anything, I had something to eat. It was rare to run into a nice person out in the wastelands, the desolate areas outside the city where survival was a constant struggle. They weren't out very often because they were more out to kill you rather than break bread with you. On several occasions, I ran into a soldier or an officer patrolling who had tried to tempt me with food to get me to go with them. Probably to the labs that they had, but they always said to a settlement. I would take their food, but only if I held them at gunpoint. I didn't want to end up in that place. Just the thought of it sent chills down my spine. The 'bomb zone' was the area in the city center that was hit the hardest during the war, a place where danger lurked in every corner.

After eating, I wandered out and returned to the store I'd left her at just hours before. There was no sign of her, yet my senses told me she was still around. For days, I always trailed behind her as she walked along the stream toward the center of Downtown Denver. My stomach filled with dread with every step closer she went to the center. I would always catch up to her when it was later in the day. It always looked like she was scavenging, building a good foundation for a long journey. I couldn't help but feel like she was preparing herself for heartache. Going into the mountains would only lead her to heartache.

For days, we follow this routine. I watched her as late as I could before drifting off to sleep.

On the last day, right as she neared the center of Downtown Denver, I watched as she looked in amazement at the gold plates from the Capitol Building. *She must not have remembered it too well.* I thought questionably as she put the plate into her bag before she walked away from the slow decline into the heart of a bomb zone.

I breathed a sigh of relief. She wouldn't be very safe if she went into the zone or went around in the opposite direction. That was the general direction where all the government vehicles retreated because the government didn't want to lose any vehicles searching inside the bomb zone area... I laughed ironically as I thought about it. It's not like they'd ever get a car out of that depression.

There are few places to hide in this area, so I walked behind her on the street, ducking anytime she looked behind her. She gazed around with wonder, evident from how she stopped all over the place; it filled me with joy and worry. I wished I could share this time with her and tell her all the fantastic things that I've seen in the last six years, yet at the same time, I knew there was a lot that I couldn't share with her.

I was so lost in my thoughts as I watched her that I didn't hear the vehicle coming up behind me. The crunching of tires ran over the broken blacktop like it was nothing. I grabbed my gun from my side pocket and turned towards the car. I was shocked as his face came into focus. *What the hell was he doing here?*

Before I could react, there was a flash. The shot rents the silent, stifling air - too powerful to be the backfiring of the vehicle. The noise reverberated in my ears as my shoulder jerked backward. *Fuck!* I flew, landing on the harsh ground.

Shit. I tried to force myself to get up, but the pain was so intense that I groaned with the effort and fell back down. There was no way for me to help her like this, and I prayed that she had been paying attention and wouldn't get caught in the crosshairs. Blackness crept in as I started to lose consciousness.

"Sir," I hear her voice. "Sir…" but she disappeared as I faded from existence.

Twenty-Five

For what felt like an eternity—days, maybe even weeks—I was adrift in a disorienting fog, ensnared in a haze that blurred the line between consciousness and oblivion. A deep ache spread throughout my entire body, a relentless throbbing that echoed like a cruel metronome of my suffering. With each pulse, I felt a wave of intense sensation wash over me, sending sharp twinges from my limbs deep into my core. At the same time, I was gripped by a chilling cold that wrapped around me like a heavy blanket, seeping into my bones and making the marrow feel like it was caught in a winter that wouldn't let go. Each breath I took felt challenging and uneven, as the air seemed thick. A fever stirred within, intense and unyielding, engulfing me in a fierce blaze. It was as though the fires of a distant realm had turned their attention toward me, almost as if they were waiting to pull me into their depths for the times I stumbled along my journey.

When I felt like the fires of Hell had finally come to consume me for my misdeeds and failures, there was a cold compress and a loving caress that reminded me of Elizabeth. This brief respite was accompanied by a ghostly whisper of tenderness that evoked memories of Lizzie—a figure loomed large in my mind, love and longing intermingling with pain. I could almost hear myself calling out her name, a desperate plea woven through the haze, hoping she might hear the echoes of my heart struggling against the void.

I was caught in a heavy stillness—a deep, dark space that closed around me, feeling as if it might swallow me whole. With every bit of strength I could gather, I pushed against this heavy shadow, driven by a deep yearning for light. It felt like fighting through a strong current in a swirling river; each effort to move forward seemed to take an eternity. It was like trying to walk through thick mud, where every step felt more challenging than the last. I felt lost in a maze of confusion, unsure if I was genuinely fighting for my freedom or sinking deeper into a troubling dream. But then, a faint voice reached out through the haze of my thoughts—a gentle, comforting whisper that twinkled like a small candle in the heavy darkness, encouraging me to keep going. Despite feeling so weak, a spark of hope ignited within me, urging me to uncover who this mysterious voice was and the importance of their gentle call that kept me grounded in reality.

Today, something remarkable happened—things began to change in a way I hadn't expected. The fog that had so thoroughly obscured my senses started to lift, allowing me to catch glimpses of the world around me. I could hear soft sounds—the gentle rustle of fabric brushing against skin, the comforting creak of a wooden chair as someone sat nearby, and the distant whispers of a voice—all gentle reminders that I wasn't alone. A moment later, I felt the calming touch of a cool, damp cloth as it softly pressed against my forehead, easing away the beads of sweat that clung there like a stubborn reminder of sadness. The caring hands that carefully wiped my face felt like a soothing balm for my weary soul, grounding me amidst the confusion and pain I was experiencing.

As I sought to break free from the heavy shadows surrounding me, it felt like my limbs were stuck in thick mud—every move a considerable challenge against an unseen weight that seemed determined to hold me back. Yet, I continued forward, driven by a strong desire to reach that warmth, that tantalizing light just beyond my reach. With every ounce of my being, I inched closer, holding tight to the hope it embodied. I could feel it, a shimmering beacon in the heavy darkness, encouraging me to break free and embrace the safety it promised. The atmosphere buzzed with energy, a whisper of comfort swirling just beyond the shadows, urging me to keep going. I wouldn't give up; I was resolute in my quest for the light that awaited me, for the love and warmth that reminded me I still had a reason to cherish life. I would rise. I had to.

IX

Mary Beth

Twenty-Six

I wrung the cloth as I walked towards the man, who still lay in the same spot I'd dragged him to days before. As I wiped the sweat from his brow, I wondered how long until he woke up. After wiping his face, I ate more from the dry ration from his bag. I'd gone through several more cans and almost finished with my rations. I'd snagged one of his dry rations, hoping it would be more filling. I'd been sharing juice dribbles from fruit cans with him and ensuring I gave him water to keep him hydrated throughout his fever.

And he had been running a high fever, but I was sure it just broke. I had used all the water in my container that day from cleaning up the blood splatter from when I'd dragged him over to our current hideaway. He had two bottles in his knapsack that I had used to clean him up afterward and then to drink for the rest of the evening. By the following day, I had used all of his and had to search around here to find a place that had some running water still.

Between the three bottles, I had managed to keep his fever down, but after almost four days of very little drinking water and using it to cool him off, we had run out. I hated leaving him alone, but I knew that we needed the water if we were going to survive. I finished the bag before grabbing my bow and the three bottles and headed out.

As I entered the building again, I noticed that the man had moved and was sitting up against the wall. His eyes were still closed, but I knew that he was awake.

"Mister," I inquired as I came upon him, "are you awake?"

He flinched as his eyes popped open. Jade-green eyes stared back at me, and I was transported back to when I was ten, and the same eyes stared at me when I'd accidentally dropped the knife instead of handing it to him.

"Dom..." the word spills out before the world turns black.

The next time that I opened my eyes, I was lying on my back in the same spot where he had been lying, not even hours before.

"What the..." I began to shout.

"Nice welcome there, kid." His deep timber tones drifted over me. He's sitting against another wall facing me as I whipped around towards his voice.

I stared at him in shock, then anger overtook me as I exclaimed. "Where the hell have you been?" My fists balled up, the nails digging into my skin as a reminder that I was human and could feel pain. However, now, all I wanted to do was to make him feel the pain I'd been suffering.

He shrugged his shoulders as if it didn't matter and it just added fuel to the fire. "What the hell, Dom? Why'd you leave?" *Or should I say who you left for?*

"Can't explain, kid, just had to do it." His words sounded so hollow to me. I stood up. The world tilted a little as I stood. I tried to maintain my composure. I closed my eyes and counted to 20 before opening them again; the world was still this time. Sighing with relief, I paced momentarily before looking at him again. "Kid, you wouldn't understand." He tried to comfort me, but it increased my anger tenfold. I pulled my fist back. It rushed towards his head.

His hand grabbed my fist in midair, so it never connected. "I understand the anger, kid, but it doesn't change anything."

I took some deep breaths as I yanked my hand back. Walking away from him, I focused on bringing my temper under check. He's still healing, and I tried to remind myself that I can't get angrier with him, even though I would love to sock him. Then I realized that I didn't know why he was shot, to begin with, or even how he had been so close to me.

"Were you following me?" I looked at him.

He didn't look up at me as he readjusted his body against the wall, moving his wounded shoulder away from the wall.

"Dom!" I shouted, spit flying from my lips. "Where you following me? Was that car after me?" I had already been worried about someone following me since they had killed everyone else, or I assumed they had anyway.

His silence was answered enough, and I swallowed hard. "Oh, okay. So, who was it?"

"I don't know," he replied. I didn't get a good look." His words lacked conviction, but I was not in the mood to push him; it wouldn't do me any good. I mean, he hasn't answered me about anything so far. I shook my head and walked away from him.

He looked at me with this deep, intense concern reflecting in his eyes, but I ignored it. He didn't deserve to be concerned or have me concerned for him. I was so angry now. All this time I cared for him was a waste of my time, especially if he kept lying to me. "Well, I'm glad you're awake now. I'll be going now." I stated as I walked over to my belongings and started putting them together. It was just beginning to turn dusk, and I wanted to get away from him before I said or did something I might regret later. However, I was starting to doubt that anything that I had to tell him would be regrettable.

"MB, come on now." He pleaded. "Don't be like that."

"Like what, Dom? I'm just following your example."

He flinched; my words burned him like a fire before he stood and stared me down. "MB, there were circumstances you just wouldn't understand."

I shook my head, rolling my eyes, "Whatever, Dom. Keep your secrets. I've got work to get done. I care about my family." I wanted him to hurt. He'd done so much to hurt us by leaving without any information that I just didn't care what he had to say anymore. Not to mention that there was someone still looking for me. They had shot Dom… who was to say that they wouldn't return to this area soon?

Where'd I put my water bottle? I tried to figure it out, but then again, I'd passed out when I saw him sitting there. Finally, I turned and looked at him as I pulled my satchel over my head and settled it on my shoulder.

"Where's my water bottle, Dom?" I demanded.

"Don't know."

"Bullshit. Where's my water bottle, Dom?"

"If I tell you, will you let me go with you?" His words make me see red.

"You want to go with me? What the hell? Do you honestly think I want you to go with me when all you do is lie and keep secrets? I've asked you two straightforward, easy questions, Dom. You've done nothing to give me any hope that you will be truthful. I can't deal with that now. You've been gone for six years. SIX YEARS! What makes you think that I need your help now?"

Jade eyes stared me down as I pulled the backpack over my shoulder, the bow and quiver already attached.

"I think you'll want me to go with you because I've been on the same journey." He stated it so simplistically that he thought I knew what he was discussing.

I laughed. *Seriously, did he just say that?* I shook my head again as I searched for my water bottle.

"Mary Beth, I've watched you go to the same places I did. You're going on the journey."

I turned and stared at him; it was hard to stare him down when he was taller than me. "Seriously? First, I knew that someone was following me. It just happened to be you, so what? Second of all, what the hell are you talking about? A journey, what sort of bullshit are you trying to sell?"

He bit his lip. "I can't say what it is for each person to discover independently, but I want to be there for you. I want to help you with whatever I can. It's the least I can do."

"I'm not on any journey," I said the word and made quotation marks in the air with my hands as I looked at him, "I'm looking for a safe place for everyone to live. They can't stay on that settlement. They're gonna end up dead with all the ration shortages that have been going on."

"Ration shortage?" He questioned, "What ration shortages?"

I stopped short, turned around, and glared at him. "Like you care."

"I do care, Mary Beth. I've been trying to help you guys as much as possible from the outside."

I scoffed. "Whatever. You could have come back." I thought back to the rules that the General and council had told everyone.

"Those rules were lies, MB. Think about it. They were

killing everyone in your group."

"How'd you know about that?" I demanded, going over to him and popping his space bubble as I stood chest-to-chest with him.

"I was there. Now, come on, MB. What ration shortages?" His eyes were begging me for a bone. Something that would give him some hope that I still cared. And, *goddamnit*, I did. I cared more than I ever wanted to admit. He was my brother, my idol. He had been everything to me growing up because he had always known the answers, so I went against everything, telling me not to trust him.

"They've been going on for the last three years," I said as I backed away and looked at a different wall in the building. "First, there was plenty of food for everyone. You remember that, right? We even had a little extra on our plates. Then, they started taking away little things before finally cutting it down to almost an entire person's food allotment. That's why I left. Our sisters and Nick don't deserve to have their food cut when I can find something better for us. Mom and Dad have done so much for us and kept us safe in this world that I had to do something that could be as helpful." I snuck a peek at him as I finished.

His jaw dropped. "They cut food down for our family?"

"For all families with someone showing signs of these stupid marks." I turned and pointed to the bumps on my face and gestured towards his own. "At least, that's what I've noticed."

His eyes hardened as he looked at me before he looked away. "I should have come back and taken you guys," he whispered to himself, although I could still hear him.

"Yeah, you should have," I said as I located my water bottle. "But you can't change the past, Dom. *I can't go back to yesterday.*

I was a different person then. Remember Dom? You told me that." I hurdled the words at him as I walked away. I didn't need him. I could do this all on my own. The lullaby played softly in my mind as I headed out the front and down the street. There was nothing left to say to him, and I don't think I had the willpower or the ability to force him to tell me the truth. I cared too much about the boy I remembered, not the man I had just dealt with.

X

Dom

Her words echoed around me as she walked away. I stared down at the ground in misery. *She's right. I couldn't change the past.* But I could be there for her, whether she wanted me to. I'm her brother, and I know what she will be facing. She shouldn't be doing this alone. At least, not now. I spun around and grabbed my bag and cap off the ground. Slapping my hat onto my head, I pulled my bag over my non-injured shoulder and ran after her.

"You're right." I hollered. The pain would come and go as I moved, trying to grab her attention. I tried to breathe regularly as I walked, although I made huge gasping breaths occasionally. She kept walking.

"You're right," I say louder, almost screaming as I slowly walk. My breathing was heavy and stiff. "You're right. I'm an idgit." I threw a rock toward her, but not close enough. I didn't want her to try to hit me again. She almost had me back in the library ruins. She didn't even acknowledge my presence as she continued past the Colorado History Museum, the last place she had been before everything had happened.

"You're right!" I finally screamed at her. I couldn't just let her walk away. "I fucked up, okay? I let my emotions control me, and they screwed me over! I should have returned and done countless things, MB, but I can't go back. So, let me help you now." I didn't want to talk about it. I didn't want to talk about Elizabeth. I didn't want to talk about my mistakes. Not to mention, I was bound by something so mystical and eternal that I knew if I told her anything about what was coming, I'd end up dead faster than a fly. Still, I couldn't just let her walk into something without someone on her side. At least someone she knew.

She stopped, turned, slowly walked back to where I stood, and came toe to toe with me. She was so tiny, I realized, as she pulled her head back and stared me in the eyes.

"Why would I do that? Why would I let you in to help me when you didn't care about helping us six years ago? Or any time in between then and now?"

I gulped and finally opened up, giving her the words she wanted to hear. At least, the words I hoped that she wanted to hear. "I have been helping. At least, for the last couple of years, I have. Every time you went out hunting, I watched to make sure that no one came up to hurt you. And I did. You never got hurt while you were alone. I made sure of that."

"You?" The surprise was evident in her voice as her eyes widened. "You were the one that shot that man?"

I nodded as I backed up. I didn't want her to see how much that death, and the ones to follow, had affected me. It still haunted me that I had to kill a man because he was coming up on my sister, unaware. I wasn't as uneasy with the deal of the guard that had been following her, but that was a different story.

"Yeah," I sighed as I continued to put space between us, "that was me."

She deflated in front of me. "The guards always wondered

where the shot came from. I told him that it wasn't me. I didn't even have a gun. But they never believed." The words came out as a whisper.

The memory had shaken her. I could see it; she was visibly torn up about it, just like I was. It had happened just a couple of months after she turned fourteen.

"Okay," she said after a while. "You can come with me. But I don't want to hear a word from you. Not a single peep." Like that would be a problem. I couldn't tell her much of anything anyway. "That man had almost gotten me thrown into the barracks, Dominic, so you better fucking listen to me because that's almost exactly when all these problems started happening."

As she looked at me, I stood tall and straight above her. Holding my hand out, I put three fingers out, "Scout's honor." She couldn't help but laugh.

"You were never a scout," she implied.

"Okay, fine then." I smirked, "Thug's honor," as I held my fingers in the letter "C."

Wow, what a way to go. I laughed internally, bowing down to my baby sister. *Dad would never let this down if he knew about it, which meant that she would tell him everything as soon as she could.* She laughed again as she stared at me. "You wish you had been in a gang. Don't forget I remember all those kids you used to hang out with."

"Okay, fine," I sighed. You got it." I adjusted my bag and looked at her. "You got it. I'll be here as a hired hand—just like those western movies grandma always used to watch."

She laughed a little more and smiled before turning away from me. I knew where we were going, but it had to be her journey. I couldn't tell her which way to go. I couldn't do anything that would jeopardize her learning the skills needed for survival out there. That's what they told me the last time I went there to ask for help, back when I had killed the lone hunter with the predator look in his eye when he saw Mary Beth standing all alone in the field. Back when I knew that she would be leaving the settlement soon. The bumps had started to become more prominent back then, and that's when I could hear her humming the lullaby more often than she had ever done before.

That was the only advice that they gave me. It hadn't been much. But then again, they never gave me any real help when I was there originally. It wouldn't be much different for her, the journey at least. Yet, this time, there was someone there who could protect her better than I was ever protected during that time. I would make sure of that.

XI

Mary Beth

Twenty-Eight

I remembered the tears coursing down Mom's face when they finally let me out of the barracks that day. It had been the worst day of my life, even worse than when Dom had disappeared. I'd been hunting alone that morning, so I didn't expect anyone to be there. I'd been so focused on catching my prey that day that I ignored my surroundings. Obviously, it was a weakness of mine because Dom had been following me since I left the settlement, and I'd never noticed. There was a point to having him tag along. He was better at paying attention to his surroundings than I ever was. I had to shake off the memory, though. I couldn't handle the flashbacks of his body falling in front of me. It had taken me months afterward to stop seeing it finally. I never really accepted that I'd seen a dead body, and I was sticking to that story.

I forced my feet to keep going. The melody became even more potent as it forced the negative thoughts of that day away from me. *Twinkle, twinkle, little star. How I wonder what you are? Up above the world so high, like a diamond in the sky.*

My feet just automatically carried me forward. I kept my eyes on my surroundings as much as possible as my lullaby carried my mind away. I didn't understand why this lullaby had always given me peace, but it did, and I needed it now.

I looked at Dom out of the corner of my eye.

Dom had been so silent behind me that I almost forgot he was there. As we walked, his eyes roamed the streets, and his hand kept straying to his pants pocket. I was curious about what he had there and couldn't remember searching for it. The mystery was eating at me.

I tried to ignore him and my innate curiosity as I kept walking. I knew there was a highway somewhere, or at least there used to be.

When Mom told us tales about going to the mountains, she would always say that we'd take Sixth Avenue out to Seventy, and then we'd be in the mountains.

I didn't remember much of those trips, but she loved talking about how things used to be. I think it was her way of not dealing with how life was presently. She had changed in the last several years and was more focused on how things used to be in the here and now.

I kicked at the things as we walked by them. There were so many objects on the ground. I saw a sign with Tenth Avenue on it, so I knew I was close. I just wanted to get away from the library ruins. Someone was bound to return eventually, and I couldn't have a chance to be in the same place when they did.

I was determined to find something to keep us safe for the night. The buildings in this area were no better, but I couldn't afford to dwell on that. I needed to find a solution, and fast.

"How's the shoulder," I turned towards him, "Is it hurting any?"

He shook his head no and walked by me. I realized he'd changed his shirt when he woke up, as it was all in one piece.

"Sorry if ya know, I ruined your tattoo… or whatever it is," I said as I ran to catch up to him.

"My tattoo?" He turned and looked at me quizzically. "What tattoo?"

I raised an eyebrow. "Uh, the one on your back?" *Who didn't know that they had a tattoo?*

He stopped. "Oh, that one. It's fine. It doesn't mean much to me anyway."

"How'd you get that anyway?" I asked. There was no way that he got that before the bombings, and I didn't know of anyone in the settlement who would do something like that.

You told him not to say anything. Not a peep. The devil on my shoulder reminded me as I continued to egg him on. *Are you trying to negate your demand and get him into trouble?* The devil on my shoulder inquired. I smiled dementedly at the devil as I continued to egg my brother on.

"I don't remember. It's been a long time now." He rumbled, his tone clipped and harsh. "It doesn't matter."

Okay. I felt like rolling my eyes. I hit a nerve. I thought as I moved past him.

Yup, I replied to the devil, *I was trying to negate.* I wanted him to admit to whatever he was trying to hide from me. I hated it when he tried to keep things from me in the past; it never ended up being something good, and this wasn't good.

He was a grouchy pant when I tried to get information. The silence was much more preferable to the grouchiness. We didn't say another word to each other as we continued.

The buildings were all familiar to me, in a more recently scavenged way than memorization of my past. Well, at least I was heading in the right direction.

"Start looking for a safe place for the night," I hollered at him, my frustration evident. I didn't look back at him as I moved away. I was still a little irate that he had the nerve to get so defensive with me over a stupid tattoo. It wasn't like I knew he had it.

Sighing, I headed back towards the middle of the road. No place on this site looked like staying in for a night would be comfortable. I had grabbed some of the bags in one of the buildings. It was some pasta, and I was already thinking of the delicious noodles I could cook in pans I'd taken the other night.

I was glad that he didn't follow me over there. I had been talking shit about him in my head ever since he got his panties in a bunch. When I got to the spot where I'd left him, I almost danced to see that it was empty. Fuck, that meant that I had to stay there until he came back. I blew my hair up as I turned and looked at the water that flowed under the bridge we'd walked over. I was surprised that the bridge held together as well. I rubbed my face with a hand as I breathed deeply.

I wasn't patient, and this waiting challenged me. I wanted to pursue him and see what he was doing.

"Grrrr…." I growled as I tried to tamper my impatience down. It felt like forever before I saw him walking towards me from the opposite side of the street I'd come from.

"Found something."

"Finally…" I was exasperated, hating that I had to wait there like a little girl when I'd been taking care of our family since he left. I started hunting by myself not even a year after he left us. "Where at?"

He jerked his head. "Follow me," he said, turning around and heading back the same way.

Sighing, I ran to catch up to him, not that I had far to go, before I ran into his back. He grunted and abruptly tossed his head to the right side. "It used to be a hospital. There are beds in there. Probably some medical supplies and stuff we could use."

His words made me pause, "Is your shoulder hurting you?" Is that why he mentioned the medicines? Did he need something to ease his pain?

He shrugged and then grimaced. "Maybe."

"Maybe?"

"Okay, Mary Beth." He conceded. "I'm in a little pain, and it would be helpful." You would have thought I was trying to pull his teeth like he answered.

"Little, my ass," I whispered under my breath as I turned towards the building. The buildings weren't as destroyed as the ones by the settlement; they were still in ruins, but there was more to protect us than when I started.

"Okay," I agreed out loud, "Let's check it out."

"I already did."

Of course you did. Did you come here, too? I wanted to ask him, but I bit my tongue to avoid saying anything. I nodded and let him take the lead.

Some hospital areas collapsed as the weight of the ceilings pushed several floors down. We searched before coming across an area that seemed to be pretty stable. The ceilings didn't look like they could collapse on top of us at any moment. Not to mention, there were several rooms in the area. That way, we could both take a room and escape from each other, which is my personal choice. I was done with his behavior and attitude. I didn't have to save his ass. At least he could be somewhat receptive to honesty because of it, but no.

"Okay, well, I'll take this room, and you can pick another

one," I told him as I pointed to the first room on the right. "Did you search for the medical supplies already, too?" I asked sarcastically as I turned to look at him.

"No. I just did a quick sweep to see if anyone was still here and if there was anything that could be hospitable." He stopped and started laughing. "Get it? Hospitable? We're in what used to be a hospital?" He stared at me, and I looked blankly at him. "Ooookay," he dragged the word out. "Anyway, this was the first thing I found that I thought would be good for us for the night."

I nodded at him, rolling my eyes internally, and turned back towards the rest of the building. "Okay, well then, I'll quickly search the building to see what I can find. Make yourself comfortable."

I walked away and started heading back toward the areas where everything had collapsed under the weight of destruction. There are so many hallways in this building, I whined internally. This would take forever. I looked through each door that I came across. I searched through offices, cleaned closets, and waited for areas while avoiding the places where the bricks and mortar had mixed into a large mess.

I walked further away from our rooms for the night before finally discovering something I thought could help us. The word "Emergency" in red capital letters stood out as I came across another long corridor. I remembered going to an emergency room once, before the bombs, because Dom had hurt himself somehow. I couldn't remember how, but it didn't matter anyway now. We had gone to the emergency room to have a doctor care for him.

I pulled my bow and arrow out, stringing them as I walked stealthily into the unknown room. I didn't know if anyone was there, and it could even be unsafe, but I was somewhat prepared.

There are chairs everywhere. Some standing up, some overturned. It's a madhouse in here. I still had trouble believing that this was what the world was now. I looked for doorways as I moved along the walls. I stepped over chairs as I kept my back against a wall. *There!* My mind screamed at me as I looked over to my left. A door hung limply by the bottom hinge. That had to be something important. Maybe that is where they took the — what was the word I was looking for — patients.

I walked toward the door and peeped around the corner. I didn't see anyone, so I stepped through and walked down the hallway. I checked every door that I passed, and safety was first. My feet were silent on the ground or as quiet as possible. As I tiptoed down the hallway, I finally came across a room with a sign engraved with the word "supplies."

I pushed the door open and looked inside. *Oh my god.*

It was a fucking disaster.

It looks like a tornado, or something hit it and took everything down. I see pills all over the floor. Bandages and other medical supplies are strewn around the room. I scanned the room before pulling my arrow from the bow and putting it back in my quiver. I strapped the bow back over my bag before kneeling and picking pills up off the floor.

I had no clue what I was doing. No clue about what pills I was looking for or even picking up. But something has to be valid. Something has to work.

Handful after handful, I stuffed them into a pocket of my satchel before moving on. There were a couple of pill bottles, too. I grabbed them and stuffed them into my satchel, not bothering to look at the labels. *What was the point at this time?* We can figure that out after I get back.

Then I grabbed as many bandages, surgical knives, and tools as scattered around the room. I knew that I'd seen some of them before… when Mom went into labor at the settlement with the girls. Then again, when Dad got hurt at the farms, I didn't care. I was just happy to have something that could help me finally.

I stuffed them inside my satchel, too. The crunching of the pasta reminded me, as I stuffed everything in, that I still needed to cook something for dinner. It didn't matter that the noodles were breaking; it wasn't like they wouldn't break down anyway when they went into my mouth. Feeling like I'd gotten us enough for a while, I pulled my bow off again and restrung my arrow.

I walked out of the room, turning and looking around before I headed back towards the rooms and Dom.

It was too damn silent in this building.

I listened to my breathing as I walked. Counting the ins and outs as I watched the walls and halls. As I turned the last corner, my feet still as silent as a mouse on Christmas Eve, I nearly jumped out of my skin when I heard a chair scraping. I turned around, and my arrow flew from my hands as I aimed at the chair from where I stood, stopping entirely.

Within seconds, I watched as my arrow aimed true, and something slammed into the wall. I walked over to it cautiously and was amazed to see a raccoon. Not just any raccoon… Oh no, this was the size of a desk from the classroom at the settlement. It was huge! I hadn't caught something like this in months. I whooped with glee. I jumped up and down and danced with excitement. My hands floated around in the air, giving myself an ovation for the fantastic catch. I continued to whoop with excitement. Chasing away anything that might have been nearby.

XII

Dom

Twenty-Nine

I laid down on the bed in a room several down from hers. I didn't want to press my luck by being any closer. She'd made it clear earlier that I wasn't much, and that hurt. Yet, there were moments when I thought she wanted to try to mend things, but then I'd stick my foot in my mouth and ruin it. I listened to the silence around me as my mind wandered over the last several days. My shoulder was throbbing in pain, so I turned and tried to lay on my stomach instead. My heart jumped out of my chest when I heard the war cry coming from my sister. *What the fuck?* I jumped up from the bed and took off towards the noise. I raced down hallways, not bothering to check for anyone, worried that she was trapped, or worse — fighting off enemies — I pulled out my gun and quickly checked the chamber before running through the emergency room doorway.

In the middle of the room is MB as she danced and pranced around. Her long black hair flowed around her as she jumped and hooted in celebration. I popped an eyebrow as I stared her down, silently waiting for her to turn towards me. When she finally turned towards me, her dance faded as she caught my gaze. She looked down quickly to the ground before realizing that she had thrown her bow to the ground in her rush to celebrate. Her face was comical as she grimaced, grabbed it off the ground, and attached it to her backpack.

"What in the blazing hell is going on?" I demanded.

She shrugged her shoulders and turned away from me. "It doesn't matter. Like you even care." She walked over to the wall, and I was still so angry at her for yelling like that that my fist clenched.

"It doesn't matter? IT DOESN'T MATTER? WHAT THE HELL, MARY BETH JOHNSON? YOU SCARE ME TO DEATH!" I raged, and my fist landed in the wall, punching a hole straight through it. "I thought someone was in here trying to hurt you." My voice trembled at the thought of being unable to protect her after everything she's done to help me and our family. Especially now that we are together.

She stopped in her tracks as my voice cracked. She whipped around, hair like a lasso around her head. She looked at me hard. "If you cared so much about someone hurting me, Dom," her voice soft against my anger, "you're too late. I've been hurt already."

My anger melted away at the soft conviction in her voice. *She's right. I was too late.* I watched her suffer through the indifference of the settlement and the abuse from the guards.

She turned back to what she was doing.

But I decided I could try to make it better from now on. I tried to convince myself that this was the best move as I walked toward her.

"What you got?" I asked her as I approached. Apologies weren't worth anything. They were just a bunch of meaningless words.

She jerked her head towards the wall before I looked at what was before her. It was a large raccoon hanging from the wall, probably almost two and a half feet long and about a foot and a half wide. Her arrow held it in place as the blood dripped down the front of the walls like one of those horror movies I used to watch with my friends.

Well, we'll have some meat for a while. I thought as I walked over to help her pull the arrow out. She didn't even give me a chance to help as she pushed my hand away. She pulled the arrow out by herself, letting the animal fall to the floor.

"I'm not a child, Dominic. I can do things by myself, and I have been for years." She said as she cleaned the arrow on her pants before putting it back in her quiver. "If you want to be helpful, grab the animal."

I nodded. Again, there's nothing that I could say that would change that fact.

I grabbed the raccoon by the feet and motioned for her to lead us back. I must learn to accept that I can't tell her what to do, even though it's my god-given right as her older brother. I guess I'd lost that privilege a long time ago.

We walked back to the rooms in silence. We stopped abruptly in the hallway before we reached the rooms. She motioned for me to put the raccoon down. "You know how to clean one of those?" She asked me as she stared ahead, not even acknowledging me.

She was angry. Hell, she had every right to be, I got that. Yet, at the same time, I deserved to be acknowledged. She scared me. My pride firmly informed me.

"Yeah, I know how to clean one," I said, and she turned towards the rooms. I grabbed her arm with my injured side. "But at least you could admit that you weren't thinking when you screamed; you scared the hell outta me, Mary Beth," I stated calmly, even though my pride demanded that I treat her the same way she was treating me.

She turned and looked me dead in the eye. She deadpanned, "Yeah, Dominic, I know I scared you. But that's nowhere close to how scared you've made me over the years." She yanked her arm awake from me and walked away. My shoulder twinged in pain, but I swallowed the hurt as I turned and walked away from the rooms. I'd clean the animal, but I needed space from her, or I'd say something I'd regret later.

I reached the hallway towards the outside and dropped the animal to the floor before I collapsed. I pulled out the knife and got to work on the animal. As I cut into the back of the animal, I dragged the knife down until I started to see the muscle within. This would take a while, so I settled myself against the wall as I completed the task. My shoulder was excruciatingly painful. I tried my hardest not to let a sound out. If she wanted to be self-righteous, then so would I.

XIII

Mary Beth

Thirty

I walked into the room and closed the door firmly behind me. I took my bow and everything off and leaned it against the wall. I hadn't even looked in the room when I picked it up, but now, as I stared at the bare aspects of the room, I was grateful for a full bed. I was so mad that I almost cried. So, as I bit back my tears, I ran to the bed and flopped down. Dust rose above me as I buried my head into the still-soft material. The dust did it for me as the tears came pouring out. How could he be so mean? Trying to act as if he cared about me. Ha!

I stifled the sobs as I pushed my head harder to the material. How dare he try to make me feel bad about myself! No matter what happened between us, he always managed to make me feel small about myself. Like the little child I was when he was around before, but he hadn't been around in six years, so why did it matter so much to me?

I lay there, tears staining the mattress, for what seemed like hours before there was a knock at my door. I stood up quickly and wiped my eyes. Walking toward the door, I took some deep breaths and composed myself, hoping my face wasn't a tear-streaked mess. As my hand landed on the handle, I reminded myself I was a strong woman who had cared for my family for the last six years. That even if he was my big brother, he hadn't been there, and therefore, he didn't deserve the power to make me feel small. I would have to keep reminding myself of it because I was still just a little kid when it came to our relationship in his eyes.

"Yeah," I said, popping the door open.

"It's clean." His words are short and clipped. "Did you find anything else while you were over there?"

Crap. There he went again. *Let's make Mary Beth feel like a failure*. It wasn't exactly my fault that he had pissed me off earlier. "Yeah," I said, turning away from him and grabbing my satchel. "Here you go. #Sorrynotsorry." I threw the words he used to say around me all the time just as I threw the bag at him.

I swore I saw a smile fly across his face, but maybe it had been a trick of the light because he was back to being solemn in the blink of an eye. "Thanks. I'll bring it back. You got something to cook this with?" He thrust the animal at me before he turned away with the bag.

Okay. So, that's the kind of communication we were going to have. I thought to myself, as I barely grasped the bloody carcass, before I yelled at him, "You have all the matches."

He threw a lighter out of his door before he slammed it shut. The lighter bounced on the floor, and the clink, clink noise echoed in the empty corridor. I'm stuck by his carelessness. Did I really want to have him here with me? Why had I even made it an option?

I wanted to throw the animal at his smirking face; I just wanted to whelp him good. Anything that would make him admit to everything he refused to tell me.

Yet, my stomach rolled and growled, the next loudest sound

in the hallway to the fallen lighter. Yeah, that would have been nice to do, but the animal needed to be cooked so that we could eat. I was so tired of canned goods, and the thought of the fresh taste of meat on my tongue made me salivate.

Ultimately, my stomach won, and I grabbed the lighter off the floor. I placed the lighter on a table before grabbing my backpack and pulling out the mini stove. I gave it a once over before deciding that it would be too hard to cook the animal on it without cutting it down. I was getting too hungry to cut it down more to eat. I pushed it back towards my backpack as I wondered. *Hmmm, what did I need to cook it? What was I going to put it on?*

Thankfully, the guts were cut out so I could run a stick straight through it. But how would I cook it? I walked through all the rooms and grabbed broken wooden legs and clothes or rags still in the rooms before my hands were almost full. That's when I decided to go outside to cook it.

If I cooked it here, the rooms would be filled with smoke. I might be able to find something to cook it on if I went outside. I kicked at Dom's door with my foot.

"Can you grab my knife?" I hollered through the door.

His hand popped out, holding a blade within his fist, the handle up for me to grab. I looked between it and overfilled my arms, and sighed. "Could ya follow me out?" I said sarcastically to him.

He stuck his head out. His eyes had dark rings under them, and his skin was pale. He didn't look too hot, but he was the one who forced the animal into my hands. He glanced down at my arms before quickly nodding. I started walking away with the hope that he followed me.

As I walked out, I looked for something to cook the carcass.

As my eyes swept the grounds, some mesh benches caught my eye, and I smiled. At least now, I wouldn't have to try to stick something through it.

I gestured towards the bench with my head, "You can put it over there." He said nothing as he walked around me and put the blade down. He turned and went right back into the building without another word. I growled under my breath, heaved everything over there, and dumped everything on top of the bench. I was starting to regret the fact that I'd allowed him to travel with me. He could have helped grab something. I shook my head.

The angel reminded me that he would have just followed me if I hadn't. However, I started to wonder if it was an angel or if I was surrounded by devils telling me to do "good" things, at least for others. The lighter ping-ponged into the cement before I pushed the wood and sheets off the bench and onto the ground.

I knelt and started wrapping some wooden legs with strips of the sheet as I cut them. After I wrapped four wooden legs, I stopped and arranged them and several other legs under the bench before the rest of the sheets were stuffed around them. After I grabbed the lighter, my finger brushing over the edge of the metal wheel, I touched it to several spots around the material. I watched as the flames licked upward and onward toward the wooden legs. I couldn't help but wonder where he had found a lighter or if it had been hidden in his belongings I had never seen.

I sat back and watched as the fire built, leaving the carcass as it was.

Whenever the fire looked weak, or the flames lessened, I threw another leg or piece of material into it. Eventually, a healthy fire roared under the metal bench. I stared into the flames as the animal cooked. Delicious, unbelievable smells of cooking meat wafted toward me. I inhaled the aroma as I lost myself in the flame.

"Twinkle, twinkle, little star. How I wonder what you are," I sang the lullaby softly, my coping mechanism, as the thoughts of my family drifted around me. The lullaby repeated in my head, an echo, as worry consumed me. "Up above the world, so high, like a diamond in the sky."

"You sing so beautifully," his voice stopped me as I turned towards him. "You sound just like mom." He held my satchel out to me. "You found some good medicines. We should hold on to them." He stated before he sat down close to me. "You don't have to stop on my account."

I nodded at him, self-conscious now, and returned to the fire. I didn't sing out loud often because I was unsure of myself. Even his words of praise did little to ease my doubt.

The animal was almost ready to be turned over, so I reached up and grabbed the legs, doing a quick flip of the animal. It was heavy, but at least it would be good eating. I sat down again and stared into the fire.

"So, where are we going? Somewhere in the mountains?"

I jerked and glared at him. *How'd he figure that out so fast?* I nodded slowly and turned back to the fire. My hand clenched the blade as I listened to our surroundings, as it allowed my heartbeat to slow down again.

"I figured so. We're heading towards the highway. What's up with the song, though? You've been humming it all day long. "

"Do you know if the highway is still viable?" I inquired, as I avoided the question about the song.

He nodded, and I caught it out of the corner of my eye. "Yeah, it's still up for the most part. We'll need to watch out for a couple of tricky areas. You can't go to 70 from 6th, though. I had to turn off before that and walked along the base of the mountains for a while."

"Was there anything good there?" I continued, still lost in the flames, as they licked at the bench and air.

"Good?"

"Somewhere we could take the family and be safe?" *Duh, idgit.*

He shook his head no. "There's a lot of rebel bases along there. They aren't very receptive to our kind either, though."

Our kind? "You mean there's more than the ones I — we — saw in the settlement?"

"Well, yeah, where do you think Lizzy went?"

There! I knew she had something to do with his disappearance all those years ago. "Oh, so you still see her?" I asked nonchalantly.

He stiffened. *Damn, I should've just let him talk.*

We sat in silence as we waited until the animal was done. I leaned back on my elbows and stared up into the black abyss of the skies as I thought about grabbing the pasta from my bag. I decided not to because I was halfway comfortable and didn't want to move.

We could always use it later if we needed to. The delicious aroma of the cooking raccoon wafted around us like a curtain. I couldn't wait to take it off the fire and eat some. I moved it occasionally to ensure it was cooked entirely as Dom stared into space, probably lost in his little world.

His comment about Lizzy made me go back to when he disappeared. He had always left when we first got to the settlement, especially after introducing himself to her. He had never told me exactly what he was doing. But then again, I was only a kid then. There was that one time I had caught him kissing her. I'd threatened to tell her fiancé; she was almost twice his age, but he'd shushed me up and told me that I'd regret it if I ever told anyone.

Nonetheless, you told your siblings that, and you knew they would respect you for it. Hell, I know I've told Nick something similar plenty of times.

He'd disappeared a couple of weeks after that. I'd always thought that her fiancé had found out and had killed him. Being a general had its privileges and all that. I figured that was why Barnes had always been an ass towards our family. He was forced to kill Dom and Lizzy, or at least that is what I had assumed based on his behavior toward us. Obviously not.

At one point, I got up, grabbed my water bottle, and returned while the animal was still cooking. I had to have something to put the fire out when it was ready. After a while, I cut the knife into the meat and checked it for completeness. Seeing that it was cooked thoroughly, I threw some water at the fire before I grabbed the legs and took them off the burning bench.

"Where are you going?" his voice echoed around me.

"Inside. I don't want to be out here longer than I should." The air had turned chilly but steamy. Part of dealing with the bombings, I guess, because it was always way too hot to do anything but sweat. "Make sure the fire is out completely," I instructed him as I walked away with the meat. I didn't bother to wait to see if he did it. I was tired of everything. The quiet of the evening was filled with thoughts of how he had left and why. Thoughts and questions I knew he wouldn't answer. Considering I saved his life, you'd think he would be more grateful and open. Still, no. Instead, I got his attitude and disrespect.

How was I supposed to be around him when I couldn't even respect him as my brother? He couldn't even act like a brother, at least not like he used to.

I walked into my room and pushed everything off one of the tables before putting the cooked meat on it. I twirled my knife, pulled it from my pants pocket, and started cutting pieces off it. I thought we could wrap the leftovers in more sheets before we left... before the lullaby carried me away from the worry associated with dealing with my brother... I cut into the meat, making as small pieces as possible while Dom put the fire out completely.

XIV

Dom

Thirty-One

I sat staring into the fire long after she left. *God, she was so infuriating!* I shook my head as I cleared my mind. There was no way that I could talk about Lizzy without telling her everything. She would never finish the journey then. f she didn't go into the mountains, she would miss out on meeting him and not realize she was destined to find that special person. Even though I hated the douche, I wanted her to have someone like Lizzy had been to me.

I rubbed my head in frustration. I'm bound not to do anything that would put her at risk now that she was away from the settlement. Yet, if I didn't do anything, then she would end up dead. A vendetta was to be fulfilled, one of my making, and I had to stop it.

I watched as the fire burned itself out. I stood up, stretching my aching limbs. My shoulder wasn't burning and shooting pains through me, so that was one victory. Unfortunately, my stomach was growling horribly. I stopped outside her door, debating whether to walk in or knock on the wall. I mean the door was wide open. I decided to act like the brother she remembered or at least attempted and knocked on the wall. She didn't hear me as she turned around from what she was doing, her hands full of something, her head looking at the ground as she stormed out of the room, knocking me to the side.

"God, Dom," She said as she rubbed her head, "could you at least announce your presence next time?"

When did she become so sarcastic? I wondered as I nodded at her. "Yeah," I replied, sighing, "that's what I just attempted to do. Why are you being such an ass?" I guess it was something that I just had no control over. Maybe it was all those years living by myself. I jerked my head towards the room. "Can I get some food, or were you planning on eating it all?"

She rolled her eyes at me, nodding, as she walked away. "Hey, where are you going?" I demanded of her.

"Personal business, Dom, personal business, unless you think you need to hold my hand while I go..."

I interrupted her, "No, no, no!" I felt my cheeks flush as I coughed awkwardly, "That's okay, just be careful, okay?"

She rolled her teal eyes at me as she continued. "Just get something to eat and leave me alone, okay?" She hollered at me, and I entered her room. Her figure had disappeared down the hall.

The meat was placed on the table, with strips and chunks all over the place. I sighed as I realized that she did this all on her own. *How many times has she done this?* I couldn't help but wonder as I grabbed several small strips and headed back out. I had done it many times but always went for something small that could be devoured. Rabbits were preferable.

I chewed angrily at the meat as I flopped down on the bed. I was thinking of everything she had done without me to help her. *Did she allow Dad to help her?* I knew she would have let me help her, but that was before. I wasn't so sure now. *Damnit, why had I been so selfish?* I wondered as I bit into the second piece.

I heard light footsteps as she returned and shut the door behind her. I ought to leave her alone like she's asked me to, but I didn't want to. Honestly, I was afraid she'd take off without me.

I stood up and then fell back down on the edge of the bed. There was nothing that I could tell her. I knew that she had to go to the mountain, and it would be a completely different experience when she got there. It would either bend her or break her. Yet, I knew how strong she was, and I was positive that she wouldn't bend or break but excel. Not only that, but he would be waiting for her. And if he was indeed her mate, he would help lift her to new heights, unlike what I did with Elizabeth. We were destined to be separated forever because of my inadequacies.

Honestly, there was nothing that I could do to change her mind about who I was. There was no way that I couldn't even change my mind. I was a failure at evolving, and I was a failure at being a brother. But that's why I had to keep trying; I knew I had a lot more going for me if I never gave up. If I kept going even if I knew I was a failure.

It didn't mean that I could tell her about Sanctum, the evolution of humanity, and her soulmate if that was indeed what he was. If I said anything, I'd break the laws placed upon me. I just wanted to tell my sister everything and damn the consequences, but I was too responsible for that. Maybe I was too much of a coward, and the thought of losing opportunities to see or talk to Elizabeth again. I ran my fingers through my hair as I continued to debate going to see her.

After a while, I figured I wouldn't sleep well tonight, if at all. So, I grabbed my bag and sat outside my door. I could protect her tonight until she's ready and up in the morning. Not to mention, this would ensure that she didn't leave without me.

XV

Mary Beth

Thirty-Two

I woke up for the first time in a long time feeling refreshed. I couldn't remember when I didn't wake up and felt like I hadn't slept a wink. Stretching out in bed, I looked around the room and remembered where I was and what was happening. I had to get up now. I had no clue how long I slept or what time of the day it was. There was a lot to get done.

I jumped out of bed and quickly grabbed the top sheet and knife from under the pillow. Gripping the handle, I ripped it into the sheet. The shredding noises were minimal compared to everything I was trying to hear outside my door. Most of the meat was still good but needed to be wrapped if I was going to make it last. I wrapped the meat tightly with the strips as I hummed my lullaby. It was relaxing to do this, even though I was curious why there were no noises or anything from the hallway.

I finished the task before grabbing my satchel to put the meat in. That's when I remembered that my satchel was overflowing. There were still pills all over the place inside, the pasta bags, the metal bowl, my clothes—it was just way too much. Not to mention the gun that I was still toting around. I didn't know what to do with it, but I didn't want to leave it anywhere.

Yet if I didn't do anything, there would be no meat for us. It would just be a bunch of waste. I dumped everything out onto the empty mattress and started to put pills together by shapes and colors. Then I looked at the bottles that I had and put the pills that matched together in the bottles. I didn't care whether they were something we needed or not. It wasn't the most interesting thing, but it must be done. Done... Rhymes with Dom. Hmmm, the clock wheels in my head started turning. Maybe I should have him do all this. A smirk flew across my face before I dropped what I was holding in my hand and walked to the door.

I opened the door quickly, and it slammed as it met the wall behind it. Dom jerked as he sat up against the wall across the hall. Looking at him in surprise, my tracks stopped.

"What the..." I didn't know whether to laugh or cry. "Why are you sleeping against the wall? What the hell? I didn't take that time to heal you for nothing!" My frustration made the words harsh and unforgiving.

But his embarrassed look was the deciding factor. A laugh bubbled up my throat, cramping my stomach as the laughter escaped and wouldn't stop. I gasped for air as I tried to stop laughing. *Why was he sleeping against the wall? Didn't he find us this place?* It was confusing, but the look on his face was priceless.

Eventually, I pulled myself together as the laughter faded away.

"What were you doing?" I asked again. Even as he started to stand up, his guilt seemed to eat at him, and he finally looked me in the eyes.

"I wanted to be safe."

"You wanted to be safe?" I asked incredulously. "Safe from what?"

"Bandits," His response was quick, almost too quick.

"Bandits," I questioned, an eyebrow raised.

"Yes, bandits." He insisted.

"But didn't you say that you checked this place out?"

"Well, yeah, but..."

"Oh, just forget it," I sighed. He wasn't ready to tell me anything. "Just get up and bring your bag in here."

"Why do you need my bag?" His eyebrows raised.

"What does it matter?" I quizzed him. "Just get up and get in here. There's work to be done if we are going to leave here anytime soon."

It was like a lightbulb went off. I thought for sure he'd hit himself in the head before he stood up and dusted off his pants. "That's good. I'd rather put the stuff in there anyway. You don't need to be looking in it."

I cocked my brow and threw my hair over my shoulder. "I don't need to look in it?" I asked disbelievingly. "You are still concussed because I've been in your bag before, idgit." Just for that smart-ass comment, I would take his bag and rifle through it again. When he reached down to grab his weapon from the floor, a wince spread across his face, and uncaring of his feelings at that moment, I yanked the bag from his hand.

He fell backward as the bag was pulled away, landing against the wall. I almost felt bad, but then I remembered that he had left our family and me for years without any kind of notice that he was okay.

Yes, I spent days taking care of him, but at the same time, it felt so pointless. He hadn't cared much about us, considering he never returned to the settlement. I was angry, and my anger overrode me at that moment.

As he pulled himself together, the pain etched across his face and the glimpse of metal in his hand caught my eye. *What did he have? A gun or a knife?* I couldn't decide; all I knew was that he must have grabbed it during his fall.

"Give me the bag, Mary Beth," he demanded.

"Oooh, my full name," I teased him as I held the bag up for him. "Get it if you think you can."

The thought of the pills and meat fell away as I teased my brother. It might have been years, and I was angry, so it felt so good to tease him again, especially since I had the upper hand.

He reached for it, still leaning against the wall, and I pulled it out of reach. He growled as I held it out to him again. "Come on, Dominic." I could play the full-name game, too. "Get the bag if it is so important." He pounced at me, the gun pointed down, so it wasn't a player in the game as it was finally revealed. Jumping out of his way, I backed up. It was surprising, to say the least. He must not have been in too much pain.

Turning, I ran into my makeshift room, dumping his bag on the bed beside my stuff. I'd quickly looked through his bag when he was sick to see if there was any food (as well as to steal some), but this felt like something else. Something that he was hiding, and I was done with it. I wanted us to be siblings or enemies; my mind couldn't take the flip-flop anymore. Maybe it was my anger talking, or perhaps my rational side, but there would be no more secrets, or we would have issues.

He'd hidden enough from me with his words but couldn't hide whatever was in his bag. I glanced behind me to see that he stood frozen in disbelief, bordering on horror, as everything spilled out.

There wasn't much in the bag, but there were a couple more of those dry good rations, his water bottle and filters, another couple of pieces of clothing, and a book. I didn't remember the book from before. It must have been in his pants that faithful day.

I picked it up and started to open it. The black-and-white drawings flashed as I started rifling through it before he pulled the book out of my hands.

"That's not yours, not at all, Mary Beth. I asked you not to look." He held the book to his chest like a lifeline.

"Oh, take a fucking chill pill, Dom. It isn't like I will make fun of you for drawing. You've done that all your life." This was weird for him, or it used to be. I couldn't decide anymore and just left him alone as I went back through the stuff on the bed.

Besides that book, nothing else in his belongings held much interest. There wasn't anything there that I would have wanted to know more about, so I started packing my bag. After a while, I glanced at him and back down at everything spread over the bed before looking at him again. He hadn't moved an inch and sighed in impatience. I debated whether it was worth it to tell him something before I gave up. *So much for having him do everything!*

Rolling my eyes, I grabbed the gun from the settlement; unease rolled through me; I didn't want to carry it. I wasn't the type of person to use a gun. It made me feel too much like a criminal. I stuffed it into his bag before filling it with other stuff. He already had one gun, so he could carry one more.

With all the bags done, I grabbed his bag and threw it at him. He dropped the book and grabbed the bag mid-air. I laughed to myself. Served him right for not helping. I didn't want to think about the fact that I was partly to blame for that fact as he bent down, grabbed the book, and slammed the door behind him. Rolling my eyes, I put my bags on, ensuring my bow was securely harnessed before taking off after him. I was half-of-mind to just let him leave. But then again, he's my brother, and blood always came first for me.

"Dom, come on now." I hollered at his retreating form. "This is ridiculous! I didn't see anything." I ran as I tried to catch up to his long strides. It was still early enough in the morning that it was comfortable to walk.

He walked before me for a long time, staring ahead, silent, just walking. After a while, he slowed down enough that I joined him.

"What was that about?"

"It's personal. That's all."

"Yeah, well, everything seems personal with you. When'd you become such a stick in the mud?" I inquired. My anger had cooled down some but still bubbled under my skin, ready to be lit again.

He sighed. "You wouldn't understand."

"Try me."

"I can't."

"You can't? Or, you won't?" I felt my temper rising. *What was it about him that just made me want to punch him? Or worse.* Closing my eyes, I inhaled as I stopped in the middle of the road. I hate the fucking secrets that he's keeping. *Why won't he just tell me?* I let the air out in a whoosh as I opened my eyes and looked at him. I stared as he continued to walk, his feet carrying him toward the mountains. I shook my head, debating whether I wanted to keep going with him or if I was ready to give up and try to find something around here that might be safe for our family. I laughed bitterly. There would be nothing safe here. I realized belatedly. He'd been shot at just a few blocks in the other direction. I had no idea who had done it or when they might return. I took off after him, my bags jiggling as I ran toward him.

He didn't talk to me as I caught up, yet again, silence reigned around us. My anger continued to boil under the surface before I realized that he hadn't had anyone to talk to, to confide in, in probably years. I mean, I assumed that anyway because Lizzy had been nowhere around when he'd been shot, and he refused to talk about her or even mention her. He was a bloody mess when I even slightly mentioned her.

The sounds of crickets chirping, our footfalls, and the scurrying of unseen animals echoed in the vast land around us as we traveled over bridges and under falling structures. Each step was packed with anticipation of whether or not it would be safe for us to walk over. Or, at least, for me, it was filled with anticipation and dread. I wondered whether the next step would be my last step as I focused on the ground in front of me. Cars littered the ground, broken windows, and doors ajar, as though the people within them didn't even stop completely before opening their doors and running off. I wished that I could remember more about that day. A couple of times, we encountered wreckage, the cars wrapped around each other, wheels flung across the highway, and glass-like glitter upon the floor.

We walked like this for hours, only stopping when one of us went to the bathroom. That's when the other person would stop, too, lean against a vehicle, and sip water from a bottle. I kept my eyes open for another water source as we walked the entire time.

It was completely silent, almost too quiet, because there was nothing to say—at least, not on my part. I didn't know what to say, and my mind was filled with so many thoughts that it was hard to determine whether or not I truly wanted to find out the truth from him.

When one of us got hungry, the sounds of a bag opening and the whispers of cloth unfolding would alert the other person, and either he or I would hold out a piece of meat to the other.

The silence was killing me. I hated it. There was never silence at home. Hell yeah, I was mad and wanted to talk about it, but I also had no idea how to address it with him.

He wanted to have his boundaries, and I wanted to know everything. *I had no boundaries.* He had been gone for so long that I just wanted to know. I wanted to be able to talk to my brother the way that a sibling should be able to, but he just didn't want to—or at least, that is the way it seemed to me. Again, either we were siblings, or we were enemies. There was no in-between.

As the sun started to set, I started looking around. We needed to figure out a shelter for the night. The cars around weren't beautiful by any means, but I thought that maybe one of them would make do for a shelter for the night. Nothing was better than still being out in the open while we were still this close to the city.

"Dom," Breaking the bubble of silence, I commanded his attention, "we need shelter."

"We'll be fine if we can just keep going."

"No, Dom. We need to stop. I need to rest." I stopped and stared at him. His long legs continued to carry him forward.

He sighed as he stopped and turned towards me. "This isn't going to be safe."

"Then, we'll take shifts." I attempted to compromise.

He sighed, as though he knew it wouldn't happen, and pushed his hat up a little as he rubbed his face before he pulled it down again. "Fine, find a car."

I had already seen one, and it looked to be pretty roomy. I mean, for a van, it had to be roomy. I pointed it out to Dom. He looked at it from where we were before he nodded, and we walked over. Opening the door, it creaked heavily as it peeled away from the rest of the vehicle. Sighing with relief, I climbed into it. Dom watched me and our surroundings until I was safely inside before he walked around and opened the front passenger door. The sound of the door echoes in the emptiness of the little valley we've stopped at.

"Get some rest, Mary Beth." He instructed me as he pulled his gun out. "I'll wake you up when I feel sleepy."

"Are you sure?" I asked through my yawn, distorting what I said. He nodded. I shrugged off my bags and put them on the floor, rummaging through them for my blanket. "Oh, by the way, I stuck another gun in your bag." I tossed out the information. My blanket fell around me as I yawned again. "Just in case, you know, you forgot that I did it."

He nodded, but his look was quizzical. He had obviously forgotten, and I couldn't help but laugh sleepily. Closing my eyes, I drifted off to sleep.

Thirty-Three

The deafening sound of thunder jerked me out of the light slumber that I had fallen into. The smell of gunpowder overwhelms the tight space of the car as the glass shatters. The ricocheting of Dom's gun echoed in my ear as I struggled to sit up in the backseat, only to be pushed down again by Dom's heavy hand. I could hear his tone and the decibels of his voice, although it was hard to determine precisely what he was saying.

"Stay down!" His words are finally decipherable as my head and chest compressed against the bench seat. He ducked under the window as best as he could before his gun peeked out of the window and fired aimlessly, or so it seemed.

"What the hell, Dom?" I screamed as I fumbled, my shoulder popping out of place as I searched for my bow and quiver. "What's going on?"

It was a void; I knew that the words were coming from my lips, yet I didn't hear them resonate in my ears until some time after they had already faded. My hand landed on the bow, pulling it out of the case, and I felt my confidence level rise. I felt in control, even if my surroundings weren't. That's what my bow always did. I kicked the bag with my foot, pushing it against the other door, as I rolled to the ground. Pain jabbed me in the side as the center of the vehicle hit me as I fell, and I shook it off as I took stock of the car around me. There was another window towards the back of the van that was broken out; luckily, it hadn't been the one above my head. I pulled the lever on the side of the bench seat, twisting my body around so that I could kick the back of the seat down, and pushed the bottom of the seat with my butt as I made room for myself to sit. The bullets continued to fly all around me, and I hated that I felt like I was too slow. I should have been moving quicker than this. I blamed the little amount of sleep on my sloth-like movements. Dom's voice floated around me as he kept talking, my ears adjusting to the noise of gunfire. At first, I struggled to understand what he was saying, but eventually, his words started to make sense.

"… were walking up to the vehicle with weapons. I didn't know who they were. Hadn't seen anyone around us in hours, even days, ya know, I just reacted."

"So, you shot at them?" My eyes widened as I leaned against the seat, where he continued to fire out the window unseeingly. "What were you thinking?"

"What we didn't know them. They had guns, and I don't know… Maybe I needed to keep you safe!" He yelled at me as another bullet wedged itself into the metal of the vehicle. The pinging of metal on metal reminds me that I didn't have time to argue with him. As long as the bullets were firing, we needed to stay safe.

"Well, crap!" I tried to string the bow with an arrow, but there wasn't enough room. *Duh,* I could hear myself say, *You can't string a bow in an enclosed car!* "Which way are they?"

"To the left… they were coming down from somewhere up by the mountains it looked like." He peeked out the window as he aimed again. "It looks like I shot one down, but there's still one out there."

I nodded and pushed the van door open, and as it slid to the back, I jumped out, landing behind the back driver's tire. I gripped the bow and arrow hard, making the metal a cold reality. Leaning around the vehicle, I looked through the darkness for the person who was shooting at us. Another flash of gunpowder from Dom exploded from inside the car, and I moved to take a shot. I followed the noises from Dom's, letting my other senses take hold, and knew exactly where he had been aiming. That had to be where the person was hiding. Sliding an arrow into the bow, I felt calm as I stepped around the vehicle, eyes closed and aimed. I didn't want to see where it landed; I trusted my shot, so I jumped back into my hiding spot, reaching blindly into the car for another arrow.

But I could see it. I could see my arrow even in the darkness of the night. It was insane. Nothing like this had ever happened before. In my mind's eye, I watched the arrow as it sped toward the person. I saw the light blonde hair dirtied and pushed under a baseball cap. Dirt smeared all around his face. I thought I had to be imagining because there was no way I could see this. I tried to shake it off, but this wasn't the time to get lost in my imagination, and yet I'd never shot at a person before, at least not willingly. *How did I know what this person looked like?* More importantly, how did I know that my arrow was on the way to taking out the shoulder that led down to the hand holding the gun that was currently shooting at us? Again, I tried to shake myself away from the freeze-frame I was mentally encased in. Even as my mind was frozen with this image, I felt the arrow under my hand and could grasp it. Dom may have started this, but there was no way I would lose it.

"Arrggh," a loud yell pierced the night as the sounds of a body slumped to the ground reached my ears. Again, everything became clear even though I was still facing the other way. I could almost feel the ground move from the thump of his body falling backward, even though I knew that it was impossible. My arrow had hit home, but then again, I rarely missed. I almost smiled as the image started to fade.

"I'm going after him," I yelled at Dom as I strung another arrow into my bow. I took off running towards the spot I'd aimed at. I held the bow at ready. The weapon was lofty in my hands. I ran past at least two vehicles before I came upon the person. Blood pooled around them, my arrow sticking out from their shoulder. Similar to where Dom's injury was. It was almost ironic. I gasped internally. There was no way that I knew where I had hit him. *No way.* Yet, his dirty blonde hair stood out from under a Colorado Rockies hat, the dirt smeared under his eyes.

They laid the gun a few feet away from him, and I pushed my bow down a little but still held it at the ready; there was nothing he could do at this point. It was an uncomfortable feeling, and I pulled at my muscles, but I wanted to be prepared. It was necessary when faced with the unknown.

I kicked the gun further away as I crept up to him. Dom said that he had shot one down, but that didn't mean that there wasn't someone else out there who was waiting for them to return.

"Who are you?" I demanded. "Did someone send you?"

He coughed; blood dribbled from his lips. "I'm no one, so you'll never know."

"What the hell does that mean?" I shook, and my bow

wobbled with the intensity of the vibrations. Anger coursing through my veins, I shook.

"What…" he coughed again, "What do you think…" His voice was raspy, and I lowered my bow even more to step closer. My arrow must have hit closer to his heart than I realized as more blood spilled out of his mouth. "What do you think it means?" His words echoed around me. I could see other spots on his clothing where the blood started to course down. He coughed, the blood spewed out, and I retook stock of the man. The arrow stuck out from his shoulder, but there were several other spots of blood blossoming over his stomach. I couldn't determine if something vital was hit or if it was a combination of my arrow, where it had landed, and the gunshot wounds he'd taken, but the man had to have been near death's door. Obviously, Dom had gotten him several times as well, but he kept going. *That took courage or stupidity.*

"Did someone send you?" My voice quacked and shattered. *Why did I sound so unnerved?* I need to act like I was made of steel. I tried to remind myself as other thoughts drifted through my head. *Was he sent here for me? Was Dom right? Was the settlement going to stop at nothing to make sure that the unwanted died?*

"Yes," the man whispered, his voice and aura weakening. I had never noticed it before, but a color of light surrounded him, and the blackness was fading into nothing as it closed in closer and closer to his skin. It was very dim, and I only had an idea of what it was from all of the books I'd managed to read before being kicked out of school. I had to lean in to hear what he had to say, "… and whoever else you have with you. They want you both dead." He chuckled drily, the blood splattering against his face as his laugh died halfway through. "They want your head resting on a platter." He grinned wickedly, turning his face into a massacre of blood and evil.

It was so graphic, and I couldn't help but wonder who would want me dead that much. Or what was so important that my death was warranted on a platter?

"Who is it?" I demanded, my hackles finally raised to the point that I pulled back the string subconsciously and aimed at him again. Dom came up slowly behind me, cautiously, as I stared down at the person. He looked down at the man before he gently pushed my hands down as he sided against me.

"Well, whoever it is. They won't get her this time." He said as he aimed. I didn't even see the gun still residing in his hand before the man's head exploded, chunks flying everywhere, I jumped back in shock. Blood, brain matter, and bones splatter all over the place. There was a gaping hole in the front of his face, and I felt like throwing up. I braced myself on my legs. I'd been close to the man when he had fired. Looking at my legs, I took some deep breaths as I noticed that, luckily, I avoided my legs being completely covered with the remains of his brain. Then I realized what an odd thought that was and wondered if I was in shock.

As I turned and stared at Dom, his eyes were flat and black as he stood there immobilized. "What did you do that for?" I asked, anger and delayed shock coloring my words.

"He was going to die anyway," Dom deflected as he turned around and started to walk away. "You saw the blood he was spitting out."

I turned and looked back at the dead man. My stomach rumbled, nausea eating at me, and I decided against grabbing my arrow. There was no way that I wanted to hold my arrow from his body with all of his blood over it. I could feel the stains of his death echoing onto the surface of my arrow, and I didn't want that to follow me.

I turned to follow Dom back to the van before my stomach tore through my mouth, and the contents of it landed on the ground. My bow clutched to my stomach as I heaved, my hair dripping down the sides of my face, catching drops of my vomit in it.

Dom sighed as he turned back towards me. He patted me on the back gently before he took my bow from my hands and rubbed my back slowly as I continued to spew until my stomach completely emptied itself. After dry heaving for a bit, Dom wiped my forehead with a cloth from his pocket.

"Sorry, kid, I was giving him mercy." His words sounded empty like he was trying to believe them himself.

"That wasn't mercy, Dom." I managed to choke out, walking weakly back to the van. I reached for my water bottle blindly as I opened the passenger side door, my eyes twitching. I swished the water once it was in my hand before continuing, "You shot first. That was murder!"

"Murder is what happened when you left the settlement, MB. Murder is killing someone to make sure that they will never walk or see the light of day again. *That is murder.* Mercy is releasing those souls already suffering; he was suffering, Mary Beth."

His words stayed with me as he walked away. I didn't know why, but I was frozen. His words were repeating in my mind as the sun slowly rose. When I finally felt like my body was under my control again, I used some of my precious water to clear the chunks of vomit from the long strands of my hair before walking over to the vehicle Dom had disappeared into. He was passed out in the back seat with my bag as his pillow. I tried to remember when he grabbed my bag after getting my water bottle, but my mind came blank.

I had genuinely frozen over his words. I watched him as he slept, his words echoing yet again, reminding me that I was no better because I had shot at the guy as well. I shuddered as a wave of revulsion hit me. I wanted to yell something anytime to wake him up. I tried to fight. No... I needed to fight. He was in the wrong. *He had to be.* I just couldn't live with it otherwise. I couldn't reconcile with myself, and I was quite sure of that.

Yet, he had been right. They had murdered everyone as they left the settlement... which led me to my next thought. *How was I going to get our family out and to safety without having them murdered, too?*

That was... if they weren't already.

XVI

Dom

Thirty-Four

She was so frustrating! I had just killed another two men to keep her safe… giving them mercy because there was no way that I could live with letting that man lie there and eventually die by drowning in his blood. There was no medical help for the shape that he was in.

But could she see that? NO. What had turned her into such a cynic? She had never been like that before. I smiled as I watched a little pigtail girl fly towards me, ghosting through my body as the memory faded. I pulled that little girl's smiling face to the forefront of my mind; instead, all I got was the scowling face of Mary Beth the way she was now. I scowled in response. The young woman she was with now wasn't my baby sister. She didn't respond in the same ways that MB had as a little girl. No, instead, she was a stranger wrapped up tightly in the skin of my little sister.

I struggled with the negative thoughts about her as I tried to stay awake. Honestly, I did. I walked around and tried going back and explaining myself to her, but it was like talking to a wall. That didn't help with my negative image of her in my mind. Eventually, I just collapsed from sheer exhaustion in another car. It wasn't like she was going to move anywhere. I half wondered if she was in shock but dismissed the idea as ridiculous because she had seen death before. *I mean, she was a hunter.* Not to mention, I had no patience to wait for her to come out of whatever trance she was in, especially with all the thoughts I had racing around in my head about her. I drifted into dreamland with the little girl and the young woman overlaying each other in my mind.

The next thing I knew, the peeking light of the rising sun heated my eyelids, turning everything into a murky red as the fleshy part of my eyelids lit up, and I struggled to wake up. I blinked, everything hitting me at once as I saw her. She had moved at some point during the night, thankfully not so induced into a shock coma. The hazy sun hit her hair just the right way, and a tiny sheen of glossy black reflected off it. Yet, as she stared out the front window with all of our belongings piled in the driver's seat next to her, I couldn't help but wonder how long she'd been sitting there. *Did she sleep at all?* The echoes of being a big brother and all of the times that I took care of her when Mom couldn't resonate through my head. I wanted to say something, anything, yet the air, coarse and thick with unsaid words, reminded me of the tense situation we had left the conversation in last night.

"Hey," my voice, gravelly and deep, echoed off the tin metal of the roof as I sat up in the backseat. Stretching out a little as my senses awakened.

She was silent as she got up and walked out of the car. *Okay,* I thought, *so we're doing the silent treatment. So mature, Mary Beth.*

"Mary Beth," I tried again.

"You are such a fucking asshole, Dom. You know that," she went off on me as she walked back to the car and sat in the seat next to me. "What dickhead idea gives you the right to decide who lives and dies? You're so much worse than an idgit. You are a downright stupid motherfucker." She stared straight ahead, her fists clenched as I watched her breathe like she'd run a mile.

Despite the beatdown she was giving me, I chuckled. "Where did you learn to cuss like a sailor? I know that it wasn't Mom or Dad. They would have washed your mouth clean." Maybe it wasn't the right thing to say then, but it was all I could think of.

She turned around in the seat faster than a speeding bullet, and the echo of her hand across my cheek resonated in my ears. "Don't be an ass, Dominic. You are the only one that ever cussed around Mom and Dad growing up. So, if anything," she tossed her hair as she settled back into the front seat, "you should blame yourself for teaching such an impressionable young child into cussing so that she could be just like you." The words sounded so childish as they exited her lips that I laughed again.

"Damn, MB, who knew that you were holding that much hatred inside of you?" Even though my cheek burned, I guess I was aching for a fight with her. Something to make it right between us, and if fighting me was the only way she would forgive me, by saying every little hateful word that crossed her mind, then I would let her. *Anything that might make this right.*

"Dom, you're such an ass. You are full of this mystical bullshit that you know something, and yet you refuse to share." She turned towards me again; this time, her whole body leaned into the seat as her icy glare landed on me. "Why do you continue to act like such a goddamn know-it-all? You told me that you'd help me... but how the hell are you helping me by killing the person who was telling me that someone was after me?"

Her face caught somewhere between guilt and sadness, and I wondered what she felt so guilty about. But I didn't have time to think about it before she went off on me again. I just had to tune her out. She needed to vent and rage, and I was the handiest thing available right now to do it. *It didn't mean that I had to listen to it.*

Again, I wondered how much I would be putting her in danger if I told her the truth. How much risk would I put myself in… how much trouble would I put Lizzy in if she knew exactly what we were heading for? Yet, I hold to the conviction that if MB found out what she was and where she was going, she wouldn't ever believe me, or even worse, she would decide that she didn't need me anymore.

"Dom, I'm sick of your shit. Either give me something or leave." Her last words are a slap to the face as I'm jarred out of my contemplation.

"What?" I demanded, sitting up and leaning into her. My face even with hers. "What did you say?"

"I said," MB enunciated each word slowly, "either tell me something about this whole shit and shebang or leave." Her mouth dropped slowly down, her eyes dead as they stared into mine. "I don't have to deal with your crap anymore. You left. Remember? That means your rights as my brother were terminated the day you left."

The words are a knife in my gut. I don't know what to do. In many ways, I'm tempted to return to the settlement and check on the rest of our family. I mean, she's already almost halfway there. Yet, something is keeping me from leaving her. She didn't leave me, even when I was shot and bleeding to death, not even when I was brooding, although I'll never admit to, and through all of my half-truths. *Hell, I mean, MB was still waiting for me here while I slept.* Obvi, MB was pissed off at me, and yet I can't determine if it is because we're siblings or the fact that she's that much of a good person that she waited until I woke up. But I'm not. I am not as good a person as she is because I wouldn't have stayed if I was that pissed off with her. *At least, that's what I want to believe.*

"MB, you couldn't handle the truth if I told you it." I deadpanned.

"Dominic," my full name rolled off her tongue, "Lashay Johnson, you don't know what I'm capable of handling."

"You're about to have your entire world implode," I told her, "everything we knew about the bombing, everything we knew about the world outside of the settlements, was a lie told to us by the government. So if you want to keep our family safe, you should trust me because no one else will keep you as safe as I am."

Shaking my head, I exit the vehicle, grabbing the bags on my way out. I extended her bags to her, waiting for her to decide if she would give me a chance to show her my trustworthiness and that, as her brother, my only intention was to keep her safe on this journey. After what seemed like hours but was only minutes, she stormed out of the vehicle and yanked the bags out of my hand before strapping it around her shoulders and mid-section before walking off. I followed after her grudgingly, and we continued, but it was just like nothing had ever happened. We just walked until someone needed to stop. By the time that night fell, we were out of the foothills, and the base of the mountains loomed ahead of us. I didn't have to wonder or guess which way she was going to go as she walked determinedly one way up the mountain roads. She went the one way that I never thought she'd go.

XVII

Mary Beth

Act III – Summits of Fate

Thirty-Five

I'm fuming. I'm so mad. Yet, I don't know what to say to him, so I hold my tongue. It won't do me any good to go off on him again. Obvi, he didn't listen to me before. I told him to tell me the truth, and he continued to evade it; I mean, come on, does he think that someone is going to kill him or me if he told me what exactly we were heading into? Not only that, but what about our family? He said that if I wanted to keep them safe… Was I genuinely keeping them safe by being away? I was so conflicted by all the mixed emotions and thoughts in my head… yet… just yet… Maybe he was telling me the truth, but I knew it wasn't the complete truth. Something was missing… Something vital.

The melody of my lullaby replayed on repeat in my head, trying to comfort me even though there was no comfort in sight. The tune, the tone, wasn't the same as the one I've listened to all my life. It wasn't my voice, or even my mom's, that I heard. I swear it wasn't, but the strange voice was still comforting. I was disturbed by all of it: the bloodshed, my suddenly 'psychic' ability to follow my trajectory, the fight with Dominic, and now a weird voice in my head. *But was it odd? Or had I been hearing it for a while and only now realized that the voice wasn't one I knew?* Something strange and abnormal is happening, but I couldn't trust Dom to tell me the truth if I asked him about these new developments.

The world was eerily silent around us. The absence of any other human presence, except for Dom, was unsettling. I found myself unexpectedly leading our journey, a responsibility that weighed heavily on me. Shouldn't I be more concerned about our isolation?

As we ascended the rolling hills, memories of the city flooded my mind, and my breath quickened. Some time ago, we had veered off the highway; my instincts guided me towards something to the left—a mystery I felt compelled to unravel before continuing our journey.

The ground around us started to change colors, going from the dirty brown and yellowish-green dead lands of the plains. Instead, it was turning reddish-brown, more red than brown. There were boulders, crumbling rocks, and sand, all of the same colors around us. Ahead of me, on the road I had decided to travel, the rock structure had almost completely collapsed against the blacktop of the road. There was a hole, perhaps just big enough that we could both go through. As I began to walk through it, I prayed to the nothingness that existed, or whatever holy power there was, that I made it through the hole alive so that I could continue to look for a place for my family. Coming out on the other side, I released the breath I'd been holding unconsciously and took a deep breath as I stopped.

I stumbled as Dom unceremoniously bumped into me as he came through the same hole.

"Don't you know that you need to move your ass when you have someone following behind you?" His smart-ass remark fell flat as I marveled at our surroundings. Everything around us was a mesmerizing shade of red. Despite the destruction, there was a strange beauty to this place.

I knelt, ignoring Dom, and grabbed a handful of the red material surrounding us, watching it fall like sand between my fingers. My skin brightened considerably as it turned red like powder, sliding like fine silk as it slipped through my fingers back onto the surface.

Dom stood over me, his expression blank. He stared at me as I continued to gaze in wonder around us. "What was this place?" I whispered reverently as I grabbed another handful. I watched it quickly fall, feeling each grain, each crystallized piece, slip slowly between my fingers and fall helplessly to the ground.

His eyes were dark and deceptive, filled with a darker emotion I couldn't place as he stared at me.

My hands, now covered with the fine powder, turned a majestic red, and for the first time in my life, I didn't care about wiping the color off. It was enchanting.

Whatever this place was, it had a calming effect on me. I could feel the worry of everything as it started to slip away. *Why did this place so hypnotize me?* I had relaxed so much that I was in a space where I didn't care about the dead man and the bloodshed that had just occurred hours ago; it was like it had never happened until it randomly crossed my mind. Hell, I didn't care about my family at that moment, either. This place so entirely absorbed me that my body drifted away, falling into space as each little granule of sand disappeared into the pile beneath me.

I was so lost in the magnificent silence and endless wonder of the peaceful landscape that I didn't hear anything around me. I existed outside of time and space. All was funneled into the lullaby, as its sounds filled my ears, completing the haven in my mind. Everything outside of it was as silent as the drifting sand going out of my hands.

A gust of wind flung the scarlet sand, burning my eyes as it scattered across my face. The wind was so unexpected and gone as quick as it came that it jerked me out of my reverie. I glanced around, rubbing the sand from my eyes, but nothing was there. Even the sky was empty. I glanced at my brother to see hatred and anger burning in his eyes. *What the hell? Why did he look so angry?*

I frowned, stood up, and walked over to his hand waving in front of his face. "What is wrong with you?" I demanded, his eyes still dark and angry. He said nothing as he stomped away, heading several feet before me. I gasped as he walked away. He was so filled with anger in a place that I found peace that I could feel myself changing from calm to something unknown.

Pulling in deeply, I took in the stale mountain air, my mouth and nose working in synchronization to try and refocus. I wanted to return my center to the hazy peacefulness the sand had placed me in earlier. But I wasn't at peace anymore. No, now I was confused. Confused and angry. *What had I done for him to be so angry? Was there nothing in what I had just done that should have caused him to have such a reaction?* I pondered over his response as I took in the surroundings. Every inhale, every exhale, one by one, each action took in the air and released it. Each moment, I could feel the air change a little bit by a little bit. Those tiny changes are often unnoticed by the average person. But I wasn't the average person. I could smell it.

The thick, oppressive smell of ozone fell around us as the skies darkened. I could hear the rumbling and rolling of thunder, sounding miles and miles away, but it was all a lie. I knew it was closer. Yet for such an unexpected sound and a flash of lightning echoes across the sky in the distance, I knew it meant trouble. I shuddered as a fire ignited within me. We needed to get to cover now. It was about to pour, and there was no telling where the acid level would be this time; there never was.

I ran towards Dom, who had wandered further in. The thunder rolled through me as another rocked the ground. "Dom," I sputtered out, every exhale a harsh sound. "We need shelter. Now!"

He looked at me quizzically before taking a deep breath; I could see that he could smell it, too, as his expression changed. Rain was coming, and it was coming quickly.

His eyes flashed panic as he looked around. "This isn't the place to be during a rainstorm, Mary Beth." His words belittled the environment. I could see a lot of spaces that we could go to.

"I don't know about that," I exclaimed as though he was being stupid. "I just followed my instincts, and we came here. I mean, look around us. There are plenty of places that we can hide."

He shook his head and started back up the pathway where he had wandered off—the one I didn't even notice was there. "Sure, MB, there has to be something here, but what?" His words sounded sarcastic, but I knew that he was being honest at that moment.

The pitter-patter of raindrops echoed me, and I pulled my hood closer to my face. There was no way that I was going to get acid marks on my face, yet as the first drop fell, I hissed in pain as it landed on my exposed hand. It was the acid rain.

Shit. Again, I ran faster; there was no way I would be caught in it. I worried about my gear as I ran faster. Each minute in this would destroy everything I had. I was running wildly in the increasing darkness when Dom yanked me towards him, my gear swinging violently as I was tugged into a broken building. The few details I could catch as I was pulled inside recklessly was another door on the opposite end, as he pulled me through the one he opened.

The stench was unbearable as if someone had never flushed a toilet. Or, as I remembered it, going to a port-a-potty at the park, which hadn't been cleaned in weeks. But this was much worse. This was years of abandonment. It was copper at its' worst. I gagged on the smell, curling in on myself as I collapsed against the wall. The wind whipped against the sides of the building, the scattering sounds of rain pattering against the bricks; it would almost be a soothing sound if it weren't eating away at the bricks and if I didn't feel like I was suffocating on the horrible smell I was currently being tortured with. *Why did he have to find the only building that was a bathroom to be our safety?*

The thunder rolled louder this time as though right above us. I shivered, grateful for the building but still disgusted by the smell, hoping against hope that it would be a short storm. Dom released my arm, and I fell completely to the floor as he walked away. Even with him not facing me, I couldn't help but remember the look of hatred in his eyes moments before this all started.

The rumble of thunder rolled over us as loud as a gunshot. I curled into my stomach as I tried to hold the need to retch. My elbows touched the bare brick as my legs came up, and I became as small as I could with everything still on me.

Gasping in shock and pain, I expanded again as the world came into sharp focus. I was in the rain longer than I intended. As I lurched away from the wall, I cradled my arms close. There were red dots of blistering skin everywhere, and I wondered if I had any cream in my gear that could help with them. I hissed in pain as it came into sharper focus how much the acidic water had hit me. I looked around me to see if this bathroom had any form of helping me in my current condition. I was unsure if Dom would ever notice me considering how much of an ass he was being currently.

There was enough left in here to be usable. I was glad as I gingerly moved towards a sink. My skin burned, and I hoped I could clean up some if there were still water in the faucet. The mirror above it reflected the filthy me reflection at me as I stared into it. The bright red blotches from the rain showed up on my arms; luckily, not much showed on my face. My ears burned, though, so I knew that some of the rain must have burned through my hood and hit me in the ears. I worried about how much of my hair would be gone, but in the end, it wouldn't matter; my hair would always grow back.

I thought I could do nothing for my ears as I gently took my gear and leaned it against my knee. Reaching inside it, I searched blindly for the bandages I had put in there the previous day. Each movement was torture, and I struggled as I tried to wrap my arms. I wasn't going to ask Dom. *Oh no, there was to be no disturbing of Dom.* I didn't trust myself not to ask him what the look was about again because the thought still boiled my blood, and I just knew that he would lie to me.

Biting back my tears and gasps of pain, I wrapped my arms slowly, starting on my right side. My necklace was heavy on my chest, and I was comforted by its' weight against me.

It was a slow process, and I was almost done with my right arm when Dom decided to come over. He gently took the bandages from my hand and finished the covering I'd been working on.

"I'm sorry, kid." The words fell gently as he grabbed my left arm, and an involuntary gasp escaped my lips. His actions are kind, opposite to his actions and behaviors over the last couple of days.

"For what?" I asked, trying to figure him out. *Was he apologizing for the dirty look, the killing of that man, or for making me hurt involuntarily because he was wrapping my arm?* I just couldn't figure it out.

"For not keeping you safe," he muttered as he tucked the bandage into the beginning of the wrap on my left side. "I should have been paying attention to the weather."

"You can't blame yourself for everything, Dom." I said, huffing, "Besides, you did keep me safe… I guess you could call it that… Back with that guy. Although I'd still like to know what you meant. Anyway, I'm the one that took us this way, right, so shouldn't I be the one to blame?" I tried to lighten the mood and said with a laugh, "Look what MB did again. She got us stuck somewhere else."

"Oh, stop it."

"What? That's the way it's always been. I'm the wrong one. You left me behind, after all, so maybe I'm naturally just a screw-up for not knowing anything." I started it so matter-of-factly, so deadpanned, that it was almost hysterical.

"Yeah, I did leave you," he replied somberly, "but it wasn't because you were a screw-up. No, that was me. Besides, you still haven't left me behind, have you? I think that makes you the better person in this case."

His words caught me off-guard as he pulled away, my arm dropping listlessly to my side. His words were almost brotherly.

"We'll stay here until it's over. Then we can move on," he nodded as he spoke. The howling winds and the pattering of the weather falling outside echoed around us before he looked at me, "Is that okay with you, kid?"

I nodded as I looked down at my arms. I don't know why, but it almost felt like we were close again. But I knew it was up in the air; there was no way to be confident whether I could trust him. Yet, at this moment, it was a good point. It felt good to be somewhat on the same page while we were stuck in a storm.

Thirty-Six

The sun was coming up, and I could tell from how it impacted the heavy layer of smog that filled the air when the rain stopped.

After a couple of hours, I became immune to the nasty smells from the bathroom. I eventually fell asleep close to the door. At least a small breeze of fresh air came in that way.

Dom was still passed out under the sinks when I got up this morning. I let him sleep in as I cracked the door open and looked outside. The grounds were still wet, but it looked like it had stopped raining. I wondered if moving out of the room was okay but was unwilling to give up my only shoes to find out. So I closed the door and went into each of the stalls, even those that had managed to maintain a door on them after all these years, as I looked for something I could toss out the door. Finally, I found some rocks that must have been kicked in the room at some point in time and picked one up. It was thick enough that if it was still too acidic out, I would know how acidic it was, and I would use that instead of any of our supplies to determine that fact.

My footsteps were silent on the floor as I returned to the door and cracked it open again. Throwing the rock out into a nearby puddle, it wasn't more than half an inch deep, I waited.

Minutes passed, and the rock still looked similar to when I threw it out. Sighing in relief, I figured it had to be at least safe enough to get out of this hellhole I'd been stuck in for the entire night.

I whistled loudly at Dom, seeing him jerk in his sleep, before yelling, "You going to sleep all day, Sleeping Beauty?" He woke up so fast that he knocked his head into the sink, and I laughed outright at his stupidity. *Who in their right mind sleeps under a sink?* I thought as I walked through the door and around the more enormous puddles as I returned to the way Dom had been yesterday. It was a pathway on the side of the mountain, heading somewhere, and I was bound and determined to figure out where it went. I glanced behind me as I took leaps and bounds over the puddles to avoid losing my shoes sooner than necessary. I saw Dom slowly following after me. He rubbed his eyes, I guessed from annoyance, as he stared after me. I might as well be in a playful mood. It wasn't like being angry and upset always would get me anywhere. *Besides, that was Dom's job.*

I raced around the pathway until I came to the end. There was a large boulder, and as I came bounding at it, I could hear the ricocheting of bullets hitting the rock. I dropped and rolled to the base of the boulder, looking around wildly to figure out where the bullets were coming from.

Goddamnit, I thought, *Back to fighting... that's all I've done since I left the settlement... It was a never-ending cycle.* I peered around the boulder to the other side. Another group of people with weapons drawn was up away on the broken downstairs.

Is this ever going to end? The thought passed hurriedly through my head as I pulled my bow and arrow from my gear. Sliding the gear to the ground, I slid the arrow into the bow and stood up slowly. As I stood, I picked a target among the group and aimed toward her. I could hear the hissing of the air as the arrow sliced through it. I slid back behind the rock, the bow string vibrating against my leg. As it whizzed through the air, I attempted to focus, to see if I could be one with my arrow. As I closed my eyes, I watched its' trail as though I was a camera attached to it. I jerked my eyes open, freaking out a little; I mean, that was crazy, right? *Who could do something like this?* I closed my eyes again. It was such a new experience for me, something so unexpected, and yet it felt as natural as breathing.

It curved, almost unnaturally, as my target came into view. No wonder I had never missed a shot when I was intentional and focused. *I was the arrow.* I truly felt as though I was one with my weapon. The crunch of bone as the arrow wedged itself deep within it, the bouncing and vibrations of the arrow against the flesh and muscle as it attempted to slow its movement after the impact. Each movement had to have caused another jolt of pain to slice through the woman's head. Her howl of pain echoed against the red stones, jolting me out of the vision.

Dom darted out from a nearby rock and swept next to me. He gave me the "Have you lost your mind" look as I strung another arrow into my bow. Obvi, but now was not the time to discuss it. I needed to focus, but it was already challenging to focus on the here and now when I was transported away whenever I shot my arrow, so I had to make this short and sweet.

"Who the hell are they?" I asked him, thinking maybe he might have recognized any of them.

"Hell, if I know, kiddo. Why'd you shoot at them?" His

question was a challenge, in my own words, not even two days ago when he killed a man lying helpless in the street.

"I didn't shoot at them first," I snapped at him. "Did you not hear the gunshots when you came here?"

He looked at me like I was crazy, and for a moment, I felt like I was. Then, another shot rang out as a bullet buried itself in the rock that we were facing. "You know what," I told him, "I don't care if you know them. I'm getting out of here alive, so here's hoping."

I jumped out again with another arrow at the ready. I let it loose as I focused on the only man in the group. If he went down, maybe the rest of them would surrender. I didn't know for sure, but I had to try. I pulled back on the string, which vibrated as I pulled harder before it flew through the air. This time, I didn't need to close my eyes for the trajectory of my arrow to know the path that it would fly, knowing that when it landed, it would be in the exact spot, killing the man instantly.

I decided this would be a bloodbath, but it won't be my blood. No, I was stronger than that. Gunshots rang out as the battle ensured. Each time I strung my bow, the arrow rang true as it embedded itself in my opponent's body. Dom was right alongside me. Each time I came out with my bow, he shot at the other group, protecting me while I was vulnerable. We felt so in sync we worked together to defend ourselves, and I truly felt that familiar connection we had been missing. I just hoped that it would stay.

XVIII

Dom

Thirty-Seven

The next couple of days passed in a blur as I continued to follow her. We had been moving non-stop since leaving the amphitheater. It was like we both were more aware of all the negative things that could happen if we stopped for more than a few minutes. It was exhausting, not to mention that we were both aching from wounds that barely got cleaned after the bloody battle we went through. We, no, she, had decimated the other group. I probably only got in a few shots that landed. It was like she was a madwoman, arrow after arrow, and they flew through the air until no one was standing. I had contemplated the idea of pointing out that she had killed a group of people compared to the one that she knew of that I had killed. Yet, we had moved so well during that fight that I didn't want to break the fragile foundation we both stood on. So, we gathered our stuff and walked away from the site after she had collected all her arrows from the bodies.

Now, days later, we still didn't talk much. The only words spoken were whether we needed something or if we had to stop somewhere. But a lot of that was my fault.

It ate at me. The dead silent air. It just ate at me. It reminded me of how I continued to hold the silence of the knowledge

I possessed. The knowledge that could benefit Mary Beth if I would just share it with her, yet Lizzy's crystalline clear blue eyes haunted my dreams. I couldn't speak if I wanted to maintain her safety in the Sanctum. Not only that, but I knew he was coming. He had already been here twice. The flash of the black wings and the gush of sudden air right before the battle at Red Rocks was a clear indication that he would soon be joining us. Not to mention when he had seen her at the settlement.

The walk was tenacious; each rock and pebble that snuck into my shoe reminded me of why I hated coming through here the first time. The rugged, cold grounds and even colder winds taunted us with a bare gust every once in a while, yet the steady chill that made my bones ache impacted me the most. The benefit was that the animals were more plentiful here, and over the last several days, we've managed to capture enough to feed ourselves for a while. Cooking them was interesting, to say the least. It was funny as hell the first time that Mary Beth had to stick the stick through the animal's carcass. Since we had cooked the animal over the metal bench at the hospital's remains, she hadn't had to do it then. We'd made a campfire with other sticks to hold up the carcass while it cooked. But it was deadly silent. It was almost too much to bear.

Yet, I didn't know what to say to her, and there was nothing that I could tell her that didn't sound wrong when I thought about saying it out loud. She hadn't talked to me about anything since our disagreement on what murder was. Outside of the bare minimum when I'd apologized to her. I wished I could just tell her everything, but there was so much, and there wasn't enough time anymore.

She was so fucking headstrong too. Stubborn more than I remembered her being. I had to yell at her the second night after we left Red Rocks. She had itched her arms during our walk. I guess I hadn't been paying enough attention to her then. She had caused her whole arm to start bleeding again. It had been so bad I swore that I thought she'd cut herself somehow when I had looked at the gauze.

I'd yelled at her about her being so irresponsible and that she didn't care anything about herself. She'd just given me this look, and I could feel the shame and guilt eat at me because I swore I could tell what she was thinking.

I tried to do everything possible to keep us camouflaged during our walks. I'd sent out illusions as much as I could. It was the one benefit that I got from this stupid mutation shit that the bombs had caused. I didn't want another run-in. *Twice was enough for me.* I didn't know what she thought about us being without another attack, considering that I was pretty sure she had seen those people a couple of hundred feet down from where we were standing on the mountain that one time. I had to keep the illusions up, though, without her realizing it because of him. I swore that I'd seen him dancing above us, his black wings whipping along the hazy skies, but just as I stopped to look and get a good position on him, he disappeared again.

She looked at me crazy every time I stopped but didn't say a word.

Not a word since we left Red Rocks. There had been one point, at the beginning, where she had tried asking me something about hatred in my eyes back at Red Rocks, but I deflected it back to her actions with that group. That just pissed her off. *It was better that way.* At least, that's what

I kept telling myself. *If she could hate me, it might make it easier to believe she would be happier at the Sanctum without knowing I could never go in with her.* I ignored her as much as I could. It hurt her feelings, but she was close to finding the answers. I didn't want to jeopardize Lizzy's standing by saying something I couldn't.

I was stuck in this complicated position. I didn't know what to do. I was torn in half about her. More than anything, I wanted to rebuild my relationship with her and be the brother she remembered me as, but I wasn't. I was bound by so many laws and powers that if I even tried to start explaining things to her. Well, let's just say it wouldn't end well. I had Lizzy to think of, stuck inside Sanctum without me. I couldn't imagine life without knowing that she was okay and that I couldn't improve my relationship with Mary Beth without jeopardizing Lizzy's safety. Because, in the end, Mary Beth would be gone too, and I'd be stuck alone in this world again. So, I didn't, and after a while, she didn't try anymore either. *What a long and very awkward journey this has become.*

XIX

Mary Beth

Thirty-Eight

My shoes were ill-prepared for the rocky terrain that I was faced with. Each day, my feet ached more and more. Yet, I scanned our surroundings with a determined gaze, resolute in my quest to find a place to stop and find something better than ratty sneakers to walk with. Not that Dom noticed. He was too busy watching the skies. *What the hell? What could possibly be in the skies the way that they are?* For the most part, Dom walked by my side, but after that snide comment about me being a madwoman for killing that group, my anger was so raw that it was better if I didn't talk to him. I tried to walk ahead of him even with my ravaged feet and aching soles. Only stopping to check on him. He was so secretive. I couldn't tell if he'd changed and had become that kind of person or because it was because something else was holding him back.

God, he was so infuriating, and it frustrated the hell out of me. It's like he's deliberately doing it to piss me off. I just wish he'd open up to me. Still, every time I thought about talking to him and giving him that opportunity, to be honest with me, he did or said something else that just showed what a lost cause that was.

Around me, though, the mountains changed the deeper we

went in. There was actually some nice color here. It was shocking! The mixture of the trees, some still lush and green while others were gray and withered, contrasted my eyes, and I couldn't help but wonder how long they had been here. More importantly, how much longer were they going to make it in the dismal aftereffects of the bombings? Not to mention, every day, I wondered and imagined that everyone could enjoy it if I found us a home here, but it didn't feel right; this wasn't the place yet.

My mind was all over the place, torn between confusion regarding the weird behaviors of my brother and my utter amazement with the mountains. They seemed almost untouched by the war. My brother's weird behaviors were swiftly becoming normal, a fact that I couldn't quite reconcile with.

We've visited many mountainous areas; they initially seemed terrible but gradually improved. Each place we stopped for a few minutes brought back memories of everything we'd experienced over the last week. We first started traveling through the mountains after leaving Red Rocks, or at least that's how Dom referred to that area. There were such dark and dank areas. It is filled with browns, dirty yellows, but occasional greens. It was depressing; all I could think about was Nicky, the girls, Mom and Dad— anything but what we were actually doing to keep myself from becoming too depressed. The loss of my family was a constant weight on my heart, a pain that never seemed to fade.

Finally, I had to stop. Looking at Dom, I demanded, "We need to find a place, any place, that might have shoes." I lifted my foot, showing him how the bare skin of my sole peeked through the bottom.

So that's what we did. We searched through empty cabins, shacks, trailers, and everything we encountered. Never straying too far from the main course. Anything that was of use we took, sorrow filled my heart that there was no one left in these places, and I wondered how viable it was to live in one of these. *Could it be an opinion for our family?* And yet, each time, my answer was no. This was not the right place. *Not yet.* Finally, we found a collection of hiking boots in one of those places. My aching feet were so thankful to have found something solid that I nearly wept with relief when I put them on my feet. My feet were bloody at that point, and I had to bandage them, but the boots helped immensely.

Dom was silent throughout the entire thing, only pointing out what he thought I might need. It was so brotherly of him that I almost forgot his manic-depressive behaviors. When he wasn't saying anything, it felt like a brick wall was walking beside me when I did feel the need to talk. When he was talkative, which was a rarity in itself, it was about all the negative shit that would make me so mad that I threw acorns and pinecones at him. There was no in-between for our relationship; either way, he ate at my nerves, going from being short and silent to being inconsistent and inconsiderate with everything he did. There were times that I looked into his eyes and swore that I was looking at my brother from the time before the settlement when he was happy and carefree. Hell, even when he was with me at the settlement, with our family, he was as happy and carefree as someone could be during an apocalypse. It was so hard to reconcile the hard-ass stranger that acted like a dumbass idgit with the brother that was everything to me. The brother that had made me feel safe in a time when none of us would ever be safe. I was torn between the memories of our past and the reality of our present, unsure of which version of Dom I wanted to be around.

Honestly, I was at a point where I didn't know which Dom I would get or even which one I wanted to be around. It was a lot easier just to sit there and ignore him, or at least my attempts to. At the same time, I missed having one person, my best friend, who always made me smile as a child.

Twinkle, twinkle, little star. How I wonder what you are? Up above the sky so high, like a diamond in the sky. My lullaby drifted through my mind, the one thing constant, consistent, and my companion when there was no one else to turn to. It kept me sane.

Every step seemed to bring me closer to this one mountain. It called out to me. I had no clue where or even if I was in a habitable place, but it felt right. It made my blood sing. With each movement we made, the lullaby would get louder and louder in my head to the point that it was almost indistinguishable. The area was beautiful compared to where I was before, but it still wasn't right. *Why was the song so consistent now? What did it have to do with where I was?* Was this some pre-ordinated bullshit, fate as they liked to call it, or was it because I was making it up on my own to try and get as far away from the settlement as possible?

Yet, the song never stopped. I would go to sleep with it pounding in my head. I would wake up and have it playing mid-sentence in my brain. It was a compulsion beating at my brain, telling me to keep going. It was like it was telling me that all the answers I wanted were at that mountain. The one that I hadn't reached yet.

Thirty-Nine

The twigs and branches brushing against each other echoed in the silence as Dom started a fire. He had grabbed materials for it while I prepped my bedroll. His arms were full of twigs and branches when he came back, and I could already feel myself warming up as he put them together in the middle of our little campground and started the fire. I revisited that morning as I laid back on my bedroll as the last lights of the day faded away and twilight took over.

I tried climbing the side of the mountain after a fishing expedition in my boots, which had been worn down by the amount of walking we'd done over the last several weeks. It was a challenge, but I was determined. No matter how many steps I took up the incline, I always fell twice as many. My feet had been sopping wet, soaked clear through the boots, my pants clinging to my legs in spots, and I heaved big lungfuls of air with each step. It was a losing battle, but I refused to give up. I couldn't even breathe by the end of it. I had figured I was never getting up and was just about to quit and stay there until the incline dried. Dom, on the other hand, had no such problems. He stood at the top of the side, peering down at me as I struggled.

"Need a hand up?" He inquired, just as I was about to

announce my defeat, although I would never say it in a way that he'd know I was quitting. But I was so frustrated by the entire thing that I felt like he was inconsiderate, considering how he said it.

"No," I said sarcastically, "I'm researching the best way to get up… Of course, you idgit." I went with my anger. It was the only way we seemed to communicate anymore. *Anger and sarcasm to the rescue!*

He shrugged his shoulders, leaned down, and offered me his hand to climb out. Even with my smart mouth, he still helped. That's when the lullaby stopped; it stopped for the first time since it started in its consistent repetition in my mind. What I had begun to suspect would be a never-ending relay had stopped. I woke up to it every morning and fell asleep every night. I fought singing it day and night, but it would never leave me alone. And now it was just gone. I felt so confused.

The song had been something that nagged at me. And, if I couldn't understand it, there was no way I would let it go and not worry about it. *Didn't they use to say that crazy was doing the same thing, over and over again, and expecting different results?* Well, I heard the lullaby over and over again, expecting different results, and now it was gone. Did that mean it was something "mystical," or was I crazy? The song had been playing in my head for so long that I felt like I was searching for some all-important, all-encompassing place my brain had decided was the spot for my family. *I was not going crazy. I wasn't.* I swore to myself, even as I debated with myself whether the song stopping was a good thing or a bad thing. The emotional struggle was real, and it was tearing me apart.

What if it was a push towards the unknown, I was following the unknown, doing something that I had dreamed up… Or was it just something I kept telling myself because I was lonely? I missed my family, and thinking that finding this "perfect" place would make things better for Mom, Dad, Nicky, and the girls might be why I kept hearing the song… But that didn't feel right. Something else was leading me, so even though I could have stopped anywhere and found a good place, a safe place, for my family, it just didn't feel right.

But I have to admit, I hadn't been as diligent as I should have been as we walked. I had been too focused on finding this unknown place in the mountains that the song was leading me towards, or at least I assumed it was, so I hadn't paid the attention necessary to my surroundings otherwise. I could have been happy with any of the places we had found, but in reality, I haven't considered a place good enough for us to live in. I should've stopped and looked around, maybe even found something viable for everyone to live in, but nope, my body had a mind of its' own and kept moving forward. It was a damn compulsion, and it was throwing me off of my game.

But I wasn't the only one that was following the compulsion. At least, I didn't think so because Dom was on a roll, too. He hasn't stopped for anything but going to the bathroom and sleeping for the last few days. If Dom weren't following a compulsion, then he would have stopped me at any of the spots that were viable for our family. Dom wanted them to be safe as much as I did, so why did he keep pushing us forward? So, was Dom following the same compulsion as me? But how could he? *Was Dom hearing the song, too?*

I tossed in the bedroll, thinking about the rest of the day. Each day, honestly, it was like the food slid down our throats as we walked. The days were endless, and the nights seemed short. We had to get there, where there was, I didn't know, but I wasn't going to stop until I knew we were there. Each day, each mile, was another step, another moment in time that kept me from my goal. I just wanted to go faster. I needed to get to wherever this song was leading me because I had the feeling that the song wasn't going to stop until I stepped onto that mountain, that one just out of my grasp. But now it had stopped, and I couldn't figure it out. *Was it because of Dom? Or was there something else...* Our sense of purpose was unwavering, driving us forward despite the challenges.

He mostly followed my lead, but his approach to the journey was markedly different. He didn't share my relentless drive to move day and night toward our destination, lacking the same sense of urgency that consumed me. Even though he seemed to move with the same sense of restlessness that I had.

"Are you in a hurry?" I asked him at one point.

His response was abrupt, almost as if he had been caught off guard. "No, not at all," he paused, his words hanging in the air.

He did seem like he was in a hurry, though, or something... and it was always so weird. Either he was in a hurry, or he was searching for something. There were these moments, these little quick pauses where he would look around, his face filled with—I didn't know how to describe it—a mixture of hatred, joy, and fear. There was no way for me to determine what made him look that way, and I had tried multiple times to figure it out.

He thought he was being so sneaky. He would pause, only for a little bit, when I was busy or when he felt I was busy. He tried to hide it from me.

Not that it meant much. Dom hid a lot from me.

But then again, I had nothing better to do than figure out what he was hiding when I wasn't trying to figure out the song. But the song had kept me busy. It had occupied my mind twenty-four/seven for the last several weeks. But now I had made it into my job to figure out what exactly he was attempting to keep away from me. I looked over at him from where I laid down on my bedroll. The fire blazed in the middle of the clearing. He stood near the fire, his own bag in hand. I ignored Dom as he motioned towards the trees, and I pulled my bag closer. He sighed heavily as he walked around me and returned to the trees.

I tried to look around, trying to see whatever it was that he saw when he made his little "unobvious" stops while we walked. I made sure that there was nothing evident about my movements. There was no way he realized I'd been looking, too. Yet, I never saw anything around when he stopped.

It started with a quick stop where I'd try looking around, doing a good surroundings observation of our area. Still, he just glanced up and around as quickly as possible before moving on. Obviously, he didn't want me to stop and look at whatever he was searching for or whatever he thought was around us. I couldn't see whatever it was that he thought he saw. Indeed, I wished that I could have because maybe I'd understood him better and we could start talking again. Talking like the brother and sister that we were instead of the rage that seemed to drive us further apart.

I shook my head.

In all honesty, I didn't think that we were ever going to get to that point of sibling dependency. We were too estranged to be as close as we used to be. I was just getting used to that because, despite how much I wished we could be closer, I didn't think he would ever feel free enough to be honest.

I'd lost track of how long we'd been out here. I knew it had been weeks, but I couldn't tell how many weeks. I knew it would take that long to go back and get them whenever I got to where we were going. So wherever I found for us to live had to be good. I had to make it hospitality, something livable. So that would take time, too. Then, they would have someplace to go when we had to return on the same journey. I couldn't help but wonder if they would even want to take the chance to come with me or if they would try to persuade me to come back and stay. I knew that there was no one that I could stay. I probably would be killed on sight. Indeed, how would I even get to them? *How could I get the message to my family that I found a spot where we could all live happily?*

The thoughts were depressing, and I tried to pull myself out of it as a fledged bunny ran by.

It seems silly now to think that I thought I could find a place for everyone to live and be back quickly. The thought sneaked back into my mind. *So much for letting it go.* Obviously, it isn't something I could do, at least not right now. We were in a position where there was nothing else for me to do but think as the skies darkened ever so slightly.

I told Nick I'd find a place for us, but it didn't seem like I'd ever be happy with what I saw. Not that the last place we stopped to rummage or any other place along the way hadn't been pleasant. Honestly, this feeling won't leave me alone; it was a driving need to keep moving forward. None of the spots were precisely how I had imagined a new, safe place for our family to stay.

Was I even being realistic? I wondered if Nicky thought I was dead because I hadn't been back. *Did I traumatize him by having him help me? Did they punish him, and if they did, how badly did they punish him for allowing me to escape?* I wondered if everyone was okay after my all-or-nothing mentality.

The questions overloaded my mind, filling the emptiness left in my head without the song. The sun dropped out of the hazy and opaque skies, and darkness overtook the lands as I moved and sat in the bedroll.

I tried to be vigilant while searching the clump of trees around us, but each tree still reminded me that we were secluded and secure. Something setting me on edge.

However, even though it felt like nothing was out there, my heart was pounding fiercely. There just had to be something out there. I wouldn't feel this way if there wasn't.

I'm sure Dom had disappeared several minutes ago to relieve himself, but the silence was oppressing.

I wanted, no need, to hear his voice, something to tell me that what I was feeling was misplaced. That my hunting instinct was wrong for the first time. As the little girl inside of me, I also wanted us to talk things out. I wanted my brother back. Yet, I knew it wouldn't happen.

He wasn't a perfect speaking partner. I mean, he used to be. He'd always tell me these great stories about the world before the bombs fell.

How we used to have cell phones, and music was everywhere. Now, you only hear music in passing or if someone is singing to you… Now, it was illegal to have anything that would play music or pre-recorded things. Hell, we couldn't even have anything that had live discussions; those were only done through the loudspeakers at the settlement. Not to mention that I couldn't remember the cell phones very much. I remember Mom carrying a silly little box on which we played games. I sighed in remembrance. I missed those talks. Hell, I almost forgot what Dom used to be like. He used to be the best big brother there was, I mean when he wasn't being a bully. But what big brother or sister didn't have moments of being a bully? True, when he wasn't being an ass, which wasn't often anymore, Dom had been a fantastic brother when I'd been younger.

I looked deep into the fire's blazes as the crunching of leaves under the heel of his shoes echoed around me. As he reached the clearing, I sighed with relief even though my stomach was still tied up in knots. No one else was around, and we hadn't had any more run-ins with rain either. I was extremely grateful for that fact, as my arms probably wouldn't be healing as well as they are if we had.

The acid had eaten away some of the skin on my arms. The bandages that Dom helped me put on while we were in that bathroom at Red Rocks had been pretty soaked through by the time we finished fighting those bandits or whatever they were when we had left the bathroom protection.

I rubbed my hand over my arms, desperate to relieve the itching without actually itching. The first time that I itched one of my arms, it burned like I was being set on fire, or at least what I assume being set on fire would feel like. Dom had cussed me out royally that afternoon when he had to redo my bandages because they had bled through so thoroughly that they had stuck to my skin. We had to use some of our water to get it off.

He had called me an idgit for itching my arms and being self-centered. I felt like laughing in his face when he had done that. He was a pot calling the kettle black.

Each day, I tried to be respectful to him, the little girl in me wanting to please her older brother. Despite the fact that he was an idgit, I mean, he's the one who was not talking to me and acting so conspicuous, but he was still my brother, and I loved him, scabs and all. My mind wandered as I looked around me, letting Dom set up his bedroll on the other side of the fire.

It was peaceful up here, but the need to travel further ate me. It was a consistent feeling that wouldn't leave. Dom walked back toward the trees, taking something with him, and I tensed, not knowing where he was going, but tried not to let it get to me. We had to be at a plateau because we'd been walking flatly for the last few hours. I thought to myself as I moved my bow and quiver off my bag and onto the ground before reaching into my bag.

I knew there had to be something more out there, but I didn't know what it was or even where. By the time I'd pulled out my blanket and some of the meat from one of our latest kills.

Dom had killed a turkey of some kind this last time, or at least that's what he had called it. I still had no idea what it had been.

As Dom returned to the clearing, I fell backward onto the bedroll, the piece of dried meat in my grasp.

"Are we going to talk today?" It was the same question I'd asked him every night for the last week, or what I assumed was a week; I'd lost track of how many times I'd asked him the same question.

After adding more twigs and branches to the fire, he sat down and started pulling some food from his bag. He looked at me once he had something in his hand to eat.

"I don't know… are we?" That had been his response the last couple of times, too.

"I don't know… Are you going to tell me where you went after you left?" I'd been trying to get him to answer this question the last two days, and I was sure he'd break eventually.

"Nope. Sorry, kid. That's classified information."

"Dom. I'm not a kid anymore." I felt like ripping my hair out! "I can take whatever you have to tell me."

"No, kid, you couldn't. But someday you will."

I cocked my eyebrow. That was something new; he hadn't said anything like that before. *What was it about this area? Was it making his blood sing too?*

Twinkle, twinkle, little star… the words dropped in my head before disappearing again as I took the last bite of my food. Standing up, I sighed and turned away. I pushed my bag with my foot under the nearest tree, holding the bow and quiver in my hands as I walked. As the bag slapped the tree trunk, I knelt and put my bow and quiver in front.

I turned back to look at Dom and nearly jumped out of my skin.

"What the hell?" The words escaped my lips as I stared at the angel standing behind Dom. I couldn't decide if I was hallucinating or if he was there. I must have been crazy because this had to be the same guy I'd seen before. *But how the hell?*

Dom certainly looked at me like I was crazy.

"What?"

I kept staring at the angel behind him. "There's something, or someone, behind you," I said as if I couldn't believe my words.

Forty

I watched him as if he were going through slow-motion. He stood up and turned around as though he knew what was there. This was strange, but it didn't register with me at the moment because as he came face-to-face with the angel, from one second to another, the angel went from standing behind him to lying on the ground out cold. It happened so fast that there was no way to understand precisely what went through his brain because I couldn't tell what happened.

"Dom!" I screamed as I ran towards them. "What did you do?"

I was freaking out. I'd never seen an angel, but Mom firmly believed in them. It was already dark out, and I didn't know what was happening with the angel, but I was shocked that Dom had hit an angel. He should have been hit by lightning, as Mom had always believed because he went against God by hitting something so magnificent. The firelight rose and fell behind me.

"Get the fire roaring," I demanded as I fell to the ground. Mom always said that God was vengeful, so I was just waiting for something to happen to Dom. *Damn, I'd just gotten used to the idea of him being back.* He just had to take a chance and do something stupid that would have retribution from an APB or All-Powerful Being.

My emotions were on a teeter-totter. I couldn't decide if I was angry or upset.

As my knees hit the ground, I gasped in shock as I saw the angel in the firelight, but was he indeed an angel? His wings were gone, and it was just a man lying on the ground. I shook my head; I had to have hallucinated something because there were no wings, it was just a man, but he looked so damn familiar to me. I sighed with relief. Maybe Dom wouldn't be struck down by an APB because it was just a regular man. As I checked his pulse, I pushed back the questions in my mind. As I felt the rhythmic beating against my fingers, I took a deep breath and turned to see if Dom had done what I had asked.

He tossed some of the dead logs into the blaze as my eyes landed on him, but the look on his face. His eyes furled, and he had a nasty grimace on his mouth. It was clear that he was angry. It came off of him in waves.

"What is your problem?" I asked, standing up, only to lean down again and try to pull the man towards the building flames. The teeter-totter of emotions landed. Anger had won that battle.

"He is," Dom said firmly. Looking at the man, his hatred burned as brightly as the fire in his eyes.

"You don't even know him…" I paused, "Or do you?" I asked, glancing back and forth between the two of them as I continued to drag the man. *He was so heavy!* It felt like I was pulling a dead horse.

I dragged the man over so that he was close enough to the fire but far enough away to be safe and took a closer look at him in the drifting light of the fire as it fell across his face. *He was a breathtaking man.* However, he couldn't be much older than me. His skin was a light tan, like he spent most of his time outdoors under the opaque skies, long enough that it changed the basic color of his skin. His hair was dark, not black like mine or Dom's, more of a brown-black color. Thick eyebrows stood out as he lay on the ground. The soft stubble on his chin and cheeks just called out to me. There were even the little black bumps, like the markings Dom and I had been plagued with since puberty hit. It was like I had been plunged into a daydream as I took every inch of him.

I didn't even know who he was, but his beauty reminded me of someone, but it couldn't be. I shook my head and stepped back. *Why was I daydreaming about a man that I'd never met before?* More importantly, why was I daydreaming about a man my brother disliked?

I walked closer to Dom and looked at him closely. He was still burning with anger, almost palpable compared to the heat of the fire. "Who is he?" I demanded.

"He's no one. Truly! We should leave, though, before he wakes up," he said as he moved away, heading towards his bag, his back towards me.

"Bullshit!" I cursed at him. "Who is he? You're acting so fucking suspicious."

"No one," he deadpanned, turning back towards me with his bag in hand, the anger in his eyes dying. It was like his soul was disappearing right before my eyes. I stepped back, squared up, and looked deep into his eyes, trying not to let the deadness in his gaze unnerved me.

"He wouldn't be a nobody if you didn't know him. You would have helped him if you thought he was harmless, and you would have killed him already if he was a threat to us." I said, thinking back to the men that we had killed in self-defense before we had got to Red Rocks.

"You're right. And I would have killed him if you hadn't stepped in." The words dropped so matter-of-factly that they jolted throughout my body as I went into shock. *Had this been something he had been planning? If so, how did he know that the man was following us, and why hadn't he said something to me before now?*

"Why?" I asked, the word barely a whisper out of my mouth as I gazed down at the sleeping man, "Why didn't you just keep going then? What did I say that meant you had to stop? You haven't listened to me before." It was true. He hadn't listened to much of anything that I'd said to him since we'd been reunited.

Raggedly, his breathing struggled to gain any steadiness, his temper warring with the deadness I could see creeping in. I watched silently as he struggled between the warring emotions before finally gazing down at me. The answer lingered on his lips. "I do listen to you, MB, but it doesn't mean I'm allowed to follow through with what you ask of me. For you, I would do anything. I would kill him in an instant, but I couldn't." He admitted before his shoulder sagged, the bag falling off his shoulder as he moved further away from the light. "I couldn't do that to you. Not willingly, and especially not without your permission."

"To me?" His words echoed around in my head, shock, and heat running through my veins, "You wanted to kill him, but you wouldn't without my permission. What do you mean? What is he to me? Who is he, Dom?"

"Levi." The name echoed around us, and a shiver ran down my spine. The voice from my lullaby stated the name so clearly. I could feel every letter as it inched along my skin. I turned around, shock clearly showing on my face, as his eyes landed on me.

The man was conscious and leaning on his elbows. His steely gaze trapped me, and his piercing black eyes burned holes through me. "I'm Levi, and I'm your mate."

The world faded away as everything turned black. *My mate? What the hell does that mean?* Dom would have killed him if he was a threat, but he didn't, so what did that mean? As the world around me began to spin, countless questions swirled in my mind, each one heavier than the last. I tried to grasp at the fleeting thoughts, desperate to comprehend the confusion enveloping me. My heart raced, but the words escaped me, trapped deep within my throat. Suddenly, my legs gave way, and I crumpled to the ground. The last thing I remember was the chilling sensation of darkness creeping in, swallowing my thoughts and leaving me in a profound numbness as consciousness slipped away.

XX

Dom

Forty-One

Shit! My bag slammed down as I slid to catch MB before she hit the ground. "You asshat!" I shouted as she landed in my arms. I picked her up in my arms and walked over to her bedroll. Placing her down gently, I turned and glared daggers at him. "What the hell are you doing here?" I demanded. Righteous anger burned through my veins as I did my best to breathe deeply. More than anything, I wanted to rip his fucking head off, but I had more important things to worry about. I pulled her blanket up over her legs and shrugged my jacket off. Placing it over her arms and torso, I saw my sister and noticed the fine details I'd been missing. Her nose was upturned, just like a little pixie, and her bumps weren't a deterrent like mine. Oh no, hers were like they sculpted her face into perfection. Seeing how much she had grown, the young woman she was turning into, I knew why he had come for her. It was the same reason I had gone after Lizzy.

"I could feel her getting closer." His words reinforced the thoughts in my head. He stood up, his figure much taller than I had encountered him all those years ago. He was almost as tall as I was and looked as smug as hell. I bit back the urge to punch him again, swallowed it down, and had it come back up full force when he walked over and reached for her face. "I felt her when you guys first came into the mountains. I had to see."

"No," I said, pushing him away. "You didn't. You knew she was going to come one day." I didn't mention the multiple times I'd caught him peeping on us during the journey here. I could. I had every right to call him out on breaking the pact his grandfather had placed on him and me when I'd been cast out of Sanctum all those years ago, but it wasn't worth it. He would never admit to it.

The day at the entrance to the Sanctum rushed my mind. When Lizzy and I arrived, he'd been on watch for arrivals that day. We'd felt the connection, familiar but not the same. He had supported his grandfather's decision as a fourteen-year-old kid, but his position in the Sanctum had power. The power that could have been helpful. *He was a jerk and would always be.* Each time I came close, he would be the one to "greet" me and send me away again. My hatred for him burned righteously inside of me. The pact had been made, ensuring that I'd keep her safe until she was ready to come, and he'd keep Lizzy safe, although I could never see her again. He should have never left the mountain to come down to the settlement, he should have never landed in the hunting grounds and talked to her, he should never have done any of the things that he'd done so far, but he had, and I hated the fact that he could get away with it and I never would.

"Yes," he replied, his sure steps echoed in the barren landscape as he walked away. "I knew she'd come one day, but I just couldn't contain myself anymore. I just had to see her. Especially," he paused, "since I felt her long before now." He reminded as he moved towards her again, drawn to her like a moth to a flame. I stopped him, a brick wall of hard muscle, before he even got close.

The desire to punch him again, the feeling of his flesh being whiplashed by my fist, echoed like a ghost through my skin. This had been our pattern the last time we'd seen each other, and I wasn't surprised that not much had changed. "Touch her, and I will knock your ass out again."

He stopped mid-approach and looked at me, dazed. "You realize you have no say in what happens with her and me?"

His words were arrogant, and my fists were already ready at my sides. I gripped the sides of my pants to remind myself that I didn't need to follow through with my most basic urges. "She doesn't even know you. She doesn't even know anything about what's going on." I said, facing off with him. "I've been a bastard to her because of the stupid laws that Sanctum enforces."

"Those laws are keeping your beloved safe."

"Don't YOU DARE try to bring her into this! This is about you and your stupidity. You are breaking the laws now, no one else." I screeched at him, fighting to contain myself. "We would have been there in days. Days, not even that. You are the one that said 'mate,' she heard it, and now YOU will have to explain. I am no longer bound by the pact that was made. You broke it first." He was an idgit, plain and simple, but now I was no longer held under the laws of Sanctum due to his stupidity.

"Yes, you would have been. But now we can go even faster because I can carry her."

"No!" I yelled. "If I can't interfere by telling her everything, neither can you! You can tell her there is more to know; you can start with the basics, but don't force her to try and transform before she is ready. Don't force her to fly before she can handle it." This was the cause of my ostracism from the Sanctum. I had been forced to transform before my body was ready. I had been forced to convert to save Lizzy, and it had caused me to be disfigured. I could never fly properly again.

The words kept coming, diarrhea of the mouth, as my blood reached a new boiling level. Eventually, I lost the ability to speak as my patience waned, and I prepared to take another swing at him. This time, though, he was ready for me and dodged the blow.

As we sparred, it escalated into a full-blown fistfight. The fists turned into kicks, and we ended up rolling on the ground somewhere along the way. I was so lost in the hazy red—the anger, jealousy, rage, everything mixed—that I didn't hear her as she woke up.

"What are you doing?" She screamed at us. She jolted up from where I'd laid her down—so lost in the haze that her words didn't mean anything like my fist connected with his jaw again and again.

She stood, throwing things at us for God knows how long before we stopped to notice her. Levi had paused momentarily, long enough that I got in one last good punch before she could pull me off of him.

Blood dripped down my face. I wiped my eye to get it out of it. Sweat dripped down my back, and my muscles ached from the exertion of fighting with him, but it was worth it. He was faster, but I landed more hits than he did. *Thankfully.*

I looked at him out of the corner of my eye. His chest was heaving, and there was blood all over him. *About fucking time,* I thought as I smiled. *About fucking time.* I felt victorious for the first time in a long time.

"What are you smiling at, Dom?" Mary Beth demanded as she took in the sight of both of us.

"Nothing that you would understand," I said as I turned and returned to my bag. I collected it further away from the fire than where it had landed. "Nothing at all. Let's send him on his way. He doesn't need to be here. Then, we could talk about this in the morning, okay?" I asked her, praying she would follow my lead and forget he told her he was her mate. I walked around the fire and back towards where I'd initially been sitting. It was close enough to the fire to keep me warm but far enough away that I didn't have to worry about being next to him. I began unpacking, pulling out the things I needed to clean my wounds from the fight before setting up my spot to sleep. I hoped my nonchalance convinced her to go with my suggestion.

After I unrolled my bedroll, I turned towards them again. She stared at him like she was dying to touch him but was afraid that he would just disappear if she touched him. The same look of adornment resided on his bloody face as he stared at her. The sight of it made me gag as I tried to cool my boiling blood. He didn't deserve my little sister. Hell, he didn't deserve anything. Yet, I knew she wanted him to stay by the look in her eyes and how she was staring at him. I couldn't help but wonder if that was how I had looked all those years ago when I had to leave Lizzy behind.

"MB," I said, attempting to gain her attention. "MB," I repeated. "Damnit, Mary Beth!" I finally ended up screaming before she turned and looked at me.

"Send him away. We don't need him." *Not yet, at least.* "Remember, we are trying to find a place for everyone. He can't give that to you. He can't do anything to help our family." I gestured towards myself when she finally looked at me. "I told you that I would help you."

"We can't just send him into the dark, Dom." She chided. "He can stay the night. Maybe then you two can explain why you were fighting…" Her words trailed off, and I could only assume she meant to mention his careless response earlier. She looked so earnest and honest—at that moment, she looked just like Mom. I couldn't decide if I wanted to laugh or cry.

"There's nothing to say, MB." I sighed as I laid the bedroll after wiping down my face with a wet cloth from my jug of water. "He's an arrogant jerk, hell-bent on destroying my life…" He coughed loudly as I said this, and I glared at him evilly. I continued as though he wasn't even there as I turned and looked her in the eyes. "He isn't a good man," I told her, begging her with my eyes to send him on his way, even though I knew that he would never harm a hair on her head. *It didn't mean that I had to like him.*

She sighed and looked at him again.

His black cesspools absorbed the night around him as he stared at us. There were so many emotions reflected in the endless darkness of his eyes.

"I think I'm old enough to decide for myself, Dom." Her words were like knives.

"Fine." I threw my hands up in the air. I couldn't believe it. She truly wanted that boy around more than her own family. "But I'm done talking about this."

She nodded, and I flopped backward onto the bedroll and glared up at the night skies. Anger filled me again. I didn't want to hear anything anymore. There was no point; she would never believe me, and it was his fault: *his and that stupid place.* I tuned them out, as best as I could, as she tried to offer him things to make him comfortable for the night. He didn't say much to her. Which I'm actually quite thankful for. It was quiet, but I knew it was eating at her, and she didn't know what he meant or what was happening when she woke up.

The light and heat from the fire warm my side. I knew she had no reason to trust me; I'd given her no reason over the last few weeks, but I couldn't help but pray that she would trust her family more than some random man who appeared out of nowhere. I knew I had done nothing but lie and keep secrets from her. I was bound by laws and things out of my control, but no longer. I'd have to be honest with her on the morning, come hell or high water. He had already broken the pact.

I couldn't help but pray that he decided to fly away by morning light, as eventually, sleep came. I knew what I needed to do. Though I may not like the man, I knew he wouldn't hurt her. His life depended on it, just like mine was in the hands of...

"You know him, do you?" MB asked me, pulling me from my thoughts, looking back and forth between us as she pulled some more wood from the pile I'd made at the corner of the campsite. Like our mom, she tried to keep the fire going, always willing to help someone else—even when she knew nothing about him. I glanced over at her. My mouth was tight; I didn't want to say anything to her that would encourage her to talk to him more.

"Who is he?" She demanded, stopping in front of me. I turned and faced the other way. Walking around the bedroll,

MB stood at the other side and glared down at me. Finally, I sighed and stared at her.

"He's no one. We should leave him and go." I deadpan as I adjusted the bag under my head, trying to find the sweet spot where I could finally fall asleep.

"Bullshit!" She tossed at me. "Who is he?"

"No one." I sat up, forcing her to step back.

"He wouldn't be a nobody if you didn't know him… And you would have killed him already if he was a threat to us." MB reminded me of flashes of the people we had gone through and the conversation that we just had. I had gotten rid of plenty of people to ensure she was safe. She knew I would do anything to keep her safe while she was with me.

"You're right. But again, I would have killed him if you hadn't stepped in. This conversation is done, MB. I've nothing else to say right now." I counted to five as I took some deep breaths; I needed to relax before she figured out how to get me to talk before Levi owned up to his words. He needed to explain before I could even say anything. Or I would end up telling her everything, hoping she would decide against going to Sanctum and we could return and get our family.

XXI

Mary Beth

Forty-Two

The silence was deafening as the fire crackled down. The man was over by the trees now. I had tried my best to get him away from Dom. He had a bag with him, so I left him alone to tend his wounds. Dom refused to let me anywhere near him once I said that the man could stay. I hoped his wounds were okay, but if Dom wanted to act stupid, that was on him.

As I walked back to my bag, I slowed and stared at it. My fists clenched and unclenched as I thought of Dom's odd behavior. *Okay, so obviously, he knows this guy, whoever he is or whatever he was...*

I was still debating whether I had imagined seeing wings on him. Not to mention that I could swear that I'd seen him before. The uncertainty was like a fog, clouding my thoughts and leaving me in a state of bewilderment, a puzzle I couldn't solve.

There was so much to consider that I just felt so overwhelmed! A part of me wanted to go over and demand that Dom gave me answers, right here, right now... but the other part of me knew that if I went over there and forced his hand, Dom would just shut down completely on me, just like he had when I'd questioned him minutes ago. It didn't get me anywhere then, and it wouldn't get me anywhere if I continued to push it.

I looked over at them as I sat down on my blanket. The man had sat back up after Dom had stopped talking and was cleaning his face now. Now and then, I would catch Levi as he glanced over at me... It was like he knew I had been watching him. The smirk that covered his face made me flush as I turned away.

I could feel the heat from my blush and hoped it was dark enough that he didn't know it was because of him. I fiddled with some things in my bag, avoiding the temptation to look at him again. It was like this guy took over my every thought. I had to remind myself that Dom was here and forced myself to look at Dom instead of the man who truly occupied my thoughts.

Dom, my older brother, was fast asleep as far as I could tell... not that it is easy to see his face. *What a brat!* First, he punches that angel/man (*Levi, my heart autocorrected me*), and then while I'm passed out from shock, something happened between them that made Levi, my heart pumping the syllables of his name, reminded me again, and Dom fight... Not just an argument of words, but an actual fistfight! *What was up with that?*

I still hadn't figured out what caused me to pass out, either, and that troubled me. I'd never fainted before in my life. I tried to consider all the factors. I mean, the guy seemed so familiar to me, but maybe I was just projecting my desire to see someone out here... We had been walking heavily the last couple of days, and water was getting scarce again... There was no way to understand what had caused the fainting spell, and I hated feeling clueless. I needed to feel in control again, but the situation was slipping out of my grasp.

I continued to rummage through my bag. *Where is it?* I wondered as I looked for my necklace. Trying to focus on something other than what was going on around me. I had put it in my bag a few nights ago because of the quick rise off I did in the stream, but I'd forgotten to put it back on, and right now, it was the only thing that seemed like it would make everything better. At least, that's how it had always seemed in the past... And, maybe, I was trying to get my mind off of my stupid brother and Levi.

Thinking back to that night, I'd been so excited when I had seen that stream and wanted nothing more than to wash up. I had been filthy with dirt and grim from the walk, and it had looked so inviting. I had hoped against hope that the water wasn't too acidic; luckily, it hadn't been, so I had been able to clean up.

I sighed as my finger traced the chain unseen in the bag. Smiling, I lifted it from the bag and held it in my hands, dangling in the air.

I was still so frustrated with everything—Dom, his hidden agendas, trying to find a place for everyone, not knowing who Levi was but knowing that Dom knew him and hated him on sight... but I could let it go for a little while. Lifting the necklace in one hand, I dragged my hair across my neck to the other before putting the necklace back on.

As the weight of the necklace settled on me, I stared into the blazing embers of the fire and avoided looking at Levi.

In all honesty, I was too scared to look at him again. Levi, my heart whispers again, reminding me that it wasn't forbidden to say his name. Even though, in my head, I felt like I needed to. There was an undeniable charm about him that just drew me in. He had to be around Dom's age, or close to it anyway. Maybe that had something to do with it. It wasn't like the boys at the settlement had been flocking towards me ever since the damn mutations had appeared. It's more like they ran from me faster than a bear chasing honey. *But Levi was different.* He was intriguing, and I couldn't help but feel a pull towards him.

I wondered if Dom saw the strings that were drawing me into Levi. The appeal that he presented to me? If he somehow knew that this guy would be my downfall... *Or maybe he was my salvation.*

My face flushed in shame, and I frowned at the thought. *What was to be so ashamed of?* I mean, yeah, I didn't want my older brother knowing or seeing me in that way... wanton, hormonal, a girl lusting after some guy... Especially some guy that I just met, who had been going at it bare knuckles with my brother. That's not who I was, not who I wanted to be. Ever since the mutations, I had felt like an outcast, and the last thing I wanted was to give my brother another reason to look down on me.

Maybe that's why he was so on edge about... Levi... I finally whispered his name through my mind, and shivers sliced through me.

But how could Dom know? When could he have possibly known about a connection? Did he hear him too when he said that he was my mate? Was that why they had been brawling? Levi, I shivered again, he hadn't even been around us for an hour. Was there even a connection between us? What was this about him being my "mate?"

I thought back to our conversation. Dom did know something, something that he wasn't willing to tell me. But what and why? What was so important that Dom had to keep hiding it from me?

I couldn't decide on my feelings regarding Levi, allowing myself to finally say his name without guilt. I couldn't decide how Dom knew what was happening. He wanted to hurt Levi. My breathing stopped as I repeated his name. I turned, drawn to look at him for some unexplained reason, but I quickly looked away as soon as he saw me. I thought back to what Dom had said about him when I asked him if he knew Levi.

Thoughts went tumbling through my head. Faster and faster. Spinning like a cyclone, whipping me with each new thought, idea, or possible connection to what had happened.

I had to stop.

I needed to wait. I needed to let things happen in their own course of time.

I was getting wound up over this, and there was no way I would get anywhere tonight. I'd been staring into the fire for so long that I finally felt empowered and looked towards Levi. But to my luck, he was already laying down his back towards me and the fire.

I sighed, put my bag on top of my blanket, and grabbed the second blanket that I had piled at the end. I turned and laid my head down before pulling the blanket over me.

I stared up into the opaque skies, yet they weren't empty. I could almost swear that I saw the twinkling of a star. I stared harder as I tried to determine if it was a star, my eyes getting heavier and heavier as I searched the sky for another glimpse of something shining in the thick darkness that oppressed the world.

XXII

Dom

Forty-Three

The morning sun shone through the hazy skies as the light hit my face. *Damn, how can it be morning already?* I felt like I'd barely gone to sleep. Stretching out, I tried to pull the cranks out of my neck from the stiff ground. It was something that I'd been doing every day for years; at least, at least, that was the way I felt. Looking this way, and as I sat up, I finally noticed I was the last person up. *Double damn.*

Scrambling out of my blanket, I yanked myself up and searched for MB. I could give two cents about Levi, but MB was my sister, and I just knew something was going to happen, and I wanted, no need, to be there. My protective instincts were on high alert. I looked over to her bedroll, hoping and praying that Levi hadn't convinced her to take off without me this morning. Thankfully, everything was still there, and a sigh of relief escaped. At least he hadn't taken off with her in the middle of the night... I had worried throughout the night that he might try something like that, but I guess not.

Maybe it earned him one brownie point in the pot filled with horse manure from all his other stupid acts. *Maybe... or maybe not.*

I didn't even look to see if his stuff was still there. He could be at the bottom of a ravine, and I probably wouldn't care, but I did care about MB and whatever he would tell her.

"MB," I called out, moving away from the makeshift campsite. "Mary Beth."

My heart started pumping; I wondered if she was hiding from me with him because she would usually respond to me by now. Maybe something had happened, and I didn't know about it.

I glanced through the fir trees and my surroundings as I walked down the hill. I was still calling out for her when I saw them. Stopping in my tracks, I just stared at the two of them. They stood there like they were in a trance at the bottom, near the edge of a lake, staring at each other. What bothered me was how they were staring at each other, gravitating as though the magnetic poles were attached to their hips as Levi's hand strayed towards her waist, and I snapped out of my daze, a growl escaping, my brotherly hackles raised. I growled low in my throat as I headed down the hill towards them.

His soulless black eyes turn towards me, obviously hearing my displeasure at him trying to touch my baby sister. His hand fell back, and he turned and whispered something to MB. She laughed quietly and then turned towards me. The joy etched on her face must have been the happiest I'd seen her in a long time, and my heart stopped for a moment as it was overfilled with joy. I never thought I would see her as happy as she was then, even though it was with him. Now that I had finally gotten to see her as carefree as she used to be as a child, I didn't know whether I still wanted to hit Levi or thank him for putting a smile on her face for a moment.

She called up to me, "Good morning, sleepyhead. I was going to check on you this morning, but then I remembered you wanted nothing to do with me last night, so I left you alone." Her tone might have been friendly, but the words were icy.

"I'm sorry," I said to her as I walked down to them. He brings the worst out in me." I jerked my head toward him and said, "Can we talk now?" My regret for my past actions was palpable, and I knew I had some explaining to do.

She frowned as she absentmindedly nodded slowly. "So now you want to talk?" Her tone was questioning, and I knew I had some explaining to do.

"I've wanted to talk for a while, but I had been bound by laws and things out of my control. With his arrival, I kind of have to speed up the process and tell you sooner than anticipated and with a little more freedom than I had before." I reached for her hand and asked, "Can we walk and talk, please?"

She took my hand reluctantly and turned towards Levi. "Thanks for showing me this. It's beautiful."

"Not as beautiful as you." He smoothly replied as he nodded. "I'll go back and start packing up. I've got some other great places to show you."

She nodded, and as he walked away, I could see her eyes following him, and I could feel the gag reflex activate in my throat. *Disgusting.* Did she need to stare at him like that? How can she even want to stare at him like that, with the bit of time she's known him?

I reverted a little as I stuck my finger down my throat and gagged as he walked by me. He smirked at me, tempting me to punch him again, but I held back.

MB stared at me, shame at my behavior reflected strongly in her eyes. I squeezed her hand in apology and pulled her towards the lake.

The waters weren't as toxic here as they were down by the settlement, so I feel comfortable taking her down here. She followed me down, and her inquisitiveness about my behavior changed, evident in her willingness to let me lead her by the hand. I felt like I was fourteen years old and taking her to the school in the settlement for the first time.

I let go of her hand as we reached the embankment and looked for a good spot to sit. The hazy sunlight reflected off the calm waters as she sat beside me. Her hair was braided today and brushed against me as she landed on the ground beside me. I had to agree with Levi; she was beautiful. I could admit that even though she was my sister. Not that the lake wasn't beautiful, it had stopped me the first time I came here, but she was my sister, and she shone at that moment. My admiration for her was undeniable.

Silence reigned because she wasn't going to start the conversation. I had expected it to happen that way, but it didn't make it any less painful for me to be the one to open up first.

"So…" I sighed, "you remember when I left?"

Her laughter is hard and forced, "How could I forget Dom? You put me in the middle…" She paused and then swore. "Exactly what I did to Nicky… only I didn't have someone wanted elsewhere." She looked hard at me, "Where is Lizzy, Dom? Why do you refuse to talk about her? Is she… dead?" Her words faltered as she asked about Lizzy—one of the unspoken issues between us. The main unspoken issue, in all honesty.

I shook my head quickly. "No, no, no…" I quickly denied it, "She's fine… I mean, she was the last time I saw her." It hurt to talk about her; my pain was so deep that it was like a chasm opened inside of me each time I said anything about her.

I swallowed and released my breath. "I brought her here… back then… we kept moving through everything… We didn't look nearly as much as you have… It was a compulsion, like singing in our blood, in our heads." My words faltered. It was hard to speak, and I had to pause as Mary Beth took in my words. "We were driven to come here… but it didn't stop here at this lake."

She shook her head in agreement. "I know what you mean… I've heard the song Mom used to sing to us before bed. *Only it isn't the same.*" She paused, the words spoken softly, as though she didn't understand why the song was different but understood that it was, "But I feel like I need to be here. And… that guy, Levi, he feels like he belongs too, and I don't understand that." Confusion streaked through her face as she tried to piece together the little bits of information and things that had happened since we started walking together.

"You wouldn't." I agreed. "He is one of the reasons why I'm still alive, and he's one of the reasons I can't see Lizzy." I paused, controlling my breathing as the chasm expanded, "I have mixed feelings about him, MB, but I know that he has good intentions; at least, I hope I know." It felt like sand coming out of my mouth to admit he had good intentions. I wanted to lie and tell her to avoid him, but I couldn't.

"But, if we keep going, there will be changes, Mary Beth. The changes are not always pleasant, and there will be no going back if we keep going. I know you want to find a place for Mom, Dad, Nicky, and the girls, but they can't go any further than this place. They probably won't ever be allowed in…" My words trailed off. "But, if you want to be with them and not learn anything more, you'll need to send Levi away.

If you want to know everything," I sighed. "Well, we must keep going with Levi to the top." I pointed to the top of the mountain from where we sat. Her eyes followed my finger as we looked upward. "I can't tell you what is up there, but I can tell you that I can tell you everything when we get there. I'm not allowed to say anything more than this; I have so much more that I want to tell you, truly, I want to. I want you to understand everything. You deserve that. Not just because you're my sister but because you are an amazing and talented young woman, and I know you will do something great." I brushed a strand of hair away from her face, my finger brushing against one of the teal bumps on her forehead, "You know I love you, right?" The compulsion to say it made me bite my cheek as I returned the conversation to her.

Tears filled her eyes, and she reached for my hand by her eyes. "I love you too, Dom. I don't understand why you've been so difficult. I don't know what happened, and I don't want just to give up knowing what you went through. You're my brother, Dominic, and you deserve to have someone there for you. We all do. You and I both know I wanted a place for our family. I can bring them here eventually." She paused, taking a deep breath in, her eyes wandering toward where Levi stood up at the top of the hill where our makeshift camp resided, "but I need to know how I know him and why this place is so compelling." Her eyes filled with wonder, joy, and a sense of longing I recognized from my own relationship and I knew that it was hopeless to ask her to forget about him and to stay here. To try and find a place for our family and live peacefully in this valley.

I sighed and nodded as her words trailed off. "Okay, whatever you want. I'm there for you."

XXIII

Mary Beth

Forty-Four

Dom and I sat in companionable silence for a while, gazing at the lazy waves that came and went with the air over the lake's surface before we decided we needed to get moving. It was nice to have a moment like this with my brother after all of the hardship we'd been through over the last several weeks.

Everything I heard this morning kept overlapping in my brain. Levi told me he wouldn't leave us, that I was almost to the end, and then he could talk to me. Dom told me that there was more to the story… They were telling me the same thing, that something big was coming, and somehow, I already knew that. I thought about everything we'd already been through as we returned to the campsite. It felt like everything had been leading up to this, from when Dom left the settlement until now. Only now, I had to figure out precisely what that was. I wasn't as mad at Dom anymore, either. I was still a little upset that he had kept and was still keeping things for me, but it sounded like he had a reason, and I understood doing things because you had a reason. I mean, it was the whole reason why I was out here. I'd left the settlement because I wanted to make sure that Morgana and Eliza had food. With everything going on, I decided that I could wait a little longer for him to explain.

Not to mention Levi... He woke up first this morning and had been sitting there, staring at me, and by the time I woke up, I'd been startled to see him sitting there looking at me. I would swear that I heard him calling me before my eyes opened. Yet, when I looked over at him as soon as I was awake enough to do so, he just smiled.

Who was he? There is something about him that I just knew... I mean, KNEW... I could almost recall seeing him somewhere before, but as soon the thought entered my mind, it would slip away like ships in the night. And when I woke and found out he had been staring at me, I didn't feel like I was being invaded or watched.

No, instead, I felt like I was at home, which was weird. *Mega weird.* More bizarre than I was finding it, I had seen it as cute that he'd been watching me when I woke up. When he suggested that we go somewhere and that he had something amazing to show me, I just went with him with no hesitation, no questions asked. I didn't think about Dom, Mom, Dad, Nicky, the girls... not anyone... just him and his dark eyes staring into mine. Even the bruise starting to show on his jawline couldn't distract me from wanting to go with him. I must have been lost in my thoughts because the next thing that I noticed was Dom's hand being held out in the center of my face.

He had stood up first; his hand was an offer, an olive branch. I took it, glad that we were finally returning to being somewhat normal with each other. There was so much that I didn't understand about this area, him, Levi, the world... and indeed, all I ever wanted was some normalcy. Grasping his hand, I brushed myself off, only to notice Levi standing at the bottom of the mountain, waiting for us. Our bags were clearly in his hands and gathered around his feet.

The sun beat down on us; it wasn't at its' hottest yet, and we could probably get to the top of the mountains before the sunset. I knew I didn't want to be climbing when it got to its hottest, so I hoped there was a shady spot to stop on the way up. The terrain was rugged, with steep inclines and loose rocks, making the climb challenging. Either way, it wasn't just me and Dom anymore. We would need to find a way to work together without killing each other, especially considering how Levi and Dom had gone at each other yesterday.

"Oh, so you packed our stuff too, huh?" Dom asked sarcastically. *My case-in-point.* He was annoyed with Levi, and while I kinda understood why he was, at the same time, I didn't. He said that Levi was one of the reasons he was still alive, but he hated him. The passionate hate was evident in his eyes. I nodded and headed over to grab my bags and bow from Levi. Trying to think of a way to get them to get along. It was a complicated dynamic, with each of us having reasons for our feelings and actions.

"Thanks," I whispered as I grabbed my bags from him. It was just the barest of whispers, skin on skin, and I was a puddle of mush inside. My heart raced at the brief contact, and I struggled to maintain my composure in front of the others.

Who was he? The confusion was overwhelming. I could have sworn I saw wings on him last night, but there was no evidence to support that. And his voice felt so familiar, as if I had heard it just before I saw him standing behind Dom. Maybe I had even seen him before today. *Was this place playing tricks on my mind?* It was so invigorating here, almost magical, but there was an unsettling undercurrent that I couldn't shake.

Dom ripped his bag away from Levi and turned toward me. "Well, are you still sure you want to go up?" I nodded in affirmation, and he turned to Levi.

"Don't do anything stupid, or I'll make you regret it." Dom threatened him, his voice so calm and collected that you would have thought he just asked him about what we would do next.

"As if," Levi replied, his voice deep and silken as it whispered across my bare skin. "This is the most important moment of my life."

Levi's words stopped me in my tracks. *This was the most critical moment of his life. Now? Why?* It was all so confusing. I needed to reach the top to find some clarity. I shook my head; the boys were just so confused.

Turning away from them, I started climbing the side, looking for well-worn tracks that would lead me to the tip of the mountain. After some searching, I found a trail that looked like it had been used for many years, more than a decade or so since the bombings.

I adjusted my bag on my shoulder, ensuring the quiver was in easy reach, before placing the bow over my shoulder and hiking it to the right spot for a quick pull-off. Feeling like everything was good, I took off on the trail, letting the boys trail behind me. I didn't understand them and wouldn't understand them anytime soon. So, there was no point in trying. The sun wasn't blazing hot as we walked up the mountain, and a cold breeze began to blow my braid the higher we went. I'd braided it at one point during a stop on our journey, not wanting to have my hair caught up in my backpack. It was too long to get caught in it, and it was heavy and black and would pull heat towards me. I pulled my cloak around me tight, letting the hood fall over my head, desperate for shade, before looking back at the boys.

After a while, I could swear that I was feeling droplets of rain on my hands. Fear shook me. *Was it going to rain acid again?* I quickly turned and faced Dominic. "It's raining," the shock was evident in my voice, shaking it as I made the statement.

He nodded, "Yes, it is. This one isn't as bad, though." He said it calmly as if he had been through it before. "It is clearer up here than down back by Red Rocks and the settlement."

The words shook me. *Was it clearer up here?* Did that mean Nicky and the girls could play outside longer without worrying about getting hurt? So many overwhelming thoughts ran through my head because I was starting to feel hopeful. Suddenly, the song came over me. Calming me down in a way that it had never done before.

Twinkle, twinkle, little star. How I wonder what you are? Up above the world so high. Like a diamond in the sky. But it wasn't my voice. In fact, I was sure it was Levi's! I turned and looked at him, staring down as he smiled at me.

"Everything will be fine, Mary Beth." Levi says calmly to me, "Don't you trust us?"

The strange thing was that I trusted him, maybe even more than with Dom. That was scary. How could I trust a man that I'd just barely met?

I nodded and turned away, letting the rain fall on my face. I tip my head back to let it fall on my face for the first time since before the bombings without fear.

The first few droplets were refreshing as they landed. I

could feel the trails they left on my face as they fell down my face and throat. I sighed in contentment for the first time that I could remember.

Shaking my face clear, I looked around me; I mean, really looked around me. The trees weren't as dead here. The grass was a little greener, and the air was fresher than anything I could remember. *This was heaven.* I was sure of it. But what did I do to deserve it?

Dom and Levi were ahead of me at this point. Fighting to be the first one that led us. I could hear them arguing from where I stood, making me laugh. They were such kids, fighting over being first, yet they weren't. Something else didn't add up, and I couldn't wait for one of them to explain everything.

I ran to catch up with them, not wanting to get too far behind, meaning that I wasn't paying attention, not really, to my surroundings because I had to focus on catching up to them first. They were stopping just as I caught up to them. They were looking around us as though searching for something, but what?

It was so obvious, considering that I had stopped paying attention, that I had missed something, and I didn't hear it at first, but after a while, I could hear the whirling of a droid in the area. *A droid?* How could a droid make it out here? I was amazed that something had made it this far.

"Is that..." I began to ask.

"A droid?" Dom finished, "Yeah, it is."

"That's not good," Levi said as he scanned the horizon. "Nothing should be out this far."

I frowned; how did he know that? Had he been here a long time? He had been here for four years because Dom had left us about that time ago, but it was still weird.

"Come on, guys." Levi said, "We need to get going before it gets any closer."

We stepped up and hoofed it up the rest of the trail, the sound of the droid always trailing behind us. Finally, we reached a peak that looked out over the lake, where Dom and I had just this morning sat down and talked. Yet, there was so much more to see here than the lake; it was breathtaking.

Forty-Five

Ragged breaths forced their way through my lungs as my ribs burned with the effort. We had climbed for so long, and it felt like ages since we last stopped. The air was thinner up here, and I was unaccustomed to the altitude, making the climb much more challenging than anticipated. Yet, I pressed on, fueled by a determination that refused to waver.

The smell was sweeter here; the stench of death and decay smells that my nose had become desensitized to over the years were absent in the wilderness surrounding us. But that wasn't the only difference. No, the grounds were softer, and I could swear I saw greener plants than I'd ever seen in many years. I wanted so badly to stop and touch it. *Would it be soft? Or rough?* So many more things than just this place needed to be explored. The unknown beckoned, and my curiosity was piqued.

My mind was engulfed in thoughts, so many swirling around in my head, but there was no possibility for any of them to be answered any time soon, of which I was sure. Confusion reigned, and I was left grappling with unanswered questions.

We had been on this journey for so long, and Levi's arrival

the previous evening was the pinnacle, the defining point of my trip. I just knew we had to climb to the top.

This man, Levi, was everything I had ever imagined, and yet, it was nothing like what I had expected. His mysterious air, the way he wouldn't answer my questions, was too much like my brother's behavior, Dom. Dom had never wanted Levi to be around me, based on his punch that was so well landed just the night before. Dom was never one to keep his word, but he was being so tight-lipped about the situation. I told him I would trust him as we finished this journey, but I so wanted to understand their relationship better. However, being in Levi's presence calmed me in a way I never had before. Levi was a mystery to me. He had promised me that there was a place for me and my family if I was willing to go to the top, and that's what I was doing, even though I was questioning it and my sanity at the same time.

Besides his promise, there was this nagging, aching feeling inside me, hence the questioning of my sanity. It felt like I was on fire, and the only way to quench the fire in my bones and blood was to see it all from the top. *What is up here? Why does it feel so familiar yet trapped in a never-ending web of deceit?* I was at a point where I didn't trust my instincts, and I just had to go with the flow, but I was still struggling with the thought of leaving, going back, and finding somewhere on the plains for my family. *Why did it have to be this place?* The weight of my family's future, the uncertainty of Levi's intentions, and the burden of my mutation and how it impacted my family at the settlement all weighed heavily on me, making every step toward the top a struggle.

My legs started to burn as the hill became steeper, and we stepped off what appeared to be a well-beaten path into uncharted territories. Not that any of where I was now was something charted, even now, to me. Using my bow as a walking stick was never as tempting as here. My body burned, my lungs ached for air, and I thought this climb had no end.

Finally, I couldn't take it anymore and had to stop. Falling to my butt, I turned and looked out at the hills and lands below me. It was so alarming to see the destruction and the ugliness of the world when I was in a spot that was almost beautiful in comparison. The world differed from this height, and I saw it for the first time in ten years. It was amazing.

Who knew that the bombing would make so many changes? I thought as I gazed out from the mountaintop. The haze that took up the skies from the ground wasn't as thick up here, and I took a deep breath, trying to refill my lungs from the long hike up the size. We weren't close to the top yet, but my body ached, and my lungs burned, so we needed to stop. I didn't care if either Dom or Levi had a problem with it. They kept secrets from me, making me nervous about being around them both. I could hear Dom huffing behind me, and I laughed internally. At least I wasn't the only one that needed a break. A chuckle followed my thought, and my eyebrows raised; that wasn't my laugh. Nervously, I turned around and looked at the two men behind me. Dom had never laughed like that, not even when we were kids, so I knew it wasn't him. I glared at Levi, and his shit-eating grin widened.

"What the hell?" I exclaimed, looking at him as he broke into laughter that echoed the one I just heard.

"What? What's wrong?" Dom demanded, turning around and looking at us. He had been doing something else and had no clue what was happening.

"He spoke in my head." I deadpanned.

"Oh," his shoulders dropped, "that."

"What do you mean that?" I got up and went over to him, getting in his face, "Dom, what is going on?"

The laughter died down, and I felt a hand on my bare shoulder, my favorite cape lying in the middle of my back, pulling me away from being in Dom's face.

"He can't answer you, doll. Let's just say you and I have a special connection. I hear things, and you hear things, too, right? Like the song?" *Wait a minute, how did he know about the song?* That song had been my saving grace for years, keeping me sane when my mutation broke out and I became a pariah in the village. "Only when we reach the top will you get the full answer." He finished, his hand still lying on my shoulder. I wanted to shrug him off; I wanted to be full of anger and rage, but it was like the storm brewing in the sea of my emotions had died down, and a calming wind was sweeping those emotions away, leaving me only bewildered and in awe.

I forced myself to pull away and turn towards the plains of the Rockies, my homeland, before me. I could see where all the craters from bombs exploding lay in the wastelands of Colorado. That was what I had used to seeing… I'd been seeing the dry, dead grass and barren trees for over ten years in my settlement, my little village if you will, and right now, I needed some type of normalcy, so this was it. Flashes of our journey swam through my mind as I traced the land, looking for the settlement I had once called home. I was so lost right now, and I didn't know if I could trust them or myself. *Am I going insane?* Levi walked over to my side and placed his hand under my chin.

"You're going to be fine, I promise. You're not going insane;

this will all make sense in the end."

I took a deep breath and nodded, pulling my face away from him. I decided to trust him, even though it felt like I was going against my better judgment. I had to focus on something else, so I looked for the settlement.

Where was it, I wondered, my right hand reaching for Dom behind me. Like any other time we were kids, Dom always had my back, even if I wasn't sure of his intentions. His easy grip comforted me, and we gazed down at the ruins and everything we had walked through together. I could feel our sibling bond strengthen from his easy grip and strength behind me.

Levi continued to stand at my left, powerful and agile. His fingers fluttered along my wrist, something I would never usually let anyone outside of my family do. I mean, no one had shown any real interest in me since the mutations had appeared, so it was weird to have him so in tune with me. Even now, it was like coming home. When I saw him up here, I felt like a part of me had been completed, and every little touch from him was comforting, even though I barely knew the man. My body continued to ache and burn, and I wondered if that was natural. We had been in the same spot for some time, and it still hurt.

It's going to be okay, his voice tore through my mind again, *I promise.*

Twinkle, twinkle, little star... He begins to sing my song, resounding in my mind as though he was trying to ease me. I sigh before joining in.

How I wonder what you are? I had always felt like someone had been singing to me when I was so down, and someone had been; had it really been his voice that I'd been hearing all these years?

Our voices continued the song together, a strong unison within my mind, *up above the world so high, like a diamond in the sky. When the blazing sun is gone, when he nothing shines upon, then you show your little light, twinkle, twinkle, all the night.*

"Twinkle, twinkle, little star, lost up in the skies. I hope you haven't died." The words slipped from my mouth just as the pains in my body increased in intensity. These racking, shooting pains hit me, going through my shoulders and encompassing my entire back.

I gasped as I fell to my knees. Dom's fingers slipped out of my hand; I tried to turn to him, his name on my lips, but he just stared at me, eyes wide with helplessness.

His mouth moved, crying out my name, 'Mary Beth,' but I couldn't hear anything over the pounding of blood in my ears.

Levi's hand grabbed mine tightly as I went into my stomach, the pains increasing, and my breathing raced as I tried to understand what was going on. He moved to ease me into a lying position gently, his other hand pulling me towards him.

The pains racked my body so badly, as I finally reached the ground, that tears dripped down my face, hitting the ground. Yet, I couldn't even lay on the ground on my side; rolling to my stomach, I pulled myself into a fetal position. My hands grabbed my stomach, trying to hold in the sobs that begged to be released. Levi's baritone voice tried to shush my worries, and he continued to sing the song to my mind as I huddled more profoundly into the fetal position. Tears streamed down my face, and I prayed for the pain to end.

XXIV

Dom

Forty-Six

Suddenly, she rolled to her stomach and arched her back off the ground. Her screams ceased as the most beautiful wings burst forth from her shoulder blades. Her eyes rolled back into her head. They were as stunning as she was, inside and out. The teal incandescent color radiated through the night sky as the world blackened. Her wings reminded me so much of Lizzy. I sighed as both jealousy and contentment warred inside me. I wanted to stay and watch her transformation, but at the same time, it was too painful for me to watch. Not only that, but I'd been through this before, and it didn't have a happy ending then, so why would I get one now?

I turned away as Levi grabbed her and fell back down, her wings receding into her torn and bloodied shirt. A whisper of memory as they etched themselves into her blades and fair skin, a tattoo that she would never be rid of. I could feel the tears as they streamed down my face. I couldn't decide what it was from, the joy she had transformed, or the heartache of never being able to do it myself again.

"Yell for me when she wakes up." I hollered at him as I walked away. I didn't wait for a response. As I headed back down the pathway from we had stopped, I had to breathe deeply to stop myself from crying. I just wasn't strong enough to be there for her when she was going through the transition. A flashback to another time. I hadn't been strong enough for Lizzy when she went through it. *I was a failure.*

I shook my head. I was clearing my thoughts as well as I could when the chopping sounds of wind sliced by the rotary blades of a droid reached my ears. *Where had the droid come from?* I wondered as I listened, *how long had it been following us, and when did it get so close?* As I walked around, I attempted to find the droid. Eventually, I couldn't hear it anymore, and I had to wonder where it was.

It was pitch black up here, yet I could see the stars. They twinkled down at me, reminding me that when I was feeling down, something extraordinary in the world wasn't seen anymore, at least down in the plains and lower grounds. I wandered around aimlessly for what felt like hours before I heard his call.

"Dominic! She's walking up!"

I returned to the peak, greeted by Mary Beth leaning against Levi's chest. Her eyes blinked rapidly.

"Oh my god," she moaned in pain. "What happened?"

Levi ran his hands over her hair, whispering sweet nothing, at least I guess it was sweet nothing. I wasn't close enough to hear, and I didn't want to hear as she spoke. He fell silent as she looked between the two of us like I assumed he was leaving this question to me. I sighed.

"That's what I couldn't tell you about. You'll learn more when we get closer to the Sanctum, but let's just say that the radiation from the bombs wasn't your average radiation."

"What?" The confusion was written all over her face.

I looked Levi in the eyes, "Get her up."

"She's still too weak." He argued with me.

I laughed. "You don't know my sister. Let her get up. She isn't going to believe it without proof." I had to do something that would make her feel powerful. She was a control freak, precisely like me, and wouldn't be happy unless she felt like she was in power. She hated not having some sort of power. We'd struggled with who was in charge and who had the power throughout the trip.

He looked at me like I was an idgit.

My wings never developed entirely after that first time, staying at the tattoo outline, but I knew my sister.

Even if she were weak, she'd believe it easier if she could do it herself. He grimaced but helped her stand to her feet. She trembled as she stood there, barely noticing that her shirt was ripped into pieces as her weak knees shook. Within moments, that core of iron, the piece that makes the Johnson family, stiffened her spine, and she pushed away from Levi to stand by herself. "I'm okay," she smiled at him, and he nodded as he backed away, although unwillingly.

I took a deep breath and remembered when I had come here before. Someone had been waiting for us then, and I struggled to remember how they had explained to me, over and over, after the first attempt at having my wings break out after the battle I'd been in to protect Lizzy from Barnes when he'd come after her at the bottom of the hill. "Okay, the next thing I will say will sound insane, but I want you to imagine wings. Any type of wings that you can imagine. I want you to close your eyes and see them rising and stretching out, wider and larger than anything else you've seen before." I paused as she followed through with each step, slowly closing her eyes. From the corner of my eye, I could see that Levi's eyes soon followed hers. He was helping her visualize her wings as he had seen them.

"Good," I said, following through. "Now, I want you to roll your shoulders easily. I know you still ache, but roll them gently and stretch your arms as wide as possible."

She creaked her eyes open at me, glaring but slowly and gently rolling her shoulder, her face grimacing with pain as she moved. She stretched out her arms, the movement agitating her weakened and sore muscles, but she trooped through it. Each movement of her arms stretching reflects the movement of her wings. The majestic and glorious turquoise wings were a solid reminder that I would never have my wings and that Lizzy's beautiful lavender wings had appeared here, years ago, in this exact spot.

Her bones creaked, the sound echoing in the pre-dawn light as I watched her go through the motions. I imagined the bones rearranging, knowing that she fought through the pain. She knew that she had to stay awake, had to fight through the pain, for her to go through the entire thing, or she would never understand. When her arms were wide open, her wings flapped in the background, stretched out in the dawning light of the day; I smiled joyfully. "MB, open your eyes."

Her eyes creaked open slowly, the teal of her eyes a shining beacon in the early light. She looked around to see her wings curling in around her, and a gasp of shock dropped from her lips.

"What the…"

XXV

Mary Beth

Forty-Seven

I couldn't believe my eyes. *It couldn't be. I must have died and gone to heaven.* There was no way that I was still alive and had wings. Yet, Dom and Levi were still there. Neither one of them looked surprised. I laughed dryly; why would they be surprised? Dom was the one who told me how to do it. And Levi... I don't know what it is about him, but he had led me on the entire time we'd walked up this mountain.

I reached up and clutched my necklace. The heavyweight helped reassure me, as though the presence of my ancestors was radiating through it into me.

I was utterly bewildered by the sight before me. There, unfurling from my back and curling around me, were wings. Not just any wings, but my wings. *How? Why?* The questions swirled in my mind, leaving me in a state of profound confusion.

The wind billowed around me as the wings closed in, blocking out Dom and Levi, and I reached out to touch them. The teal feathers were soft against my skin, like touching a cloud, and where I expected coarseness, there was a sleek, shiny feel. They matched perfectly against the bumps of my hand, a complete compliment as if planned by a higher power. I sighed, the air leaving me in a huff; the feathers and wings shook with the same velocity as the air left my body. *What is this?* I pondered as I pulled my hand back.

His voice, like a sudden thunderclap, pierced through my thoughts. *It's your wings.* I jerked back, my wings instinctively retracting as I turned to face Levi, my shock palpable.

"How are you doing that?" I demanded, still saying it out loud as I looked him in the eyes. He shrugged as though it didn't matter that he was in my head. The one spot that no one else should ever be but myself.

I wish I could tell you, but, he replied, *not even the brightest in our society has figured it out yet.* My wings flapped and shook as fear and another emotion, something I couldn't name yet, slammed into me.

How could he invade my thoughts like this? The fear that he could hear every thought, every secret, sent a chill down my spine. *Did he hear my thoughts about him that first night?* Shame flushed my cheeks.

"Are you guys doing that mind thing?" Dom's words slapped against me aggressively. I glanced over my wings to look at him, shock riding my face. He looked more aggravated than angry. He was referring to our telepathic communication, a skill that developed after the radiation exposure, which was the only thing that made sense to me at this point.

Dom continued, frustration leaking through his voice, "Can you at least wait until I'm gone before doing it?" Maybe it wasn't just frustration but jealousy, I pondered as I took in his appearance. He seemed green with envy as he looked at the two of us. I could swear that he sounded like he had experienced and missed it himself. I wondered what happened that would cause him to experience it and yet not have it. His jealousy was palpable, his eyes betraying a longing for the same abilities we possessed.

"Ummm, yeah." I laughed nervously as I readjusted my facial muscles from shock to nervous amusement, as though the laughter would brush the shame, fear, and even… some mild excitement away. "I guess we were." I tried to ease my own anxiety about having Levi in my mind. I knew he had said he was my mate last night. *Was that the reason he could speak to me in my mind?*

He rolled his eyes as the sun rose higher in the sky. I could almost see it from where I stood. It was glorious to feel the heat permeating my bones, warming my wings as they pulled tightly against my sides.

This reminded me, "What's going on, Dom? Don't give me any baloney this time," I demanded.

The wind ghosted across my skin. Shocked, I looked down at my torn shirt and clutched it around my mid-section. The tips of my wings wrapped around me, helping to save the bare skin of my stomach, and framed my face so that I could see both Dom and Levi.

This time, it was his turn to laugh nervously. "Well, ya know how radiation was supposedly going to kill everyone in the radiation zones when the bombs dropped? The bombs, a result of a catastrophic war with China, had created radiation zones, areas where the effects of the radiation were most severe."

His words brought back memories of being in a hospital room with Mom, Nicky, and him as we waited to see if we would be cleared to leave. I had never really understood it then, but I remembered being so bored of being stuck in that room.

I nodded, and he continued. "Yeah, well, it didn't. It did

something to our blood and DNA that changed us."

"What about Mom, the girls? Nicky?" I asked as the thoughts of stark naked white walls rang through my mind. Every little thought, each negative aspect of the hospital room, began to affect everything around me. I could feel my wings as they began to pull back. The feathers tickled a little as they rubbed against my sides, no longer attempting to help cover my bare stomach. As wings disappeared around me, I wrapped my hands around my stomach more as I fell to my knees, my wings still out but shaking as the thoughts of the past hit me like a ton of bricks.

"It doesn't affect people as much if they're older. I mean, I didn't get…" his words trail off, and he jerked his head towards me. Indicating that he was talking about my wings. "Well, I did, but I didn't." He sounded bitter. "As for Mom, I think she just got a mild dose. I have no idea about the girls, but Nicky will go through this, too. At least I'm pretty sure he will."

"What the hell is this, then?" I demanded, looking between him and Levi. Dom started to back away from us slowly as though attempting to disappear.

"Perhaps I can explain." Another voice interjected as an older man stepped out from behind a tree. "That is if you are willing to let me." His white hair was a stark contrast against the minor bumps along his wrinkled face, but even those seemed faded and old like him.

The sun was edging over the peaks of the surrounding mountains, making a beautiful horizon, the lights hitting the older man in the face. For the first time in years, the rays of an unfiltered sun surrounded me. It was spectacular. I started to nod, still slightly unsure; I had no choice. It wasn't like Dom or Levi offered additional information to help me figure this out.

If I wanted to understand what was happening with the world, my body, Levi, Dom, and my family… my only choice seemed to be an older man I didn't know. He had answers, but I was not sure what ones.

"How do I get them to go away?" my hands gesturing to the resting wings on my back. They had stopped short of going into my skin. I was afraid of when they went back in. *Would it hurt a lot when they went in?* The weight of my wings was heavy but not oppressive on my body, but I could feel the fatigue of having them out starting to settle in.

Dom gestured to Levi. "You'll have to help her with that."

He nodded and came closer again, but his actions were close and cautious. I couldn't determine if he felt shame for everything that had happened or if he was defying the older man who continued staring at us as though we were amusing him. While they were slow and almost peaceful, it was so confusing to have this sudden behavior change. It was not how he had been behaving before this older man came out, but then again, a lot of shit had been going on since we got to this point, but I continued to wonder if it had something to do with the older man. Speaking of which, where the hell did that guy come from?

His hands were gentle, although calloused and rough against my skin, as he laid them on my bare shoulders. I turned and looked up at him, and he smiled this little crooked smile at me, and my heart jumped into my throat; oh, he was a lady killer with that smile. He may have acted like a jerk around Dom, but I was still interested in getting to know him better. Even though it felt like it should be against my better judgment, I knew something weird was happening between us.

"Close your eyes," he instructed me. "Imagine you are pulling on a warm jacket or blanket. Pull it close to you. Those are your wings closing and coming in." I did as he instructed, imagining my warmest blanket wrapped around my shoulders. I could feel the feathers beating and fluttering against my skin, shrinking against my skin, and suddenly, they were no longer there.

Opening my eyes, I turn and look around at my back. My shirt was tattered, floating in the lazy wind, but nothing else was there. No more wings. They were completely gone. I couldn't understand its logic. *How?*

The chopping of the droid sounded off again, and I remembered that we had been running from it. *How did it even get up here? Where did it come from? Where had it been during the night?* I turn my questioning eyes towards the older man.

"Do you know what that is?"

He nodded and smiled grimly. "They have been tracking you and Dominic for some time now. They lost you, Dom, and me in the uphill climb, but I'm afraid they are getting closer. I hate to ask this, but I was hoping you could go down lower and distract the droid so that we can shoot it out of the air. We don't want it to get any closer to our entrance." He gestured behind him. "It has been protected for many years, and we need it to remain that way." He was dedicated to whatever was nearby as he glanced back at the man behind him and watched us.

Levi's hands were still resting on my shoulders, and I shook them away as I pulled away from him, searching around me for Dom. I felt weak, but I knew that I could do this. I was never one to back down from anything.

He stood there, looking off to the side with an angry look. He was almost entirely out of reach of the older man as if he had been sliding backward since the older man had arrived. *Why had he hidden this from me, and why did he seem so angry that we were here now?* The questions and thoughts drifted through my head. The wings were a wonderful feeling. I remembered feeling every wind drift through the wings when they were spread out… But Dom said he couldn't tell me how to close them, that he wasn't able to. Then I thought about the bitter look on his face. Something had happened when he'd left all those years ago. *Why did it seem like he wanted to run away from this geezer?* I had never seen Dom act like this, and it brought up a shit ton of questions.

I turned, looking at the older man again, steadying myself as I adjusted to not having the wings out around me. "If we get rid of the droid, we can go into your haven? I'll even shoot it down myself."

"It's called Sanctum, and you may. He, however, may not ever come back in."

Back in. The words rocked me, and shock tunneled through my body. "Why can't he?"

"He gave up his entry into it a long time ago."

My eyes trailed over to Dom. His fists white-knuckled at the proclamation.

"But he can remain within the area while we talk." I felt like this was a concession, and I was never one for concessions; it was all or nothing for me.

Dom nodded grimly, as though he had expected this answer, and gestured for us to return to the mountainside further down. My cloak was a torn mess on the ground where I had fallen originally, and my shirt was barely held together by the bottom. I shook as my hands held the edges of the torn back together.

"Okay, we'll go and get it." I turned to Levi and said, "Stay here. There is something you aren't telling me, and I can't trust you right now. I hafta do this without you until I figure out how to trust you—or if I can." The thought seemed to rip me apart inside as it crossed my mind.

I had to step away from him and figure out what was happening. I just had to because I could hear him in my mind and knew there was something there. That something made me feel at ease with him, and I'd known him for less than a week; hell, less than a day, it was insanity!

He nodded; the argument warred over his face as he struggled with my directions.

"I promise I'll be back." The words dropped before I could even think them through. He smiled brightly at my proclamation.

I walked over to Dom as he grabbed my bag, bow, and quiver and put his arm around my shoulder to help hold my tattered shirt together as we walked away, showing that brotherly love I'd been dying for all this time and was only now getting as I knew he was going to be torn away from me again. This was the closest we had been since before he left, and I felt the love for him swell within me again as he showed his concern for me by helping me with my shirt.

"Can we stop somewhere quickly so I can change it?" I asked him. He nodded as he began to rummage through my bag for another shirt. Finding one, he held it up to me, and I grabbed it, letting go of my shirt from one hand in the back but keeping my shoulder hold. We walked a little further away from Levi and the older man, barely enough that we couldn't see them anymore, before he stopped and turned around to give me a little privacy.

I'm thankful he was aware enough of my need for privacy as I peeled the shredded thing off my shoulders and over my head. My bra was destroyed, but I was sure that I could make it without it for a little while; at least, I hope I could. Throwing the two items onto the ground, I quickly pulled the newer shirt over my head and then reached down and picked up my discarded clothes.

"Thanks," I spoke as millions of thoughts ran through my head. I wanted to ask so much but didn't know where to begin. "Should I go in?" I decided to go with the most straightforward question. He knew more than me at this point, and I, strangely enough, wanted to have him with me during this. It was traumatic enough that I had wings sprout from my back, but he was the only thing I knew with certainty wouldn't lie to me about what was going on, although he'd lied to me throughout the journey here. His face, when everything happened, was evidence enough that he was affected by this too.

"Yes, you should. We can talk afterward, but they can explain it better than I ever could." He said as he turned around. "Let's destroy that thing so you can go with them and maybe, hopefully, come back out." He sounded as though he didn't think I'd come back out.

I nodded, trading him for my bow and quiver from him after giving him my tattered shirt remains. We walked down the mountainside in silence as we stalked the droid. The sun, finally, was peeking out from the haziness of the skies, and I saw it for the first time in what felt like forever.

It was beautiful.

The light reflected off the clouds as they drifted over the world's edge. I became so lost seeing the sun that I ignored the surrounding sounds. Dom nudged me to the side and tilted his head to the side.

"Do you hear it?" Dom asked, and I slapped myself mentally. I needed to get my shit together, I wasn't being the best hunter that I could be, and I'd been taught by the best. He had been the best besides Dad.

I nodded and notched my arrow into the bow. Lifting the bow, I aimed it towards the sky, scanning the horizon until I saw it. The droid flew almost haphazardly around the mountain, looking for something or someone. I closed my eyes, allowing my new ability to be triggered, as I pulled the string tight as the arrow came back, before opening them as I released a breath of air.

Something was hanging down from it. I could see it, barely, as it floated along the side of the mountain. A horrible feeling entered my stomach, premonition or what, I didn't know, but there was something terrible on that droid, and I was sure it had my name on it.

I had to know what it was—what was hanging beneath it. I breathed in again profoundly, knowing that my arrow would fly true in this instant. As I released my bowstring, the air exited my lungs. With my newfound extra ability, I watched the arrow fly through the air toward the machine, lending it strength and trajectory.

My hunting instincts kicked in, and I took off, knowing exactly where it would land.

Dom ran behind me, slowly but surely, as I gained speed. The arrow hit the metal, and the sound echoed around me before the droid came careening down. I wanted to be by it as it landed; as I neared the spot, the sounds of metal crashing and breaking echoed around me as I watched the droid crash. I slid next to the ground where it landed, the dirt and gravel tearing at my jeans, and even some tiny metal chunks tore through my pants, biting into my tender skin. Metal was scattered around me, but I paid no attention as I found the enormous pile and started digging through the wreckage. It had been holding something, and something in my heart told me I knew exactly what it was. Finally, as I reached the last piece of droid chunk, I saw an envelope underneath, my name bold on the white paper.

I pulled it out, landed on my butt, and just stared at it. Dread and trepidation filled my veins. I'd seen this type of envelope before... it was the kind that the council used to send messages to families after a death or when someone left the camp. I had to look at it before Dom got to me.

When I finally realized he was there, he was panting, leaning on his knees. "Well... why'd... you... run... off?" His words stumbled out between his breaths as though he hadn't seen the envelope yet.

I shrugged. "I don't know," I whispered, even though my gut told me I did, "I thought there was something on it."

"Well... was... there... something... there?" He struggled to get it out, clearly not as in shape as he thought, as he tried to regain his breath.

I nodded absentmindedly and tore into it. There wasn't much there, but something fell into my lap as I pulled the envelope apart.

Looking down into my lap, I saw something metal shining up at me as the morning light hit it. The charm I had left at home winked at me as I stared down at it. I tore into the letter, afraid to see what was in it.

IF YOU EVER WANT TO SEE YOUR FAMILY AGAIN, I SUGGEST YOU BRING YOUR BROTHER BACK SO HE CAN FACE HIS JUDGMENT.

The words burned as the letter fell from my hands, joining the charm on my lap. *What was I going to do now?*

TO BE CONTINUED...

About the Author

Jillian E. Thompson is an accomplished mystery writer known for her character-driven plots and engaging storytelling. The author of the young adult novel *Melody of Redemption*, Jillian has also written numerous short stories and poems, showcasing her versatility across genres. Her love for writing began early, fueling a lifelong passion.

When she's not writing, Jillian balances her creative work with her role as a special education advocate. She's been in the field for over a decade and is pursuing a doctoral degree to empower educators.

Jillian lives in a bustling household with her husband of 18 years, their two children, four dogs, a cat, and a collection of reptiles her family adores. Whether crafting mysteries or navigating family life, she brings depth and heart to everything she does.

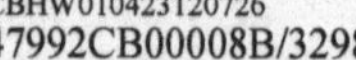

* 9 7 9 8 3 4 9 3 0 9 1 7 5 *